"HERE WE GO AGAIN!"

"You have heard of a great boar of ghastly aspect, who brings famine and pestilence in its wake," said Avice, as Quadroped and his friends neared the edge of the crowd. "That is not true. The traitor pig is nothing but a small white piglet." Avice pointed directly at Quadroped, Fairfax, and Morrag. "And there he is!" he shouted. "With his evil companions, about to make good his escape! Catch them!"

PRAISE FOR QUADROPED'S PREVIOUS ADVENTURE
the PIG, the PRINCE & the UNICORN

"A delightful surprise,
by turns charming and totally wacko!"
Craig Shaw Gardner, author of
An Excess of Enchantments

"Karen Brush has a fine command
of character and story,
her style is engaging, and you find yourself
thinking about the book long after
you've finished reading it."
George Alec Effinger, author of
When Gravity Fails

THE DEMON PIG

KAREN A. BRUSH

AVONOVA

AVON BOOKS • NEW YORK

THE DEMON PIG is an original publication of Avon Books. This work has never before appeared in book form. This work is a novel. Any similarity to actual persons or events is purely coincidental.

AVON BOOKS
A division of
The Hearst Corporation
1350 Avenue of the Americas
New York, New York 10019

First AvoNova Printing: December 1991

AVONOVA TRADEMARK REG. U.S. PAT. OFF. AND IN OTHER COUNTRIES, MARCA REGISTRADA, HECHO EN U.S.A.

Printed in the U.S.A.

RA   10   9   8   7   6   5   4   3   2   1

Mushrooms are a vegetable
That you eat when you are able
You won't know them when you seem them
But you'll know them when you eat them;
If in Heaven you awaken
You will know you were mistaken
And the thing that you have ate-en
Ain't the thing ya should've et;
Must've been a toadstool,
Tough luck.

—Anonymous Camp Song

My thanks to all those who helped Quadroped survive his second adventure: my father and brother, both Charles F. Brush; Lily Chu; Oscar Collier; John Douglas; Amy Goodhart Raeburn; Ian Harding; Catherine Hills; Sylvia D. Karas; Jane Rodgers; Marie-Louise Sorensen; and Non Vaughan-Thomas. Also to Elizabeth Carlo, for her definition of wind, and Steve Goringe for comments on *Quadroped I*. Humble apologies to Matthew Johnson for omitting the Marxist slug.

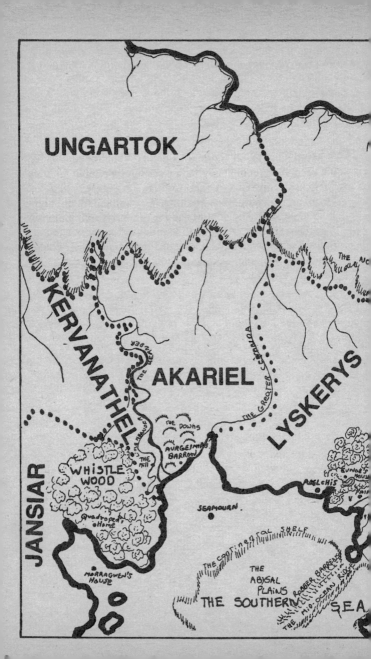

Preface

There was once a Great War between the nine mortal Kingdoms and the magical land of Ravenor which lasted for one hundred years. Ravenorians being nearly immortal, and the people of the Kingdoms being averse to conquest, it would have raged one hundred years more had not a Prince of Essylt trapped the Black Unicorn, Ruler of Ravenor, in the unfinished realm of Chaos.

Once every century the Gate into Chaos would start to open, and a Key Bearer would have to lock it again. The last Key Bearer was a young pig called Quadroped.

From the moment Quadroped found the Key his life was in danger. Glasgerion and Reander, Princes of Essylt, were determined to get Quadroped to the Gate alive. The four Warlords of Ravenor were just as determined to stop him.

Quadroped reached the Gate alive. In a terrible battle, Reander fought and slew the four Warlords. The way was cleared for Quadroped to lock the Gate and save his country from war.

Life has a sorry tendency to become complicated. In the course of his travels, Quadroped had discovered that the Warlords of Ravenor were not so much evil as desperate. The Black Unicorn had created Ravenor; it could not thrive without him. When the Black Unicorn had been locked into Chaos, Ravenor had become a wasteland, its people had suffered and starved.

So Quadroped struck a bargain with the Black Unicorn. He could go free if he would forsake his revenge and agree to make peace with the Kingdoms. The Gate was opened; peace was made. And the first fruit of this fragile new friendship was the marriage of Prince Glasgerion to the Ravenorian Warlord Morragwen.

And now our story begins anew, but not precisely where we left off. It begins in those moments *before* the Black Unicorn was freed. The four Warlords of Ravenor have been slain. Morragwen, Manslayer, Toridon, and Goriel lie dead. Reander, Prince of Essylt, has commanded Quadroped to lock the Gate once more. . . .

Prologue

Morragwen died, engulfed in flames, in the caverns under Illoreth. At the moment of death she slept. Morragwen's spirit awoke to find herself running headlong across a beach where ribbons of blood washed down to meet the tide. Her lungs burned, coarse sea heather scratched her legs, muddy red water splattered at her feet.

The roar of the ocean filled Morragwen's ears and a salty wind howled and sang. The beach shuddered under monstrous black rollers, wreathed in foam as they came crashing in. Greenish black clouds roiled overhead like waves on an upside-down sea. Ugly vapors dripped down.

The Manslayer ran at Morragwen's side, red and black, the prongs of his antlers gleaming. Toridon, a furious flame of gold, fled far ahead. Confused and frightened, Morragwen ran on. She somehow knew that *something,* dreadful and hidden, pursued her across the sands.

Footsteps, soft and dull, told of another runner approaching. Morragwen glanced back. Goriel ran behind her, great wings pressed close and streamlined against his heaving sides. His eyes were wild. Long shapes glided after him, low and lithe, terrible in their speed. Slender beach grasses trembled aside as they passed.

"What are they?" Morragwen asked. "What's happening?"

"Who knows?" said Goriel. "Hurry."

"Why don't we squash them? We've got magic."

The Manslayer looked over his shoulder. "Toridon tried. Our magic doesn't work here."

"Where are we?"

"In some Land of the Dead," said Goriel.

"We're dead? Reander killed us?"

"So I'd guess," said Goriel. "There's no place like this in the Living Lands."

The Manslayer growled and gnashed his teeth.

How odd, thought Morragwen. *I don't feel dead. I feel uncomfortably alive.* The red hounds bayed loudly behind her. Fear returned, banishing rational thought.

The red hounds came on. Their howls drowned out the breakers' furious roar. Savage barks and cries grew louder and more ecstatic. Beside them flew a flock of chattering skulls, egging them on with raucous screams.

Then the hunt appeared, cresting the dunes that rose above the beach. White and roan horses, wild of mane, tore up the sand with sharp hooves. Foam laced their sides. Their black eyes rolled and glared, rimmed in white. Gaunt figures, dressed in gray and green, bent low over the powerful necks, urging the great beasts on. Morragwen stumbled, regained her feet, ran on. Horns sounded, loud and deep. The pack closed in.

Morragwen could hear the dogs' labored breaths between each frantic yip. The skulls shrieked. Great hounds leaped past her, red mouths gaping, racing after Toridon. The Manslayer cried out. Sharp jaws seized him upon the thigh and brought him down.

Teeth snapped at Morragwen's heels, tearing the thin hem of her dress. Heavy paws smashed into her shoulders, driving her face down into wet abrasive sand. Water rushed in, choking her, and left with a tug at her hair.

Massive jaws sought for hold on the back of Morragwen's neck. She rolled onto her back, trying to shake the dog off. It moved and came in over her chest to try for her slender throat. Morragwen brought both arms up and grasped the brute, trying to strangle it before it tore the life from her. A skull bobbed before her face, distracting her with high-pitched cries and obnoxiously clattering teeth.

Another wave arrived, submerging Morragwen's head in cold water. The dog snarled and drooled in her face. Around her, other dogs barked excitedly. One came dashing in to nip at her sides and legs. The pain was sharp. Instinctively she drew her legs up to her chest to protect her tender abdomen from their sallies.

For endless minutes Morragwen fought for life, then the hunters arrived. Harness jingled, horses stamped and snorted. The riders dismounted, calling their hounds to heel. Tall figures, famine thin, beat the dogs from Morragwen's side and bent to grasp her arms. Morragwen looked up into their hooded faces. Red eyes twinkled at her from deep within the sockets of their fleshless skulls. The Revenants smiled the eternal smile of the dead.

A tall woman, robed in scarlet, rode up and the skulls sailed off to greet her. Morragwen winced at the click and grind of the Revenants' bones as they hastened to hold the bridle. The woman dismounted, stripping off her gloves and issuing commands in a low voice. The skulls fell still and silent as the Revenants led their captives forward.

The woman laughed, a low and pleasant sound of wonder mixed with disbelief. "Warlords of Ravenor," she said. "Welcome to the Fleshless Land." The dancing skulls gnashed their teeth.

"Nieve," Goriel whispered.

Fear, in life an unaccustomed feeling, renewed its hold on Morragwen. This was Nieve, terrible Queen of the Dead. Into her power all souls of the slain were given. Morragwen shivered as she gazed into the strong well-sculpted face before her.

Nieve's beauty was unmarred by wrinkles or any sign of age. Dark hair and dark thin brows set off her pale translucent flesh. Cold thin blood tinted her cheeks and lips the palest pink. Eyes blue and clear as water, rimmed with black, glittered with secret laughter.

"I see you know of me." Nieve's smile was gracious. "My heart rejoices in your presence here. Immortals rarely venture to the Homes of the Dead. Cold Essylt's Prince is mighty indeed who can send you four to my halls. I never predicted such an outcome when the Key was taken from Essylt's vaults."

"*You* stole the Key?" asked Toridon. She flamed into yellow surprise.

"Not I," said Nieve. "I dare not venture in the Living Lands. A sometime suitor took it at my bidding. We had planned to keep it hidden until the Gate should open and the Black Unicorn return to wreak his revenge on the Kingdoms. Alas, we lost the Key. A magpie stole it and dropped it onto the piglet, Quadroped."

"I knew something was amiss when the Key was lost," said Goriel. "My sorcery failed to find it until it was too late."

"I hope you will not hold my actions against me," said Nieve. "Had I succeeded the Gate would have opened. The Black Unicorn would have been free. I would that you four were still alive, fighting the Kingdoms, sending their slaughtered souls to me. My hall is sparse of company, my people all too few.

"I never dreamed," Nieve continued, "that you would fail to slay the pig. Though he comes of ancient fairy stock he has inherited none of his people's powers nor, to my sorrow, aught of their loyalty to me. Indeed, I should be vexed with you for failing to free your monarch. Still, the pig has an almost magical aura of cuteness about him that makes him difficult to harm and, no doubt, you did your best. Your own remorse will be punishment enough. I'll not chastise you further. Instead, I'll bid you welcome once again."

Nieve clapped her hands and a Revenant shuffled forward with a great chalice of silver, chased with gold and set with blood-red stones. Nieve unhooked a silver canteen from her belt and poured a rich red wine into the vessel. Turning to the Warlords, she proffered the cup.

"Drink," she said. "It will quench your thirst and heal your wounds. You will need strength for the journey home."

Morragwen struggled against the arms that held her, but to no avail. Disjointed memories filled her head with alarming visions, making it ache. Glasgerion lay silent before the Gate, struck down by his nephew Reander. Quadroped crouched beside him, clutching the Key and looking scared: a piglet, unused to danger or strenuous thought, forced to choose between worlds.

I can't stay here, she thought. *They need me. Reander is probably forcing Quadro to lock the Gate right now.*

The only Ravenorian left alive at the Gate was Morragwen's familiar, the moray eel Morrag. Morrag could never defeat Reander. If he tried he would only get himself killed.

"You must stop resisting, my dear," said Nieve. "You are dead by violent means and are therefore in my power. At least," she amended, "for the time being. Eventually you will pass beyond this realm to whatever place it is that those who are truly dead must go. Come, the wine is sweet and cool."

Morragwen hung back and clenched her teeth tightly shut but Toridon reached for the cup. Goriel forestalled her.

"Do not drink," he said. "If we eat or drink aught in the Lands of the Dead we can never return to the living."

Nieve frowned, her blue eyes narrowed. "Warlords, you will never return. Only the Black Unicorn has the power to call you back, and he cannot. Any moment now the pig will lock the Gate. Your sovereign will be imprisoned forever."

"The Gate will open again in a hundred years," said Morragwen.

"And the Key Bearers shall lock it again," said Nieve. "Who will stop them, now that you four are dead? Reander has won peace for the Kingdoms for a long, long time. You will remain with me. Accept your destinies and drink. If you will not you will die the second death and pass on to that place from which there is no return."

"I shall not drink," said Goriel.

"Neither shall I," said Morragwen.

"Hunger shall win your consent before long," said Nieve. "But starvation will be a waste of time and quite unpleasant for you. Please drink. My land is a pleasant one for those with eyes to see. 'Tis only to those who have not drunk that this realm appears dead and gray. Beyond the dunes lie forests rich in birds, and fertile fields. Friends and relatives wait to welcome you. Many victims of the Great War have found shelter here: for Toridon, a sister who starved to death; for Goriel, a wife and twin daughters. Manslayer shall have armies at his command and many new foes to slay."

Morragwen looked at Goriel. Hope warmed his wintry eyes for the first time since she had known him. Toridon and the Manslayer both looked eagerly to him for permission to take the cup.

Goriel will drink, she thought. *Nieve has offered him his heart's desire. I am the only one whose heart remains with the living.*

"Morragwen, drink," said Nieve. "Glasgerion may come here too, in time. Many Princes of Essylt have come to my halls."

Morragwen shook her head. Reander, Glasgerion's arrogant nephew, would no doubt visit the Fleshless Land. Glasgerion, gentle scholar and bard, would never be claimed by Nieve. His soul would pass to whatever Kingdom housed the souls of the peacefully dead.

"I will not drink," said Morragwen. *Perhaps Glasgerion will rescue me,* she thought. It was a futile hope. Glasgerion knew no magic and Reander would never willingly revive a Warlord, even if he knew how. Beside her Nieve raised the chalice to Goriel's lips with slender hands. Gold bracelets gleamed on the pale bare flesh of her arms.

Goriel bent his head to drink, eyes closed. His lips had just parted when a slight tremor shook the sand beneath their feet. The beach shook itself again, a gentle twitch. Goriel's head came up, eyes open. He stepped away from Nieve. The earth shook again, harder.

"The Gate," said Goriel. "It begins to open!" His voice was hoarse and tight.

"No!" Nieve's face flushed red and her long neck was taut in anger.

The ground rippled. Nieve kept her balance and held the chalice steady. Horses reared up, dogs whined and barked. The Revenants cowered. The screaming skulls chattered their teeth.

"Warlords, drink. My armies need you."

The beach arched its back and began to crack apart. The sound of rending, tearing rocks filled the air as a great fissure slowly opened at their feet. Sweet warm air, hay scented, blew up into their faces. From far away a deep voice came whispering, faint but clear, saying:

"You served me well, children . . . there will be no more battles . . . there is too much work to be done." And then, louder and more clearly: "Get up!"

Morragwen ran to the chasm's edge and turned. "Come on," she called. "Quadro's done it. He's opened the Gate. The Black Unicorn is free!"

Toridon and the Manslayer obeyed the summons without question. Swiftly they walked to the fissure's edge and tumbled in, ignoring Nieve's pleas to stop. They fell downward like slow autumn leaves, Toridon trailing lazy sparks behind her. Morragwen looked at Goriel.

"Stay, Goriel," said Nieve. "Your children await you."

Goriel stared across the chalice at Nieve. Terrible longing twisted his face for a moment. He shook his head. His face became impassive once again, revealing all the bland emotion of a statue.

"I cannot stay, Nieve," he said. "My Lord is free and calls me to his side. Love has no power to keep me from that summons."

Silently Goriel walked to the edge of the fissure and took Morragwen's hand in his own. Together they dove, in a great clear arc, down into the dark. Above them the fissure closed, hiding them from Nieve as they fell toward safety and life.

When the sands were whole and the earth was still, Nieve turned back toward the cowering Revenants. With an oath she dashed the chalice to the ground. The ruby liquid sank quickly into the parched earth. She watched a moment, then frowned. "Wait," she said. The liquid came bubbling back from the earth and lay in an obedient pool at her feet. "Show me the Gate."

The liquid spread itself thin as a mirror, its surface took on many colors as it revealed what Nieve commanded. In the great cavern under Illoreth, Reander of Essylt faced his ancient enemy. Around them the Warlords stood, Morragwen wrapped in Glasgerion's arms. The Black Unicorn placed his horn against Reander's throat.

Nieve drew her breath. "Kill him quickly," she whispered. "Send Reander here. Let the Great Wars begin."

Then a small white piglet with purple eyes stepped out from under the Black Unicorn's forelegs. He spoke, and the Black Unicorn dropped his horn. Nieve watched in incredulous anger as a spherical Key Bearer forged peace between the Black Unicorn and the Prince of Essylt.

Nieve gazed long upon the guileless image of Quadroped. "Little Key Bearer," said Nieve, "you have cost me much. A way must be found to increase the harvest, better if bitter for you. Long shall you rue the day the Key sought you out, the day that I found my lost fairy pigs. Your sounder's covenant with me is broken and you, my pig, shall pay." In the grim land beneath the hills, Nieve, Queen of the Fleshless, brooded on her revenge.

Chapter One

Golden summer gave way to dripping fall. Mists hugged the ground. Cold winds screamed down the chimneys at folk huddled inside over smoking fires. In frozen Essylt snow turned to hail and unseasonable blizzards drove the inhabitants of the ice-city indoors. The Kingdoms were buffeted by storms, and attempts to dispel the fronts by magic met with limited success. After a month of unending battle the storms abated and reports of flooding decreased, but the skies remained leaden and refused to clear, and the damp air released another, unrecognized, foe. . . .

Far to the south three dripping animals moved slowly along a badly rutted dirt road that wound through the heart of Whistlewood Forest. Great oaks, set back too far to shelter the road, blazed red against the overcast skies. The road was littered with wet leaves, twigs, and muddy acorns. Many huge trees had fallen to the hurricanes. Others leaned at awkward angles, their splintered limbs dangling uselessly at their sides.

Fungi grew in wild profusion on the damp bark. Mustard yellow staircases spiraled up the trunks of trees. Mushrooms like stars, or delicate corals, bloomed in black leaf molds. Weird mottled toadstools, purple and brown, thrived in the dark embrace of the roots.

"Rain, rain, rain, nothing but rain," said the sharp-nosed hedgehog, walking gingerly along the edge of a deep wagon rut. "I *hate* rain."

"Acorns," said the round white piglet splashing along in the rut. "Hot, roasted, *buttered* acorns."

"Oh, for a clean fluffy towel," said the moray eel, swimming gracefully through the damp air beside them.

"Pigs," said Fairfax bitterly, "*enjoy* mud. . . ."

"But not *this* much mud," protested Quadroped.

"And eels," Fairfax continued, "like water."

"But not mud," said Morrag equably. "We are all miserable, Fairfax, but I will allow that you are the most miserable of all." He smiled benevolently upon the sodden hedgehog, revealing a mouthful of needlelike teeth.

"If I were a *magical* pig," said Quadroped, "I could make the sun come out."

"Well, you aren't," said Fairfax nastily. "And besides, the sun is dead. If she were still alive we'd have seen her by now." He paused to remove a wet leaf from his spines.

"It *has* been raining for an awfully long time," said Quadroped.

"A week, to be exact," said Morrag. "Before that we had the storms."

Quadroped shuddered, remembering the weeks of rain and hurricane-force winds. Travel had been virtually impossible. They had spent many days huddled miserably together in abandoned barns and hollow trees.

Food had been scarce. The blackberries by the wayside wore jackets of blue-green mold. Squirrels stole the nuts the winds blew down. Nor were the mushrooms a safe source of food. Loathsome species, cunningly disguised to look harmless, abounded. Despite his lifelong training in mushroom collection, Quadroped had feared he might poison his friends.

Thirst had also plagued them on their journey. Puddles abounded, springs and ditches overflowed their basins, but nowhere was the water clean and fit to drink. Clouds of brown mud, churned up by rushing water, polluted every pool.

"I'm hungry," said Quadroped.

"You're *always* hungry," said Fairfax.

"We should reach your home soon, Quadro," Morrag said. "You can eat then."

Quadroped sighed happily, his spirits cheered by the thought of home. Even if it *had* been raining for months the world was still a safe and pleasant place to live. He had freed the Black Unicorn and made peace with Ravenor. There would never be the terrible threat of war again.

"I can't wait to get home," said Quadroped. "The second crop of acorns will be ripe and Mother and Father will be so proud of me."

"Vanity, vanity," mourned Morrag.

Quadroped blushed. "Well, I *am* a hero now," he said. "I've gone all the way to Ravenor without getting killed. They can't say I'm too little to go adventuring anymore. Although," he added, "I don't really *want* to go anywhere just yet. I want to sit under the acorn tree and eat acorns."

"If you ate less," said Morrag, "you might become lovely and slender." He twisted to admire the way his tail rippled and shone in the rain. The water glistened on his smooth skin like a net of diamonds. "It's a shame that all this healthful exercise has not decreased your rotundity."

"Pigs are *supposed* to be round," said Quadroped.

"Do pigs have dry houses?" Fairfax asked suddenly.

"Very dry," said Quadroped. "With toasty warm fires and soft beds with woolly blankets."

"Ah," said Fairfax noncommittally.

"Dry," said Morrag. "But probably not very clean."

Quadroped ignored the insult. Conversation lapsed and the three companions trudged on, each content with his own thoughts.

*   *   *

The cloud-shrouded sun was low in the sky when they turned off the road onto the grassy track that led to Quadroped's home. The air was damper and chillier, the wind had picked up and blew water from the forest canopy into their faces.

Quadroped gave an excited squeal as soon as he sighted the familiar, lopsided outline of his parents' twig hut through the trees. He pricked up his ears and galloped full speed down the path crying: "Mother? Father? I'm home, I'm *home*!"

At the front door he slid to an abrupt halt and noticed for the first time that the house was dark. No smoke curled up from the small brick chimney. The windows were closed and dusty. "Mother?" he called. There was no reply. The clearing was quiet. The chattering birds seemed far away.

Bitter disappointment was slowly replaced by uneasiness. *They're probably out back and didn't hear me*, Quadroped thought, trying not to panic. *Or maybe they've gone out for a while. They didn't know we'd arrive today.*

Quadroped scampered around to the back of the house, where a neatly fenced vegetable garden sloped down toward the still weedy waters of the duck pond. There was no sign of his parents. A ring of white mushrooms had sprouted beside the kitchen stoop, their stems buried in brown rotting leaves. Worse, there were weeds growing in the garden. Then a tomato plant rustled and Quadroped found himself staring into the fiery red eyes of a large box turtle.

"Morrag, Fairfax, help!" Quadroped cried, running back toward the road. Mother never allowed turtles into the garden, they ate out the bottoms of tomatoes.

"Quadro, what's wrong?" asked Morrag, swimming quickly toward the distraught pig. "What's happened? Where are your parents?"

"Gone!" said Quadroped.

"They'll probably be back soon," said Morrag.

Quadroped shook his head. "No," he said. "They're gone and something terrible has happened to them." He explained his theory about the turtles. He felt like crying but managed to keep calm. "We have to find them," he said. "And soon."

Morrag exchanged a look with Fairfax. "I think," he said, "that we should have a talk with this turtle."

"He'll talk," said Fairfax, and scurried grimly ahead.

Morrag and Quadroped followed but decided to check the house out first. "For," said Morrag, "they may have left a note."

The back door was unlocked and Quadroped pushed it open with his nose. Morrag entered and blinked at the scent of mold that assailed his fastidious nostrils. He flicked the tip of his tail over the kitchen table. The wood shone darkly through the dust.

Quadroped looked around. *Maybe they've been murdered,* he thought.

Quadroped's house was one story high and not very big. It had three small bedrooms, a family room into which the front door opened, and a kitchen with a big table where the family ate its meals. The kitchen door opened onto the backyard with its vegetable garden and duck pond. Quadroped and Morrag went through the house room by room, Quadroped looking for spilled blood or signs of a struggle, and Morrag, more sensibly, seeking a note.

Quadroped's bedroom was impeccably neat. His mother had fulfilled a fond wish and cleaned it in his absence. The bookshelves, filled with tales of adventure, were covered in cobwebs. There was no note to be found.

After searching his brothers' bedroom Quadroped reluctantly entered his parents' room. Their bed was neatly made under its old patchwork quilt. On the table beside it lay a book, half-opened, and a glass of water with green slime growing on top. Against one wall was a small fireplace. A puddle of gray water, with an ashy scum on top, had seeped under the fire screen onto the braided rug. Quadroped went over and shut the flue. The flowers on the mantelpiece were dead and dry. His mother's collection of feathers was dusty.

Quadroped went to his father's desk and began to go through the papers and books piled messily on top of it.

He found all sorts of things, including half a dried hornet's nest being used as a pencil holder, but no note. He went through the desk drawers one by one. In the bottom drawer he found a necklace he had made for his mother. It consisted of different-colored yarns all braided together. An acorn, a piece of colored glass, a seashell, and a bit of stone hung from it. It wasn't very beautiful but she had liked to wear it.

Quadroped's vision blurred with tears. He hurried out, shutting the door firmly behind him. For a moment he stood in the hall, head down. Then he shook his tears away and joined Morrag in the kitchen. Together they went out into the garden where Fairfax had succeeded in locating the turtle.

The turtle was drawn tightly into its orange and black shell. Occasionally its sharp yellow beak opened and it hissed. It did not seem inclined to cooperate with the hedgehog whose long pale snout poked into its face.

"Where are my parents?" Quadroped asked, coming up to the turtle. "Please tell me. Are they in trouble?"

The turtle slowly extended its black wrinkled neck and glared at Quadroped. "Why should I tell you anything?" it asked.

"Hah, then you *do* know something," said Fairfax.

"I don't *like* pigs," said the turtle, and withdrew under the rim of its shell.

"We try to keep them out of the garden," Quadroped explained. "But some always get in anyway." He looked at the turtle. "You wouldn't have any tomatoes to eat at all if we didn't plant them," he said.

The turtle was not moved to reply. Morrag darted around the back of the creature and seized it up in his jaws. The turtle dangled in midair. "Talk, reptile," Morrag said. "Or I'll drop you."

"In a pot of boiling water," said Fairfax. "Yum, yum."

"Put me down!" said the turtle. "I'll tell you what I know. If you break my carapace, I'll die."

"Talk first," said Fairfax.

"Oh, let him down," said Quadroped. "You've frightened him."

"I'll do more than that if he doesn't cooperate," said Morrag, but he set the turtle down. Fairfax snuffled in disgust.

"Your parents left two or three weeks ago," the turtle told Quadroped. "They were out in the garden repairing the fence. I was watching to see if they made any mistakes but they didn't. All of a sudden they got this funny look on their faces and stopped working. They put up their ears as though they were listening to something. I listened, but all I could hear was the wind. Then they just stopped what they were doing and walked away into the woods. They didn't say anything, just left. They looked as if they were sleepwalking."

Quadroped gulped and felt a stomachache coming on. "Didn't they try to run away or fight? My father is a magician, you know."

"I know," said the turtle bitterly. "It isn't just the fence that keeps us out and the insects away from your crops. Your mother isn't too bad at spells herself. No, they just left. Although, come to think of it, I think your mother was crying."

"I knew it," wailed Qaudroped, wringing his hooves. "They've been kidnapped. Some horrible creature has lured them away. Maybe they're dead. Maybe something has *eaten* them." He wrinkled his snout in despair and the tears escaped at last.

"Now look what you've done, you horrible turtle," Morrag said.

"I haven't done anything," said the turtle as it began to crawl slowly away. "It's probably all the piglet's fault. He set the Monster of Ravenor free. His parents told us *all* about it. He's made enemies and his people are going to suffer for it."

The turtle reached the edge of its hole and turned to glare at Quadroped. "*All* of the fairy pigs are gone," he said. "And whoever took them will be coming for you as well."

"*Who'll* be coming?" cried Morrag, darting forward, but the turtle had already slipped into its hole and was gone.

Supper that evening was a dreary affair. The remainder of the day had been spent searching fruitlessly for clues about the fate of the fairy pigs or the direction in which they had gone. But the rains had destroyed any evidence outside and there was nothing inside either. When it grew too dark to do more they withdrew into the house. Morrag built a fire on the living-room hearth while Fairfax poked around in the kitchen for food. Quadroped made up the beds. The linen was damp and mildewed.

Quadroped lay awake for a long time that night. He had thought his adventures were over. *It's not fair*, Quadroped thought. *I did my best. I had to free the Black Unicorn, Ravenor was dying.*

Quadroped recalled the desolate land of Ravenor with a shudder. In the Warlord Goriel's garden, high in the Crystalline Mountains, a pair of immortal goldfish had gasped for centuries in a dried-up pond.

At least someone will be happy to be wet again, thought Quadroped as tears dripped off his snout. He wondered briefly if the peculiar weather had anything to do with the Black Unicorn's efforts to restore Ravenor.

Quadroped stared up into the darkness. Warm sticky tears tickled his cheeks. His pillow became damp and uncomfortable. He wished Glasgerion were near to comfort him. Glasgerion always knew what to do. But Glasgerion was far away in Essylt, happily married to Morragwen.

"Oh, Mother, Father, where *are* you?" he asked aloud. "Please be all right. Please come back. Please?" In the hours before dawn he cried himself to sleep.

Quadroped awoke the next morning to the sound of water dripping off the eaves and splattering onto the windowsills. It was another dark, overcast day. His head ached and his eyes were sore and red. He jumped out of bed, shivering in the damp air, and hurried into the kitchen. Someone had lit the old iron stove and the room was comfortably warm. Fairfax was laying out a breakfast of stale bread and jam. Morrag was staring out a newly cleaned window.

Quadroped jumped up on a stool and reached for the jam. Morrag forestalled him with a hiss. "Wash your hooves first, please," he said.

Quadroped went to the sink and washed his face and ears too for good measure. Then he returned to the jam. It was never wise, he reflected, licking a sticky hoof, to brood on an empty stomach. Fairfax apparently shared this philosophy for he was devouring the bread.

"Aren't you going to have any?" Quadroped asked Morrag, pausing thoughtfully before the last mouthful of jam was gone.

"No," said the eel in an abstracted way. He rippled his body and turned. "The duck pond was well supplied in minnows. When you're done eating, Quadro, we should talk."

"I'm done," said Quadroped, pushing away the jam. Fairfax continued to nibble at the stale bread but his black eyes gleamed attentively.

"I've been trying to decide all morning how we should go about finding your parents," Morrag said. "I don't think we can do it on our own. Since time *may* be of the essence I don't think we should waste it running around the forest looking for clues. Our best plan would be to head back to Essylt and get help from our friends there."

"But that will take *months*," said Quadroped.

"It could take longer than that on our own," said Morrag. "In Essylt we'll have powerful magicians like Reander and Morragwen, as well as a huge research library, at our disposal. Also, we'll be able to contact sources in Ravenor if there is no help to be found in the Kingdoms."

"But my parents could be *dying*!"

"Hedgehogs," said Fairfax, "do not fight well."

"Fairfax is right," said Morrag. "You've told us that your father is a magician, Quadro. If he's a full-grown boar he's a formidable fighter as well. What could we do against something that could kidnap *him*? With Reander and Morragwen on our side we could tackle anything.''

"You're right," said Quadroped. He looked fretful and unhappy.

"Cheer up," said Morrag. "We may learn something more along the way."

"We should go soon," said Fairfax, looking a trifle grim. "Something may be looking for Quadro."

Fairfax's observation galvanized them into action. They quickly cleaned up the kitchen, closed all the windows and chimney flues, and stripped the beds. Then they locked the doors behind them and set off down the long road toward Essylt.

The journey north proved slow and uncomfortable in the extreme. Morrag had taken the turtle's warning to heart and insisted that they keep to the side of the road. After two days of slogging through muddy, tangled undergrowth, Quadroped had had enough. His skin was scratched and stung by nettles. His muscles all ached from the effort of climbing in and out of deep ditches.

The sun had sullenly refused to shine. Each day the clouds seemed to sink a bit lower. On the third day Quadroped awoke from dreams of his family's demise to find the world shrouded in fog. Ghostly shreds of white draped over the trees or coiled, snakelike, along the ground.

It will rain until the world drowns, Quadroped thought. *If Essylt were downhill we could build a boat and wait for the roads to flood.* Fairfax lay curled against him for warmth. His short stubby spines tickled Quadroped's skin.

"I think we should travel on the road today," Quadroped said. "We've been traveling for days and I don't think we've come very far. The forest is still in sight, or it would be if the clouds weren't hiding it. At this rate we'll *never* reach Essylt."

"It's too dangerous," said Morrag.

"My parents *need* me," said Quadroped. "They could be dead by the time we reach Essylt. We *have* to move faster than this."

Fairfax uncurled and twitched his spines a bit. "Hedgehogs," he said, "hibernate in winter. The leaves have turned color already. We must reach Essylt quickly. Also," he added, "fog will hide the road today and we may get lost."

"Very well," said Morrag. "We'll travel on the road. But don't blame *me* if something horrible kidnaps Quadro." Quadroped shivered but resolutely got up and began to climb up the steep bank to the road.

They moved faster that day and soon the forest was no longer in view. By nightfall they had reached an old Water Mill on the Little Meander. The huge wooden waterwheel at its side was still, for the hour was late and the river was almost in flood. The Little Meander was high above the Mill's lowermost windows, swirling muddily around its foundations. The current looked terribly swift.

The Water Mill had a large cobble courtyard with a woodshed along one side. Warm yellow light streamed from the windows past lacey white curtains. Smoke curled up from the chimney, a gray plume against the indigo sky.

"It looks warm," said Quadroped hopefully. They had stayed in such places on the trip from Essylt and had always found a warm welcome.

"I don't like it," said Morrag. "Let's go on. We'll find a haystack somewhere around here."

"What's wrong with it?" asked Quadroped, looking carefully around the courtyard. Morrag was ancient and wise, his warnings could not be discounted. Yet everything seemed perfectly normal, neither messy nor overly neat. Not even Quadroped's sensitive nose could detect anything wrong. The air smelled of clean water, spiced with cinnamon and wood smoke.

"Nothing," said Morrag. "It's just . . . I'd prefer to go on."

"Bah," said Fairfax. "I am going to knock." He walked up the steps and thumped his body hard against the door. The soft thud that resulted could barely be heard. Undeterred, Fairfax balanced himself on his hind paws, front paws braced on the door, and tried to poke his nose into the mail slot. This maneuver also failed, for the hedgehog was rather short.

"Help," said Fairfax, "would be appreciated." His dark little eyes glittered balefully at Morrag.

Quadroped paused for a moment, but the promise of a warm supper overcame caution. He joined Fairfax on the doorstep and rapped a hoof against the door. This made more noise but the wood was thick and it was doubtful if he could be heard by anyone inside. He was reluctant to shout, it seemed so impolite.

"Come away from there," said Morrag. "We don't know anything about these people. If we must stay let's sleep in the woodshed."

"But there's a fire in there," said Quadroped. "And they're cooking *food*. You could reach the doorbell. Oh, Morrag, please try?" He looked at Morrag with mournful purple eyes. It was an expression he had perfected early in life.

"Oh, very well," said Morrag. "It *would* be nice to have a hot bath. They might even have fish for dinner."

"Ugh, fish!" said Quadroped.

Morrag glided forward and lifted the knocker in his mouth. After three short raps they heard the sound of voices and a pair of heavy footsteps coming to the door. They stepped back, suddenly nervous, and huddled together in the shadows. The door swung inward, bathing them in golden light. A tall, slightly stooped man stood in the doorway. His floury white apron identified him as the Miller.

"Who is it?" the Mill Wife called from inside the house.

"Animals," said the Miller. "Cold, wet, and hungry, by the looks of them."

"What sort of animals?"

"A piglet, a hedgehog, and a snake."

"A snake?" the Mill Wife's voice rose in a shriek. "Not in *my* house."

"Oh please, sir," said Quadroped. "Morrag's not a snake. He's a moray eel. He's been enchanted so that he can live on land."

"Ah," said the Miller, looking only mildly surprised. "It's an eel, dear."

"Oh, that's all right then," said the Mill Wife. "Let them come in."

"It feels perfectly safe now," said Morrag softly.

The Miller stood aside and held the door open as Quadroped, Fairfax, and Morrag trooped into the front hall. He closed the door after them and led them to a warm sitting room furnished with comfortably soft armchairs and a sofa. There was a fire burning in the fireplace. A plump, gray-haired woman sat knitting beside it. She looked up as they came in and smiled.

"Hello," said the Mill Wife.

"Good evening, ma'am," said Morrag formally. "Our thanks for your hospitality. I am Morrag, and these are my companions, Fairfax and Quadroped."

"You can call me Quadro," said Quadroped shyly.

"Would you like some dinner then, Quadro?" asked the Mill Wife with a smile.

"Oh, *yes*," said Quadroped eagerly. He blushed and added, "That is, if it isn't an inconvenience. We don't want to be any trouble."

"Oh, it's no trouble," said the Mill Wife. "We get travelers here all the time, especially this fall. The cold and the rain drive them indoors." She got up and left for the kitchen.

"Have a seat," said the Miller, seating himself in an armchair beside the fire. He picked up a book and began to read, ignoring his visitors completely. Quadroped, Fairfax, and Morrag climbed onto the sofa and snuggled deep into its cushions.

Several sandwiches and a slice of apple pie later, Quadroped and his friends were shown into a bedroom and tucked up in a huge four-poster bed. "Good night," said the Mill Wife, turning out the lights.

"Good night," said Quadroped softly and promptly fell asleep.

Quadroped dreamed, and knew he was dreaming, that he heard a voice calling to him late in the night, so he jumped out of bed. Moonlight pushed through the curtains, limning the room silver. The air quivered around him with half-perceived sound, as of belled feet slowly dancing. Quadroped walked quietly into the hall. The Miller and his Wife were in the living room, talking about killing their guests.

"We might as well let them go," the Miller said. "They don't have any money. The season's been good to us. It's well to let a few get away so that no one suspects us."

"But we could eat the eel and the piglet," said the Mill Wife. "There'll be famine before spring. Food will be more precious than gold. They'll keep well if we smoke them."

Quadroped walked on. The couple did not notice him. He thought that he ought to be frightened but it was only a dream and someone was calling for him. He could hear the voice clearly now, it was coming from the cellar. Briefly he wondered how he knew there *was* a cellar. Then he realized that he was making it all up anyway.

He found the door to the cellar under the staircase in the front hall and pushed at it with his nose. It opened easily, revealing a flight of steps going steeply down into the darkness. Quadroped went down the stairs, leaving the door open behind him so that the hall lamp could light the steps.

The voice was crying for help now. It was weak and ragged. Quadroped's heart ached to hear it. He hurried down into the basement. The air here was cold. He could hear the river roaring outside.

I'm below the Little Meander, Quadroped thought. He imagined water seeping through the stone blocks, eating its way into the cellar, trying to drown the prisoner. For he suddenly knew that it was a prisoner calling to him.

"Quadroped, help me."

The voice was softer, which was odd, as Quadroped was now closer, but things were always a little odd in dreams and Quadroped was not perturbed. He looked around. Above his head was a small window, half underwater. Silver light shone in. Quadroped assumed it was moonlight. He wondered how it could shine through the heavy clouds that had covered the heavens for days. In the far wall he saw a stack of empty flour sacks. The top of a short wooden door was just visible above them. Quadroped walked over and began to pull the sacks away with his mouth.

"What are you doing? Stop!" cried a faint, gurgling voice from under the very last sack, which was mildewed and muddy.

Quadroped moved the last sack and managed to make out a gelatinous blob in a damp patch of earth. "Hello. What are you?" he asked.

"A slime mold," replied the creature. "What are you doing?"

"Hello, Sly Mold," said Quadroped. "I'm moving the sacks so I can open the door. Please move, or the door will squash you."

"*What* did you call me?" asked the slime mold.

"Sly Mold," said Quadroped, a trifle impatiently. "That's what you said your name was."

"Sly Mold," repeated the slime mold slowly. "I like it. I really do! Thank you!"

"You're welcome," said Quadroped politely. "Please move."

"Why?"

"Because there's someone in there who needs help," said Quadroped. "Can't you hear him calling?"

"No," said the Sly Mold.

"Well, it is my dream," said Quadroped. He began to to push open the door.

The Sly Mold quickly oozed aside. "I wouldn't go in there if I were you," it said. "I really wouldn't."

Quadroped ignored it and walked in. He found himself in a tiny dark room that smelled particularly foul. A small slit in the mildew-spotted wall let in a thin shaft of light. Against the far wall crouched a gaunt, unshaven figure manacled wrist and ankle with iron chains. The bones of his skull pressed tightly against their thin covering of flesh. His eyes were wide and pleading.

"Water," gasped the ragged man. "Quadroped, bring me water."

The Sly Mold said, "I wouldn't if I were you."

Chapter Two

Quadroped walked closer to the ragged man. His flesh was wrinkled and gray with dust. A tattered shirt, bereft of all its buttons, revealed a chest so thin the ribs stood out. His wrists and ankles were knobby protuberances on wasted limbs. The manacles had rubbed his flesh raw. The prisoner rattled his heavy chains.

"Please, I'm so thirsty," said the ragged man in a hoarse, dry voice. "Water."

"Where can I get water, Sly Mold?" Quadroped asked.

The slime mold quivered in its agitation. "There's a bucket over by the cellar steps to catch the river when it seeps in," it said. "But this really isn't a good idea. I think you should reconsider."

"Well, I don't," said Quadroped. "All he wants is a drink of water. It must be horrible to be so thirsty when you can hear the river going past on the other side of the wall."

"Water, Quadro, water," said the ragged man, and clanked his chains.

Quadroped turned and ran over to the cellar stairs. In a

few moments he found the bucket and saw that it was indeed half-filled with water. It was too big and too heavy to carry in his mouth. Quadroped tried to push it along the slimy stone floor but the pavement blocks were uneven and the bucket seemed destined to spill.

I shall have to find some sort of ladle I can carry, Quadroped decided. The ragged man's weak cries for water were beginning to get on his nerves. He was scared that the Miller would hear them.

Quadroped looked around and eventually spied a flour measure lying beside a big barrel. "Please hush," he called to the ragged man. "I'm coming." He seized the measure's handle in his mouth.

The ragged man grabbed the flour measure from Quadroped and drank so greedily that water spilled down his chin. Flesh, white as snow, shone through the dirt where the water had run. Quadroped looked at the man. He was less shrunken and wizened now, as if the water had plumped him up and filled in all the wrinkles. He seemed younger, barely more than a youth.

"One more, one more, Quadro," begged the ragged man. His voice was stronger, less harsh, and with more of a grating whine. "Have pity on me. For years I have lain here, bound in iron chains, with the sound of the river in my ears."

"He's had enough," said the Sly Mold earnestly. "You don't know what you're doing. Young pigs should heed their elders." It flowed distractedly back and forth, making a horrid sucking sound.

"Oh, Sly Mold," said Quadroped. "Another drink can't do any harm. It's only water and this is only a dream."

He picked up the flour measure and fetched another scoop of water. The ragged man grabbed the measure away and drank with greedy slurps. In an instant the measure was dry.

Quadroped looked carefully at the ragged man. The water had certainly had a miraculous effect. His hair no longer hung limply on his brow but curled and gleamed like corn silk. He retained a porcelain complexion but his lips and cheeks shone red. His pale green eyes glittered in the dim light. His face was thin, delicately boned, full of points and angles.

"Another," said the ragged man, in a voice rich and deep. "Bring me another, Quadroped."

"How do you know my name?" asked Quadroped. He misliked the way the last request had been phrased as a command.

"It's your dream," said the ragged man.

"Then why don't I know yours?"

The ragged man shrugged. "My name is Avice, and I'm dying of thirst. A third, bring me a third little hoggling. I'll ask for no more, I promise."

"Well," said Quadroped doubtfully. The changes the water had effected were a little frightening. The man no longer seemed pitiable or weak. Still, he could not see that it would do any harm. The chains that bound the man were thick and very strong. He walked back to the bucket with the flour measure. The Sly Mold slithered after him.

"If you do as he asks," said the Sly Mold, "you'll regret it. The Miller wouldn't use such heavy chains if this were a safe, normal man."

Quadroped hesitated. There was some truth in that, and the slime mold seemed quite anxious. "Why do you care?" he asked.

"You gave me a name," said the Sly Mold. "I want to earn it by helping you. Go back to bed, it's safer."

Quadroped seriously considered doing just that. But as he stood beside the bucket, trying to decide what to do, a shadow fell across the stairs, plunging the cellar into darkness.

"The cellar door is open," the Mill Wife cried from the top of the stairs. "One of the animals must be down there. The pesky thing will be up to some mischief. We should have killed them. Hurry."

Heavy footsteps echoed overhead. The Miller and his wife began to come down the stairs, moving cautiously lest they trip.

They'll kill me, thought Quadroped, looking for a place to hide. *Help*.

"The third drink," Avice called. "Give it to me. I'll help you if I can."

Why not? thought Quadroped desperately. He grabbed up the flour measure and dipped it once more in the bucket.

The Miller and his Wife reached the bottom step and raised their lantern high. "Stop, pig!" they cried in unison when they saw what Quadroped was up to. "Desist!"

"I wouldn't stop now," said the Sly Mold. For once Quadroped took its advice.

Quadroped dashed toward the prisoner, the Miller and his Wife close behind him. Avice stretched out his hands, his mouth open, his eyes blazing with hope. The Miller grabbed at Quadroped's tail and he tripped, losing his grip on the flour measure. Water splashed forward, drenching Avice's face and flying into his eager mouth.

"Alas," cried the Mill Wife. "What have you done, stupid pig?"

"Freed Avice," said the Sly Mold gloomily.

"Woe," cried the Miller. "All is lost."

"But he's all chained up," said Quadroped. His knees hurt and he wished that the dream would end.

"Not anymore," said the Sly Mold.

The sound of bells increased until Quadroped was forced to flatten his ears. The room trembled, grew cold and burning hot. To his considerable dismay, Quadroped realized that there was Old Magic at work in the room.

Avice rose to his feet, spreading his arms wide. The fetters burst from his wrists and ankles and fell with much noise to the floor. Thin lips, blood red against marble flesh, twisted in an unpleasantly gloating smile.

"The fetters have burst," he said and laughed. "Once more Avice runs free!"

What have I done? Quadroped thought, eyeing Avice fearfully. His mind, desperately trying to perceive the forces being unleashed with its limited senses, imbued the stationary flagstones with liquid motion. He felt rather ill and very frightened as the floor undulated slowly beneath him. The air smelled faintly of mangoes. Belatedly he realized that the Sly Mold had been right; aiding Avice had *not* been a good idea.

Avice turned his cold green eyes upon Quadroped and stretched out a slender hand. Quadroped quickly retreated out of reach.

"Oh come now, hoggling," said Avice. "Surely you're not frightened of *me*? Why, you're the savior of Ravenor." He chuckled in high good humor.

I am also a small pig, thought Quadroped reasonably. *I wish I knew how to wake up.* Avice looked both merry and dangerous.

"For each of the drinks you gave to me, I shall give some gift to thee," rhymed Avice. "I do you the first favor now."

The Miller and his Wife had sidled away toward the steps. Now they turned and ran. Avice pounced, grabbing each by the back of the neck in his long slender hands. He jerked them both to a quivering halt.

"You two are coming with me," said Avice. "I know just the place for you. Several of your former 'guests' are eager and waiting to greet you."

"No, no," wailed the Mill Wife. "Have mercy on a poor old woman. I only did what my husband bade me. Take him instead."

"Ah, don't listen to her," moaned the Miller. "She drove me to a life of crime with her shrewish ways. She couldn't be satisfied with an honest profit, always she had to have more. Take her if you must have revenge."

"I'm taking you both," said Avice, unmoved by their pleas. "And Quadro is going to bed."

As he spoke he began to grow until he had to bend at the waist to avoid the ceiling. He tucked the Miller under his left arm and the Mill Wife under his right. With a clap of thunder he was gone.

The roar of the river grew louder in Quadroped's ears, until he could hear nothing else. *The wall's caved in,* he thought in despair. Water swirled around him, tugging and pushing, telling him to wake up.

*   *   *

Quadroped opened his eyes and sat up. Fairfax was prodding him in the stomach with his strong burrower's paws, roughly requesting that he rise. Watery gray light came in through the windows, and birds were arguing in the trees outside.

"Oh," said Quadroped, rubbing his eyes. "What a terrible dream."

"Get up," said Fairfax, walking on him. " 'Awake, arise, or be forever fallen!' There's breakfast," the hedgehog added. "In the kitchen."

This last remark produced the desired effect. Quadroped scrambled down from the bed and hastened to the dresser. There he climbed upon a chair and washed face, hooves, and ears in the washbasin the Mill Wife had provided. The water was freezing cold and the task unpleasant but Morrag was particularly strict in the morning.

"Where's the Mill Wife?" Quadroped asked as he trotted into the kitchen. Morrag was up on the counter stirring a bowl with a long wooden spoon. Fairfax was setting the table. Of the Miller and his Wife there was no sign.

"Gone," said Fairfax. "Go get the milk."

"Out," said Morrag. "Find me a skillet."

Quadroped hurried around looking for the desired objects. Then he helped Morrag butter the skillet and watched as the eel prepared omelets.

"Where did they go?" asked Quadroped anxiously. His nightmare had a lingering effect and he was worried about them. He also felt guilty for dreaming that they were murderers.

"To market," said Morrag, setting the eggs on the table. "Fairfax found a note. They've told us to eat what we want and not to worry about cleaning up afterward."

"Goody," said Quadroped.

"However," Morrag continued with a repressive glare. "We will of *course* wash our dishes, change our linen, and tidy our room."

"I get to dry," said Fairfax quickly.

"Fine," said Morrag. "Quadro can wash and I'll put things away. *I*," he added as Quadroped began to protest, "can reach the cupboards."

"I *hate* washing dishes," said Quadroped. He gloomily gobbled down his eggs. The joy had gone out of breakfast.

An hour later they left the Water Mill behind and followed the river road north. At least, Morrag insisted that they were going north. Quadroped was not convinced. He could smell salt on the freshening breeze and the sea lay away to the south.

By midafternoon their road left the Little Meander behind and began to twist through a hilly pastureland littered with tumbled-down boulders. Herds of sheep could be seen grazing in the distance but they never strayed very close. Water ran in rivulets down the steep slopes. The road turned into a stream, but the sandy soil stayed firm beneath their feet. The wind picked up toward evening. The road itself was sheltered by the downs but they could hear the wind whistling overhead, sending dark masses of clouds scuttling toward the horizon.

The road began to climb steeply upward. The tangy, iodine scent of drying seaweed grew stronger. At length they reached the top of the rise and the whole landscape came suddenly into view. Below them lay the downs and beyond them, fringed by sandy dunes, the gray expanse of the sea.

"I *knew* it," said Quadroped. "We've gone backward. That's the Southern Sea." He sat down and stared disconsolately ahead.

"We have *not* gone backward," said Morrag crossly. "We've been traveling steadily north. Whistlewood is on a peninsula, Quadro. That's the northernmost inlet of the Southern Sea ahead of us."

"Oh," said Quadroped. He had never paid much attention to his geography lessons, preferring to daydream instead.

They stopped that night in the lee of a rock slide, halfway up a long low hill. From their camp Quadroped could look out to the west where the sun was setting, visible at last as a great red ball half-dressed in purple clouds. After a while a silver moon sailed out to take his sister's place in the sky.

* * *

Quadroped dreamed again that night. A voice was calling his name. He wished it would go away. He was tired of having nightmares.

Quadroped got up. The voice was coming from the top of the rock slide. With a small sigh he began to climb. Loose rocks shifted and slipped under hoof. Pebbles rolled noisily down. Fifteen minutes later he staggered, breathless, to the top of the hill and came face to face with Avice.

"Oh, no," said Quadroped. "Not *again*?"

Avice grinned, his teeth shone white and sharp. His pale blond hair gleamed in the moonlight. His eyes were sea-foam green.

Avice's slender form was gaudily dressed. Long, artfully tattered sleeves rustled in the wind. Bright jewels gleamed and glittered about his person. Quadroped wished that it were daylight so that he could see the whole effect. The moonlight washed the colors away and made them hard to see.

"What did you do with the Miller and his Wife?" asked Quadroped.

"You don't want to know," said Avice. He sat down on a boulder and leaned forward, arms resting on his knees. "Did you get the note they left you?"

"Yes," said Quadroped. "Morrag made us wash the dishes anyway."

"A pity then, that they won't be back to notice."

"Why are you here?" asked Quadroped. "I don't like dreaming about you."

"I'm here to help you, Quadroped," said Avice.

"Why?" asked Quadroped.

Avice chuckled. Quadroped liked the way laughter flickered over his face, smoothing his sharp features and making his eyes sparkle.

"What a suspicious little hoggling you are," said Avice. "You set me free through acts of kindness, acts I want to repay. Do you find that sinister?"

"I don't know," said Qaudroped. "I don't think I

should be talking to strangers. Glasgerion warned me
not to.''

"You haven't heeded his warnings in the past," said
Avice. "Why should you heed them now?"

"Because I'm not sure I trust you," said Quadroped
boldly. "And I'm not sure this is really a dream. I wish
you would go away and let me sleep. I'm tired. Morrag
always wakes us up before dawn."

Avice smiled, but his green eyes narrowed. "I've two
more favors to repay," he said. "Going away isn't a favor
I had in mind. I'll take it amiss if you refuse my help."

"I only gave you a drink of water," said Quadroped.

"Three drinks," said Avice. "I don't like being in
debt."

"You're not," said Quadroped. "You got rid of the
Miller and his Wife. They were planning to *eat* us."

"Ah, but they had decided not to," said Avice. "And
it was but one favor after all."

"They might," said Quadroped, "have changed their
minds. I don't *want* any more favors. I'm sleepy."

"Don't be angry, Quadro," said Avice. "You *need* my
help."

"Don't," muttered Quadroped.

Avice ignored him. "What would you say," he asked,
"if I told you that I knew where your parents were?"

Quadroped was suddenly wide awake. "*Where?*" he
cried. "Where are my parents? Are they hurt? Tell me!"

"Patience, patience," said Avice, half closing his eyes
and leaning back on his hands. "I thought that would
interest you. They're in the Fleshless Land."

"The Fleshless Land?"

Quadroped repeated this slowly. It was a terrible, frightening name. He imagined his parents as bleached skeletons
scattered about beneath some ghastly tree.

"Are . . . Are they *dead*?" whispered Quadroped. He
took a deep breath and closed his eyes, afraid to learn the
answer.

"No, you ignorant pig," said Avice. "Didn't your parents teach you anything? Nieve has them."

Quadroped let out his breath and felt dizzy. His parents were *alive!* "Who's Nieve?" he asked.

"The Queen of the Fleshless Land," said Avice. "Ruler of all those who've been violently slain."

"But you said they were alive," said Quadroped.

"I said they weren't dead," said Avice. "They're in a Land of the Dead, but they're not just souls. They are still in the bodies they had in this world. That means you can bring them back."

"Oh," said Quadroped.

"Look," said Avice, sitting up straight, "I haven't time to explain the cosmography of death to you right now. If you want to rescue your parents you must go the Fleshless Land. Tonight."

"But I don't *want* to go there," said Quadroped.

"There is no other way to rescue your parents," said Avice. "I thought you loved them. Nieve's halls are not always a pleasant place to be, especially when she's angry."

Quadroped gulped and flattened his ears. "I do want to help them," he said. "I want them back more than anything. But I'm scared." He looked around. The night seemed blacker and the shadows more threatening.

Avice reached into a pocket and withdrew something small and round. "Here," he said. "Have a sugarplum. You'll feel better when you've eaten. It's the night that makes you so timid."

Quadroped eyed the sugarplum with misgiving. Taking food from strangers was forbidden. It looked plump and tempting, dusted in sugar crystals. He reached out his hooves and took the proffered sweet. As he munched he began to feel much better. There was something so normal and sane about food. Avice seemed suddenly safer.

Only nice people, thought Quadroped, *know how to treat pigs properly.*

"Thank you," said Quadroped as he cleaned the last of the sugar from his hooves. "Is Nieve very angry with my parents?" he asked.

"Not with them," said Avice. "With you."

"With me?"

The sugarplum turned to lead in Quadroped's stomach. All the guilt the turtle had inspired came flooding back. "Is it because I let the Black Unicorn go?" he asked.

"That and other things," said Avice. "If you want them back we have to hurry. The Door will close at dawn."

"But how can I get them back?" Quadroped asked. "I don't have any magical powers and I'm too small to fight. I don't even have my tusks yet."

"Magic and strength wouldn't help you against Nieve," said Avice. "In her own land she is all but invincible. We shall just have to persuade her to let the Drift go."

Quadroped shivered. A fairy pig herd should be a willful, wild Sounder, not a tame and fettered Drift. "But she won't listen to me," said Quadroped. "I'm the one she's mad at."

"True," said Avice. "And your rotundity and pleasant disposition will be of no help. Nieve is notoriously immune to cuteness. However, I have some influence with the lady and I believe I can talk her round. She owes me a favor or two. That will be my third gift to you. My second shall be to take you there. Now come along, and don't dawdle." He got to his feet and turned toward the top of the hill.

"I have to get Fairfax and Morrag first," said Quadroped.

"No," said Avice. "Don't wake them. No mortal may enter the Fleshless Land alive. To get to Nieve your friends would have to die, violently."

"But you said my parents got there without dying," said Quadroped. "Will I have to die to reach them?"

"You are a fairy pig and not truly mortal," said Avice. "Your ancestors came from the Lands of the Dead. You may pass freely between the worlds. It's a power not granted to many."

"If," said Qaudroped, "people have to die to go to the Fleshless Land how can you travel there?"

"Why," said Avice, "I am not a mortal man. Now come, we've far to go and much to do before the east turns pink."

"Can't I just leave Fairfax and Morrag a note?" asked Quadroped. "They'll be awfully worried if they wake up and find me gone."

"If you tell them where you're going they'll try to follow. Do you want them to die?"

"No," said Quadroped. He looked up at Avice and shivered. "This isn't a dream anymore, is it?" he asked.

Avice chuckled and walked to the top of the hill. After a moment Quadroped scrambled after him.

They walked for an hour along the crest of the hill. All around them lay the undulating downs, black and fringed in silver against an indigo sky. To their right the sea murmured and roared as it nibbled the coastline away.

Avice strolled along, humming and whistling odd fragments of songs. Occasionally he threw back his head and stood still for a moment, gazing at the million stars twinkling above.

"I've missed the stars at night," he said.

Quadroped trotted swiftly at Avice's heels, barely able to keep up. "Why," he grumbled to himself, "do humans always walk so fast?" He began to tire and to fall behind. At last he gave up and sat down.

Avice came back and looked down at him. "Giving up so soon?" he asked.

"I'm frightened," said Quadroped. "And my feet hurt."

Avice bent and picked him up, tucking him under one arm. Quadroped felt squeezed and uncomfortable. "You don't have to hold me so tightly," he said.

Avice did not relax his grip. "I'm not letting you slip away from me now," he said. "It's far too late for second thoughts."

Avice came at last to the end of the hill and stood a moment, looking down. A ring of low mounds rose from the grassy plain, a larger mound hunched in their center.

"This was a battlefield once," said Avice. "Those who fell here lie buried within those barrows."

Quadroped considered the mounds with misgiving. He

did not like the way they crouched upon the plain, nor the way the grass whispered in the wind.

I shouldn't go any farther, he thought. *I don't know anything about Avice.* He wished that his mind felt less muddy. It was terribly difficult to think properly.

The black sea growled on the shore. Avice tucked Quadroped more firmly under his arm and descended the hill, half running to keep his balance on the steep slope. At the bottom he stopped and dropped Quadroped unceremoniously onto the ground.

"Stay there," said Avice.

Quadroped stayed and watched as Avice walked forward to the perimeter of the barrow ring. There he stopped and stood, arms at his sides. The irritating sound of bells returned, half-audible over the sounds of the sea. Avice began to tremble.

Quadroped tensed, anticipating the sensory chaos that accompanied any working of the Old Magic, but the ground remained stationary. The stars forbore to wheel around or to turn pink. The air persisted in smelling clear and cold, untainted by even the slightest hint of fruit. Not Old Magic then, whatever it was.

Maybe Avice is just having a fit of some kind, Quadroped thought. Close upon this thought came the idea of escape. Avice was paying no attention to him. It was the perfect time to retreat up the hill but did he want to?

If my parents are really in the Fleshless Land this may be my only chance to save them, Quadroped thought.

He pictured his mother surrounded by a host of grinning cadavers and shuddered. It was so terrible it had to be true. Yet, if Avice were really a friend, why had he forbidden Quadroped to wake Morrag and Fairfax and seek their advice?

They wouldn't have stopped me from saving Mother and Father. Quadroped thought. Then he recalled how protective Morrag could be. Morrag would have been highly reluctant to let Quadroped go on this mission alone.

While Quadroped pondered these difficult questions the ground around the barrow mounds began to burn. The crackle of greedy little flames interrupted his thoughts and he looked up. Dark shapes were flowing out of the mouths of the mounds, moving toward him with liquid grace.

The terrible forms reached the circling fire. The flames towered up with a noise like thunder. Heat poured forth. Red sparks flew like fireflies into the midnight sky. Avice said: "The dead stand at the doors of their tombs. The Way of the Slain is open."

Quadroped watched, in horrified amazement, as Avice walked into the raging fire. He stopped and turned. Hot winds lifted his hair. Flames licked about him, dancing along his tattered clothes, playing in his hair. His skin shone red, glistening with the heat. His eyes burned red with the fire. Slowly he stretched forth his hands.

"Come through the fire, hoggling," he said. "Come into the barrow, Quadroped, through the dark and the flickering flames."

Quadroped did not move. Avice might be fireproof, pigs were not. Incineration was doubtless a violent enough means of extinction to warrant a trip to the Fleshless Land, but it was not a means Quadroped wished to employ. Dead, he would be of small use to his parents. He turned, and discovered too late that some spell held his hooves to the ground.

"Let me go," cried Quadroped.

Avice smiled a comforting smile. "Fear not, hoggling," he said. His voice was soft and soothing. "Nothing here shall harm you. Nieve awaits you in her halls of bone. Young piglets frolic at her feet, delighting the court with their squeals. Great boars sit beside her eating acorns, and their tusks are gilt with gold. Your parents are there and waiting."

As Avice spoke, visions of all he described formed in the air before Quadroped's nose. He forgot to be afraid of Avice. He forgot about Morrag and Fairfax. He even forgot all his fears for his parents. Truly the Fleshless Land was a wonderful place.

With a happy squeal, Quadroped ran toward Avice, and was swallowed up by the flames.

*   *   *

Quadroped passed through the flames unharmed. Down a corridor of fire Avice led him. On either side the risen dead pressed against the burning wall. Clawed hands, with dirt-filled nails, reached out for the intruders. Their cavernous mouths howled black rage.

Quadroped trotted blithely past the enraged cadavers, his thoughts too full of the Fleshless Land to pay such horrors heed. Avice was with him and he was safe. Soon he would be with his parents. They approached the central barrow.

The door of the tomb was open, the massive stone lintel glowed red in the flames. A narrow passage ran into the grave, lit by a thin thread of fire.

Avice entered the mound, stooping down to avoid the low ceiling. Quadroped walked in after him, ignoring the spiders whose eyes glowed like jewels, not minding the cobwebs at all.

The passage ended in a long oval chamber. Quadroped's first impression was that the barrow was clean. No bugs crawled across the damp earth floor, no roots dangled from the ceiling stones. There was no scent of rotting flesh, nothing repulsive at all. The air was motionless, antiseptic, and sterile.

Avice straightened up and gestured dramatically at the earthen floor. "Behold the ocean steed," he said. "Behold the ship that shall sail us to Death's dark shore."

"What ship?" asked Quadroped, partially waking from his pleasant dreams and gazing around the empty room. It was dark, for the passage fires stopped short at the threshold. In the dim light Quadroped could just make out a number of lumpy objects in the middle of the floor.

"She lies before you," said Avice. "Long ago her timbers crumbled into dust, destroyed by rot and insects. Now even those agents of decay are gone, defeated by time. Nothing remains of the mighty seafarer but black earth, and the inorganic materials used in her construction."

Quadroped's eyes began to adjust to the gloom. Scattered fragments of badly corroded iron bordered a long oval of blackened earth. They might once have been nails, holding the timbers of the ship's hull to her wooden ribs.

Quadroped stepped carefully onto the black earth and walked toward a pile of objects in its middle. He found the sparse remains of a man. The shaft of a femur, a rib or two, a scapula crushed and disfigured with age. A rusted sword lay where the hip must have been. A buckle loop, a fragment of glass. By the shoulder a spearhead. Over the chest a great iron shield boss, encircled by rivets.

Above the shield boss lay a helmet of bronze that gleamed through its dulling patina. On its crest stood the figure of a golden boar. Its bristles shone in the fitful light, its ruby eyes glared forth. A face-guard was fastened below the helm; it had masked the warrior's face. Now it cradled its owner's skull, preserved from decay by the metal.

Quadroped peered into the skull's ocular orbits with detached curiosity. An eye appeared. The eye winked at him and vanished again, leaving its socket empty. Quadroped jumped and hurried back to Avice, startled out of his pleasant dream.

What am I doing here? he thought. *Pigs have no business in barrows at night.*

For the first time it occurred to him that he might not survive a trip to the Fleshless Land. He had inherited none of his people's powers. Perhaps he lacked their ability to enter the Lands of the Dead as well.

Avice stretched his hands out before him, shoulder high, palms up. "Aurgelmir, hear me, heed me, and wake. Arise from your earthen bed."

A voice fragile as autumn leaves and dry, arose from the dark oval of earth. "Who are you who disturbs our rest? Why do you come here, ill-mannered man? Flee, before it's too late."

"I am the last who remembers your name," Avice replied. "Aurgelmir, I have need of your ship. Arise now and bid me welcome."

The voice moved and centered itself on the bronze boar helm. "Alas for us," sang the cranial bones. "Alas, whose descendants are dust. The sons of our sons have all passed away. The beloved are gone. Oh, sorrow.''

"Cease your wailing," said Avice. "Such lamentations become you ill. A warrior should not wail so."

"Sorrow," said the bones a trifle more loudly. "Oh, endless woe. We lie here forgotten, alone in our hall, and strangers feel free to insult us."

Avice began to tap his foot on the ground. "Aurgelmir, rise, my patience grows short! Your defiance shall cost you dearly."

Quadroped felt sorry for the pitiful fragments of bone. Avice, he thought, was not being very nice to them. "Don't cry," he said. "I'll remember you."

"Will you?" asked the bones in a slightly cheerier tone. "Will you remember what works we did? How we feasted and how we fought?"

"Yes," said Quadroped. "I'll even look you up in the library in Essylt."

"Be quiet," said Avice. "Don't encourage him."

He walked up to the bones and drew a circle in the earth around them. "Over you I'll cast a spell. To your mortal remains I'll chain you. Sealed in your flesh you will rot in your grave, writhing as insects consume you."

An ugly yellow light began to kindle in the fragile orbital sockets of the skull. The voice now issued clearly from the region below the toothy maxilla where the voice box once had been.

"Sorrow," said the skull firmly. "Endless woe. Ask what you will, O loathesome boy. What would you have of me?"

Avice rubbed out the circle with his toe. "Passage tonight to the Fleshless Land, for myself and the hoggling beside me."

The fragments danced up into the air and placed themselves in their accustomed stations. Aurgelmir's body took form around them, his ghostly flesh shrouding, but not quite concealing, the original splinters of bone.

Quadroped backed nervously behind Avice's ankles as the huge warrior solidified before him. Aurgelmir as a pile of bones had been a safe, pathetic sight. Now he seemed filled with menace.

A red woolen cloak covered Aurgelmir's shoulders, pinned over the right by a golden brooch, to keep his sword arm free. That arm, and all his upper torso, was clothed in linked mail. Over this he wore a knee-length tunic of fine white linen, embroidered with serpents on breast and hem. His legs were encased in boots of leather, their soles studded with iron that his feet might not slip in blood on the field. Leather gauntlets covered his hands. His fingers were curled into fists.

Aurgelmir rose a few feet into the air, the better to glower down upon Avice. His mouth was grim. His eyes glittered angrily from the slits in his helm.

"Are you mad, that would ask such a thing?" Aurgelmir demanded. "No man nor pig in all the world would wish to sail to that fearful land."

"Summon the ship," said Avice, "or suffer my curse. I will not ask you again."

Aurgelmir shuddered and came down to earth. "She'll sail with the tide," he said. "And ill may you find your journey."

Aurgelmir floated to the center of the chamber. Half-seen images of a rocky shore and brown, splashing water spread like mist across the floor. From the tunnel a cold, moist wind began to blow. Under Aurgelmir's feet his ship took on spectral substance.

The bits of iron rose into their original positions. Around them the hull formed. A deck coalesced. Masts sprouted up fore and aft. Shrouds dropped down from masts to the deck. Huge sails unfurled. The gunwales swept up to a high carved prow with gaping beak and outstretched claw. A war-shield hung from the mainmast, dyed red and bound in steel.

The great ship lunged against her moorings. Water slapped her tarry hull. Her decks glistened with spray. Boards creaked. Halyards rang against their masts. Sheets hissed as they snaked through pulleys. Overhead, the luffing sails snapped and thundered in weed-scented wind. All was noise and commotion. With furious, destructive energy the great booms swung from side to side as the ship was held in irons.

"Now you must board," said Aurgelmir. "The hour grows late and dawn shall close our way."

A gangplank slid out from the deck to the rocky shore and a breach appeared in the gunwales. Avice stepped lightly through the shallow surf·and bounded aboard with apparent energy and enthusiasm. Quadroped took a tentative step into the image of water and stopped, assailed by sudden doubts.

This is not wise, thought Quadroped. Avice frowned and drummed his long fingers slowly against the railing.

"Come hither, bold piglet," said Aurgelmir. "With brave heart and open eyes."

Chapter Three

Quadroped shivered as illusory water swirled around his hooves and lapped at his sides. Above him the spectral ship rocked on the tide. He felt neither bold nor brave.

I can't be cowardly now, Quadroped told himself. *I'm here and Avice probably wouldn't let me leave anyway. There's nothing for it but to go on. My parents need me.*

The thought of the dangers that might be threatening his parents gave him renewed courage. He took a steadying breath and walked forward to the gangplank.

Quadroped climbed the steep plank with great difficulty. The wood was worn and slippery, the strips of wood nailed across it were too far apart to aid him. Avice and Aurgelmir watched his progress in silence. Neither one offered assistance. The small smile that curled Avice's lips suggested that he found the whole spectacle amusing.

"It took you long enough," said Avice, when Quadroped had gained the deck. "Sit forward and keep clear of the lines."

Quadroped was too frightened to resent Avice's tone. Obediently he went and settled down in the bow. The ghost waves danced in the wind. He was cold and scared, and he had a painfully unghostly splinter in one haunch.

The mooring lines came free, snaking up into the air and snapping down onto the deck where they coiled themselves neatly. The ship began to buck and sway, fighting the last few ties to the shore. Quadroped wondered morosely if seasickness was about to add itself to his endless list of woes.

The last line was released. Wind filled the sails. The ghost ship inched forward, its keel slicing through the hard-packed floor of the barrow as though through creamy mud. Rocks and gravel ground along the hull with a shrieking sound. Directly ahead lay the wall of the tomb, studded with roots and flints. If the length of the entrance tunnel had been at all representative, that wall was some five feet thick.

When Avice had talked of sailing between worlds, Quadroped had envisioned a magical voyage. The walls would vanish away, revealing an otherworldly ocean. The wall before them was distressingly solid. It showed no signs of going away.

Quadroped grabbed hold of a cleat and looked back. Aurgelmir stood firm at the wheel, staring straight ahead. He planned, it seemed, to physically batter a path out of his tomb. This was not, Quadroped reflected, a route that he himself would have chosen. It seemed highly unlikely that egress would be achieved without grave damage to both the ship and her passengers.

The ship plowed slowly but inexorably on. Quadroped retreated to the stern. Neither Avice nor Aurgelmir appeared perturbed by the impending collision. They looked calm and a trifle bored, as though sailing through earthen walls were a mundane activity in otherwise exciting and eventful lives. Quadroped failed to find their attitude heartening. Aurgelmir was already dead, and who knew *what* Avice was.

The figurehead hit first, its gaping jaws biting eagerly into the dirt. The impact shook the ship. Her timbers groaned aloud. The ship shivered but moved on, passing slowly into the wall. Loose pebbles and soil showered onto her deck and lay there, looking very solid indeed.

Quadroped watched the heavy mass of earth approach. It swallowed up the mast and advanced to the stern. He imagined the weight of the wall crushing him from all sides. His breath came in hard gasps, as though he were already suffocating. In terror he sought comfort from unlikely sources and pressed hard against Avice's legs.

"If you're worried," said Avice calmly, "hold your breath."

Quadroped waited until the wall was upon him and took a great gulp of air. Eyes closed, he waited . . . and felt nothing, not the wind that filled the barrow nor the earth that he knew surrounded him. His lungs began to hurt. He exhaled. After a moment of temporary relief the pressure to breathe got worse. Then a blast of cold air struck him. He opened his eyes and inhaled.

Before him lay the barrow ring, and a sky pierced through with stars. Quadroped looked back. The grassy side of Aurgelmir's tomb was smooth, the grass undisturbed. No gaping hole existed to mark the ghost ship's passage.

The ship swept on, over the grass and out of the ring. Up the steep slope of the northernmost hill she sailed, her deck tilting sharply as she climbed. Quadroped was pitched off his feet. He began to roll backward. "Help," he cried.

Avice caught the tumbling pig before he could fall overboard and set him safely on his feet. "You won't escape that way, hoggling," he said. Quadroped moved away from Avice and sat down behind Aurgelmir, wrapping his front legs around a stern railing.

The ship reached the top of the hill and continued to climb. She leveled out ten feet above the ground and began to race the clouds across the nighttime skies. From where he sat, Quadroped could see the lumpy downs retreating below him. Off to the east lay the sea.

"Why are we sailing uphill?" he asked. "Isn't the Fleshless Land below us?"

"The Lands of the Dead are all around," said Aurgelmir, in hollow tones. "In the depths of the sea, in the hearts of the hills, and some in the cold of the sky. The living are but a handful, dead without number surround them. From the star-windows the souls of the Fleshless Land stare down, waiting to greet the slain."

Quadroped looked at the stars. They had always been cold and far away, now they seemed filled with menace. *I don't want to be here,* Quadroped thought. The fresh air had revived him. For the first time that evening his mind felt clear.

Quadroped reflected that his actions this evening had been unusually irrational. He tried to recall the first time that a false sense of security had replaced his natural caution, and winced. He had almost certainly been betrayed by the wretched sugarplum.

Which will teach me, thought Quadroped, *not to accept candy from strangers.*

The horizon grew pale. Aurgelmir cast a grim eye toward the east and began to haul in the sails, speeding the ship forward. "It grows late for the voyage," he said. "If the sun should rise . . ."

"If you had obeyed me sooner there would be more time," said Avice. "But never fear, we'll reach the Door in time. I've no desire to be left standing on air when the sun dissolves your ship."

The knowledge that sunrise might prevent him from reaching the Fleshless Land revived Quadroped's spirits considerably. He began to consider escape.

Quadroped studied the ground carefully. It seemed to him that they were sailing back the way he had come with Avice. If this were true they should pass directly over the place where Fairfax and Morrag lay sleeping. And, if they did *that,* he might be able to wake his friends up and alert them to his predicament. What precisely could be done to wrest him from Avice's grasp he did not know, but Morrag would think of something.

The ship's steep ascent and the wind had cleared the decks of most of the rubble from the tomb wall. However, there were still a few good-sized rocks lying about. Quadroped looked carefully around. Avice and Aurgelmir were

staring ahead and paying him no mind. He slowly eased
a rock from under a coil of rope, where it had wedged,
and rolled it up to the edge. Then he settled down to
watch for his friends.

Minutes seemed to stretch into hours and still there was
no sign of his friends. Quadroped began to wonder if he
had missed them. He had a good view of the hillside but
perhaps they would only be visible if he moved to the
other side of the ship. He resisted the urge to go see.

Quadroped's patient watch was rewarded. In the bright
moonlight he saw the familiar tumbled mass of the rock
slide where he and his friends had taken shelter for the
night. The boulders cast long shadows and, as he peered
steadily down, Quadroped prayed that Morrag and Fairfax
would not be hidden in the gloom.

After several anxious moments, Quadroped saw the two
familiar shapes. Fairfax was huddled close against Morrag's side for warmth and both were sound asleep.

Here goes, thought Quadroped, and he pushed the rock
over the side with his snout.

The rock fell down with deadly speed. By some miracle
it missed the two animals completely and landed with a
clatter beside Morrag's head. Quadroped watched with
glee as Morrag reared up, eyes glaring at the sky, while
Fairfax scuttled for shelter.

Quadroped leaned precariously over the stern and waved
his hooves frantically. A shout, he knew, would draw
Avice's attention and lessen his chances of escape. Yet,
when the ship began to pass and Morrag and Fairfax still
had not seen him, he decided to take the chance.

"Morrag, Fairfax, help!" he cried. As an afterthought
he added, "It's me, Quadroped."

As the mighty shout began to die Avice leapt forward
and grabbed Quadroped away from the rail, clamping one
hand tightly about his snout. Quadroped struggled but
Avice was too strong; his tight grip did not loosen in the
slightest.

Fortunately Morrag and Fairfax were familiar with
Quadroped's ability to land himself in odd situations. Neither wasted any time assessing the probability that he was

indeed sailing over their heads in a spectral ship. With a loud cry of *"Quadro!"* Morrag leaped into the air. On the ground below, Fairfax scuttled after the ship.

"Faster," cried Avice. "The eel is in pursuit."

Aurgelmir grumbled but pulled in the mainsheets. The ship gained speed once more.

"I thought," said Avice into Quadroped's trembling ear, "that we had decided to leave our friends behind?"

"*We* didn't," said Quadroped into Avice's hand. "You did, and you tricked me into agreeing, and they're *my* friends, not yours."

"No matter," said Avice. "The eel can't catch us now. He'll tire of the chase soon enough." He put Quadroped back down and walked away to the bow.

Quadroped returned to his post at the stern. Morrag was still in sight. The eel's tail swept steadily through the air, the powerful muscles rippling. Morrag was falling behind but he showed no signs of tiring or abandoning the pursuit.

Quadroped grabbed a nearby line and tried to tie it to the railing. If Morrag could catch the rope he would be towed along until he could pull himself aboard. The rope was thick and did not bend easily. Quadroped worked frantically with his hooves and mouth but the line refused to twist into a reliable knot. A foot fell upon the line. A slender hand reached down and plucked it away.

"You *are* a stubborn creature," said Avice pleasantly. "If you try my patience too far, hoggling, you'll find yourself in the hold. There are probably phantom rats in the hold, it is so wet and dark down there."

Quadroped gulped and edged sideways. If he fell overboard Morrag might be able to catch him before he hit the ground.

Avice herded Quadroped away from the side with one foot. "Suicides," he said, "don't end up in Nieve's halls. You'll never rejoin your parents that way." He picked Quadroped up and tucked him back under his arm.

"Let me go," said Quadroped. "I don't want to go with you to the Fleshless Land. I don't want to see Nieve. There must be another way to rescue my parents." He kicked out with his hooves and nipped at Avice's fingers.

"Oh, there are," said Avice, adjusting his hold on Quadroped. "But I promised to take you there myself and I *always* keep my promises. See? The Door lies open before us."

Quadroped stared ahead and saw a patch of dark fog or smoke, clearly bounded, lying midway between heaven and earth. It was the most dreadful and sinister phenomenon he had ever seen. Black vapors roiled and bubbled, revealing glimpses of bloody, flickering lights. He looked back and saw that Morrag was now only a tiny dark ribbon in their wake. For the first time that evening, Quadroped began to cry.

"Stop sniveling, hoggling, and be brave," said Avice, setting Quadroped back onto the deck. "Tonight you will see your parents."

"Tonight we shall sleep in the arms of the dead," said Aurgelmir cheerfully. "We shall feast and fight and fall and not be slain."

Quadroped wept on despite all this dubious comfort. The Door loomed larger as the ship raced on. There was no more hope of escape. Soon he would be a prisoner of the Fleshless Land like his unfortunate family before him.

"Woe," said Aurgelmir suddenly. "Despair! Cruel the Fates, unkind the webs they weave."

Quadroped blinked away his tears and looked to see what had evoked this lament. The ship, he saw, had slowed to a crawl, her topsails hanging slack above her.

"Why are we slowing?" Avice demanded.

"The winds are hushed," said Aurgelmir in direst tones. "They wait for the sun. Alas, day's fiery lance shall scuttle my ship. I shall become scattered remnants drifting upon still air. Oh, for my tomb where the soothing sea sings to my dead bones each night. Gone are the sheltering walls. No more shall my bones lie together, keeping company in that sacred house. Small use Hrimnir's work of earth and stone now. I am doomed to be the breezes' plaything. Scattered dust . . ."

"Stop that," said Avice, interrupting Aurgelmir's touching threnody. "Be quiet."

Avice's obvious displeasure cheered Quadroped up

immeasurably. The Door was drawing no closer. Morrag might still catch up. Then Quadroped heard the faint sound of dancing bells and his spirits sank. Avice was summoning magic.

Avice walked forward to the bow. Now he stood there, hands raised in invocation or supplication. His eyes were half-closed, his face drawn and pale. After a moment he began to chant a verse in strong iambic pentameter. The language was like none that Quadroped had heard before. It was seemed to lack all hard consonants, like the hissing of a snake or a whisper of wind.

Avice swayed from side to side like a tree in a storm. The ship began to mimic his motion. The tipping made Quadroped feel ill.

The sails began to flap. Puffs of wind hit them with increasing force. One by one the great sails filled. The ship moved forward once more, gathering speed until she created a wind of her own.

Avice returned to the stern. "We'll reach the Door well before dawn," he said. He looked upward with a repugnant smile of self-satisfaction. "The Wind Maids shall see to that."

Quadroped looked up into the rigging. Something fluttered around the mast and vanished again. He stared hard and for a moment caught sight of a slender girl hanging on the shrouds. The light shifted and she was gone. Stare as he might he could not catch sight of her again.

Quadroped gave up staring at the rigging and sat down and stared at the deck instead. Ahead of him the ghastly Door filled the sky. Behind him lay the familiar world he was surely leaving forever. The tears returned.

"I'm frightened," wept Quadroped. "I want to go home."

"Then why don't you?"

Quadroped looked up and saw nothing at all. "Who said that?" he whispered.

"I did. Over here, on the railing."

Quadroped stared hard at the air where the voice had spoken. At last he saw the shape of a young, slender woman perched decoratively on the railing, her hair and filmy draperies streaming out in the wind. Her skin and clothing blended perfectly into the background as if their colors were those of a chameleon. Only the faint shadows cast by her body revealed her presence at all.

"Hello," he said. "Are you a Wind Maid?"

"I am Asja," said the Wind Maid in a breathy voice. "Why don't you go home, piglet?"

"I'm Quadro," said Quadroped. "I can't go home, Avice won't let me. He's taking me to the Fleshless Land."

Asja was silent. Her thin, beautiful face registered a sort of shocked dismay. Or at least, that was as close as Quadroped could come to interpreting the look on that half-visible face. Another Wind Maid fluttered up to join her. They whispered together a moment.

"This is Dylja."

"Why didn't you summon us to carry you home?" asked the second Wind Maid.

Quadroped blinked in surprise. "How could I?" he asked. "I don't know how."

The Wind Maids stared at Quadroped from wide blue eyes. "But you can see us," said Asja.

"You're a fairy pig," said Dylja.

"I don't have any magical powers," said Quadroped patiently.

The Wind Maids giggled at the thought of a fairy pig who could not summon the winds. "The Storm Boys would be happy if there were more like you around," they said. "Shall we help you, piglet-without-power?"

"Yes, yes," said Asja. "Let us take you away. It will serve the Weather Master right for waking us at dawn."

"You'll help me escape?" said Quadroped. "Really?"

"Really," said Asja.

"Quickly," said Dylja. "The Weather Master's seen us."

Quadroped looked and saw that Avice was hurrying toward them. "Oh, please take me away," he cried. "I don't want to go to the Fleshless Land. Don't let him catch me, please don't."

Misty gray arms reached down and grabbed Quadroped

up. The Wind Maids' touch was soft and chill. Before Quadroped knew what was happening he was flipped over the side. With a terrified squeal he found himself falling toward the ground. From the deck of the ship, now far above his head, he heard Avice's furious cry of: "Stop! Return that pig!"

With shouts of laughter the Wind Maids dove from the railings and flew after the hurtling pig, catching him up again, giggling at his distress. They swept Quadroped high up above the deck and circled around the masts.

"Look how angry the Weather Master is!" they cried. "He wants you badly, powerless pig."

"You won't return me, will you?" asked Quadroped. "He can't make you bring me back?" Avice looked savage.

"Maybe we will," said Asja.

"He *is* a Wind Master," said Dylja. "Piglet, you didn't know our names."

"No!" wailed Quadroped. He wrapped his hooves around Asja's neck and clung on as hard as he could.

"Beware, hoggling," Avice called up to him. "You scorn my aid at your peril. Pray that I have forgiven you before we meet again, or it will go poorly with you. And Quadroped," he added, "we *shall* be meeting soon."

Quadroped gulped and buried his snout in Asja's shoulder. She laughed and swooped down low over Avice's head, then fled away, her sister following close behind. In the rigging, Quadroped heard other Wind Maids laughing as they worked to fill the sails.

Quadroped's fear of Avice was soon replaced by a wonderful feeling of freedom. The ghost ship sailed away. The Wind Maids hovered, watching as the ship was engulfed by the ugly black smoke of the Door.

The ship vanished from view. Quadroped gave a great sigh of relief. *I'm safe,* he thought. *Now all I have to do is get the Wind Maids to put me down where Morrag and Fairfax can find me.*

This was not so easily done. The restless wind spirits, though inclined to be helpful, were mischievous in the extreme. As Quadroped, delightfully, had no powers to control them they began to play with him like a ball.

"Help!" cried Quadroped as he was tossed high into the air.

"Catch him, catch him!"

"Careful, or you'll drop him."

"Oh, I've missed," said Dylja.

Quadroped went hurtling down toward the ground, squealing with fright, only to be caught at the last minute.

"Put me down!" said Quadroped. His initial fear changed to anger as he began to realize that the Wind Maids were only playing.

"It's getting cross," said Asja.

"It's no fun anymore," said Dylja. "Let's put it down."

"Oh *do* put me down," said Quadroped.

The Wind Maids descended to the earth and placed Quadroped gently upon the wet grass. They began to drift upward again.

"Thank you," called Quadroped, remembering his manners at the last minute.

"Good-bye, good luck," said Dylja.

"Remember our names, piglet," said Asja. With a last wave they floated up toward the clouds, their skins shifting to pink in the first light of dawn.

"Good-bye," called Quadroped, waving a hoof.

The ground felt wonderfully stable beneath his hooves. It did not pitch or let him fall but lay there, solid and unmoving. For a while he was content just to sit in the grass and watch the sunrise.

After a while Quadroped began to look around. He did not recognize the landscape and, he realized, he had no idea where he was. The Wind Maids had carried him far from the ship's course. He had no idea how to get back to his friends and there was no one at all to ask.

There must be someone around, Quadroped thought. He looked carefully about and his eyes fell upon several small glistening black lumps hiding among the grass clumps.

"Hello," said Quadroped.

The slugs, for such they were, made no reply. They

neither moved nor spoke. They showed no signs of life nor intelligence whatsoever.

"I'm lost," said Quadroped.

The slug nearest him twitched. Ever so slowly it began to uncurl. It moved a little closer and Quadroped bent down in case it wished to speak. He suspected that the voice of a slug might be very soft indeed.

"We are all lost," said the slug.

"Oh," said Quadroped. Then, "Where are *you* trying to get to?"

"Somewhere else," said the slug.

Quadroped digested this information in silence. He had a feeling that the slug was not talking about the same kind of lostness that he was.

"I'm trying to find my way back to the barrow," he said.

"The barrow is all around us," said the slug. "Death cannot be lost."

The second slug extended two black antennae. "The Pig Who Lost Death," it said. "It has a ring, a certain air. Shall I compose an epic, or an ode? Which one? Eh, *n'importe*. I shall begin: 'Oh pig that never Winter's touch hath felt . . .' "

"He doesn't want Death, he wants a specific set of geospatial coordinates," said the third slug suddenly. "He seeks topographical information of a highly specific nature. What was your latitude and longitude when last you saw the barrow? What time was it? What day of the week and month of the year? In what position shone the stars?"

"I don't know," said Quadroped.

"Without such information you are lost indeed," said the third slug.

"How did you come here?" asked the poetic slug.

Quadroped looked at the ring of black, featureless faces. "The Wind Maids brought me," he said.

"Wind Maids?" said the third slug. "What sort of atmospheric phenomenon is that?"

"They're not phenomenons," said Quadroped. "They're spirits. They look like beautiful human girls and have chameleon skins."

"Ah," said the poetic slug. "What depths of imagination this piglet shows."

"It's lying," said the third slug. "The wind is but a stratospheric reservoir of high isentropic potential vorticity. It does not consist of beings of any sort whatever."

"I'm *not* lying," said Quadroped.

"Deluded, and so young," sighed the scientific slug.

"Death cannot find him too soon," said the first.

"It will be a kind release," said the poet.

They all curled up to muse upon the interesting phenomenon of Quadroped. So immersed did they become in deep philosophical thought and artistic endeavor that they forgot about Quadroped completely. When the sun had fully risen, and the grass begun to dry, they all crawled away without a backward glance.

Quadroped watched the retreat of the slugs with some amazement. He had never suspected that slugs were capable of such dizzying heights of intellectual thought. Still, they did seem to have a poor sense of reality, which, considering their unpleasant appearance and physical limitations, was probably just as well.

I'd better just sit here and wait for Morrag to find me, Quadroped decided. He was tired and knew from experience that when people run around looking for each other they usually run in circles until someone stops. The weather had not yet turned to rain and a weak patch of sunlight fell where he sat. So he curled up in the grass and closed his eyes. The wind sang him to sleep.

Dark clouds gathered at the horizon, massing for an attack on the sun. The sky turned gray. Soft drops of rain began to fall upon the sleeping form of Quadroped, soliciting nothing more than a twitch of his ears. He slept on through the morning, never stirring until a loud cry disturbed his heavy slumber.

"Quadro! *There* you are!"

Quadroped awoke with a start and sat up. Morrag was skimming low over the ground toward him. The eel looked very cross but Quadroped was too happy to care. He ran forward, ears waggling with delight.

"I knew you'd find me," said Quadroped.

"Why," asked Morrag, inspecting Quadroped for signs of injury, "was it *necessary* for me to find you? No, don't tell me," he said as Quadroped burst into a confused explanation and apology. "Wait until Fairfax gets here. I don't suppose he'll be any more pleased with you than I am."

Fairfax was *not* pleased to see Quadroped. When he appeared, fifteen minutes later, he was in a thoroughly bad mood. He looked muddy and disheveled, and was audibly grumbling as he plodded slowly toward them.

"Aha!" he said in grim tones when he reached them. He sat down and eyed Quadroped sourly. "Hedgehogs," said Fairfax, "do not sprint. They do not make good long-distance runners. Hedgehogs travel slowly, at a dignified pace. They do not *appreciate* chasing after flying pigs."

"I'm sorry," said Quadroped.

"Pigs," said Fairfax, "should not fly."

"I didn't want to," said Quadroped. "I won't do it again."

"I should hope not," said Morrag with some asperity. "How could you be so foolish? Going off alone like that. When I saw you peering down at me from that ship I almost had a heart attack. What were you doing up there? What happened?"

Quadroped looked at the ground. "Avice was taking me to the Fleshless Land," he said. "To free my parents."

Morrag swayed back and gazed at Quadroped in dismay. "The Fleshless Land?" he asked.

"Who is Avice?" asked Fairfax, prodding Quadroped with his sharp, pointed snout.

"I'm not sure," said Quadroped. "I met him at the Water Mill." In faltering tones he told them how he had freed Avice. "The Miller was going to kill us."

"He could have tried," said Morrag. He hissed, revealing his teeth. "What happened last night?"

Quadroped told the story of his midnight adventures. When he had finished Fairfax had several pithy comments to make on the subject of pigs who got themselves into dangerous situations in the middle of the night.

"I quite understand," said Fairfax, "that when the Key dropped on your head you had no choice but to go gallivanting off to the Gate, but what ever possessed you to go off with Avice?"

"I find this whole business of the Fleshless Land most disturbing," said Morrag.

"Why would Nieve want to kidnap a herd of pigs?" asked Fairfax.

"They're *fairy* pigs," said Quadroped.

"They're still pigs," said Fairfax. "It doesn't make any sense. Avice was probably lying."

"I hope so," said Morrag. "Nieve is a strange and evil woman. If the fairy pigs are in her power we may not see them again. I don't think Glasgerion or Reander could help you against her, Quadro. Even the Black Unicorn would think twice before challenging Nieve."

"But I *have* to get my parents back," said Quadroped. He wished he could believe that Avice had lied about his parents' whereabouts but somehow he just knew it was true.

"Maybe I should have gone with Avice," he said bitterly. "*He* knew how to help me. He said he could free my parents."

"Anyone who can command favors of Nieve should be avoided at all costs," said Morrag. "You're lucky he let you go."

"He didn't let me go," said Quadroped with a touch of pride. "I escaped. The Wind Maids helped me."

"If Avice can raise the dead he can handle a few recalcitrant Wind Maids," said Morrag. "He let you go."

"I suppose so," said Quadroped. He sighed. He felt like a mouse in the paws of a cat. He wondered when Avice would pounce again.

They continued their journey north. Quadroped was fretful and anxious. The distance to Essylt was vast. The miles seemed to pass slower than ever. He began to annoy his friends by telling them repeatedly to hurry. When they paused for rest he fidgeted, twitching his ears and hopping up and down. All in all he was a less than ideal traveling companion.

They left the downs two days later and began to travel in a more westerly direction through fields and coppices. The road became wider and more traveled. Groups of people walked or rode past at all times of the day or night. Heavy traffic, and weeks of softening rain, turned the thoroughfare into a deeply rutted bog.

For the most part these travelers paid the three animals no mind. But once in a while a child would stop and point until his parents cuffed him and hurried him on. Often they glanced back over their shoulders, their eyes wide and frightened. Quadroped noticed these things and began to worry.

"I think people are afraid of me," said Quadroped.

"Afraid of you?" said Morrag, eyeing the muddy white piglet in disbelief. "Don't be silly, you're too round."

"Paranoia," said Fairfax grimly, "is a sign of mental collapse."

Quadroped let the subject drop but he continued to observe the people on the road. His observations did not comfort him. When travelers saw him watching them they turned their faces away and gestured, as if to ward off some evil. People moved away from him, crossing the road to avoid him.

One evening they stopped to rest in a rye field. The tall stalks provided some shelter from the cold and hid them from travelers on the road. They curled up together on the muddy ground. The rye rustled in the wind, drowning out all noises save the steady patter of the eternal rain. Before long they were lulled asleep.

The rye sang on through the night, soothing the animals, masking alarming sounds. The sun began to rise, rose red through the clouds, and still the rye spoke and the animals slept. So snug and secure were they, so sound asleep, that they did not notice when a flock of crows flew up from a nearby row. Nor did they hear the rough voices of the approaching farmers, walking their fields to inspect the crops.

The wind paused and the rye stilled. Heavy footfalls and human voices woke Morrag, and he started up in alarm. "Quadro, Fairfax, wake *up*," he hissed. "Someone's coming."

Quadroped and Fairfax scrambled to their feet, bleary-eyed and confused, just as three brawny farmers stumbled upon them. For a moment both parties stared at one another in wild surmise. Then the foremost farmer grinned affably. Quadroped began to relax. Fairfax shuffled quietly away and hid.

"Hullo, beasties," said the first farmer. His two companions nodded and smiled.

The wind came and the rye whispered. The first farmer listened. His expression grew dark and angry.

"Thief," he cried, pointing at Quadroped. "Verminous swine! Destroy him. Destroy the white pig."

"I think we should get out of here," said Morrag. Quadroped just stared at the farmer, too surprised to run. *"Move!"* hissed Morrag, and slapped Quadroped sharply across the flanks with the tip of his tail.

Quadroped flattened his ears, turned, and ran as fast as his hooves could carry him. Morrag flashed ahead, his sinuous body weaving through the rye.

"Run *across* the furrows, Quadro," he hissed. "They're too big to pass easily through the walls of grain."

Quadroped fled between the tough rye stems, his hooves sinking deeply into the soft tilled earth. The farmers cursed and plunged after him, breaking the rye, trampling their crop into the ground in their haste to catch the pig.

Quadroped ran as hard as he could but his short legs were no match for the farmers'. Before he knew what was happening the men had formed a circle around him and were beginning to close in. Quadroped ducked and wove, turning frantically from side to side. There was no way out of the ring of grasping hands.

A pitchfork jabbed down. Quadroped squealed in fright. His feet got caught between the sharp iron prongs and he fell. Before he could rise the farmers were upon him. Quadroped kicked out with all his might but the farmers had captured pigs before. They grabbed his legs, avoiding his sharp little hooves, and hoisted him off the ground.

Quadroped hung upside down and stared into the angry, perspiring face of the foremost farmer.

"What're you going to do with him, Malker?" asked one of his companions, a dark-visaged farmer called Grindle.

"Sacrifice him," said Malker. "His blood will keep the rot from the rye."

"Never heard that before," said Grindle.

"The rye thirsts," said Malker. He trembled slightly and his grip on Quadroped tightened. "The rye whispers for the blood of pigs."

"Seems to me that it's got enough to drink with the rain and all," said Grindle, unconvinced.

Quadroped raised his head, the muscles of his neck straining with the effort, and gazed imploringly at the farmers. His purple eyes glistened with tears.

"Please don't kill me," he said. "I'm sorry I trespassed. I didn't eat any of the rye."

His head fell back. He no longer had the strength to hold it up. The tension in his throat cut off the air, strangling him. Blood pooled painfully in his head.

"Seems a shame to kill him, Malker," said the third farmer, a rotund individual known as Gregin. "He looks healthy, and he *talks*. He'd be a nice addition to our herd."

Malker turned on Gregin with a low growl. "He must die. This is the Demon Pig."

"What, *him*?" said dark Grindle. He spit on the ground. "He's just a baby."

"Fools!" Malker screamed, revealing a mouthful of broken teeth. "Don't you hear? The rye is dying! The soil is angry. The sky *weeps* in anger. *This* is the evil in the land."

Malker licked his lips. His eyes were crazed, ringed in white. His breast heaved with unpleasant emotion. Gregin and Grindle stepped back in alarm.

"Don't get so upset," said Gregin. "We don't know anything. We can't hear the rye. Kill him if you think that's best." He looked at Grindle and tapped his head.

Malker relaxed a bit. "Hold the pig then, Gregin,"

he said. He handed Quadroped over. "Grindle, fetch a knife."

Grindle walked away at a leisurely pace and eventually returned with a huge machete. Its wide silver blade gleamed dully in the rain-washed light. Gregin held Quadroped's legs tightly with both beefy hands. Laconic Grindle came and held Quadroped's head down, neck stretched tight to receive the blow.

Quadroped tried desperately to move his legs or bite the huge hands that held him. But the effort was too much and he soon collapsed. He hung limply in Gregin's grasp and stared at the ground.

Malker raised the knife over Quadroped's throat and smiled. "Time to die," said he.

Chapter Four

Quadroped stared up into Malker's terrible face. *I can't die like this,* he thought. *My parents need me.* He tried again to free himself, but it was no use. He was too dizzy and sick to fight on.

"Drop that pig!"

Malker lowered the knife and turned, crouching. Morrag darted out of the rye, mouth gaping wide to reveal a thousand gleaming teeth. With a terrible hiss he threw himself at Malker, clamping massive jaws down upon the farmer's forearm. The machete fell to the ground.

"Grindle, get it *off* me!" screamed Malker. Blood came, staining his arm, and Morrag, red. Malker grabbed Morrag close to the head with his free hand and began to pull. Morrag's jaws locked harder into Malker's flesh.

"*Cut* it off," said Malker.

Grindle grabbed the machete up from the ground and ran forward. Morrag lashed out with his tail and knocked the man aside. Grindle scrambled to his feet, backed off, and tried again.

Gregin spoke up, his chubby face alight with inspiration. "The pig, Grindle. Come and kill it. Malker was right, it's evil. It summoned this eel to save it."

Grindle looked skeptical, but he held the knife to Quadroped's neck. Despite himself, Quadroped whimpered. Morrag heard the sound and dropped Malker's arm, wheeling about to face Gregin and Grindle.

"Hold right there, eel," said Grindle. "One move and I'll kill the pig." Morrag hovered irresolutely in the air and glared at Grindle.

Malker came up, his damaged right arm hanging at his side, blood running down in rivers to feed the soil. "Good work," he said. "Give me the knife, Grindle. I'll hold it while you see to my arm."

Grindle handed the knife over and took off his shirt. With patient precision he tore it into strips and began to bandage Malker's arm. When he had finished he straightened up and looked at Malker. "What now?"

"Get some rope from the barn," said Malker.

Grindle nodded and hurried off. Five minutes later he returned with a coil of heavy rope.

"Tie the pig first," said Malker.

Gregin and Grindle trussed Quadroped up tightly. Morrag swayed in agitation but did not attack. Malker never let the knife stray more than an inch from Quadroped's neck.

When Quadroped was tightly bound, Gregin and Grindle laid him on the ground and approached Morrag warily. "How do we tie up an eel?" they asked, looking at Morrag's long slippery body.

Malker shrugged and rested the knife against Quadroped's throat. "Don't know," he said. "Just do it."

Quadroped gathered his remaining strength and raised his head. He couldn't let Morrag be captured like this.

"Get away, Morrag," he said. "They'll kill us both."

"How touching," said Malker. "But you won't go, will you, eel? You'll stay and try to save your friend. I'll kill you, eel. I'll kill you slowly." Morrag hissed but did not turn away.

After a short but bitter struggle Gregin and Grindle managed to twist Morrag into a knot and then wrap him in the rope like a ball of yarn. It looked odd but it proved quite effective. Morrag was unable to break free.

Gregin turned Quadroped onto his back. Grindle seized his chin and pulled it down. Malker laid the cold blade against Quadroped's outstretched neck. Beads of sweat glistened on his forehead.

"Now, pig, you die."

Quadroped felt the knife move as Malker prepared to slice it across his throat. Dimly he hoped the knife wouldn't hurt too much, that it would be over soon, that his parents would be waiting for him in the Fleshless Land. Cool metal slithered across his skin.

Then, without warning, Malker suddenly dropped the knife and staggered back, convulsed. He crumpled to his knees, hands white and clutching at his stomach. The muscles in his neck stood out. His mouth stretched wide in agony.

"Malker, what's wrong?" said Grindle.

"The Pig. The White Boar. It's *killing* me."

Malker struggled to his feet and stood there, swaying, while his eyes swept wildly around the field. The wind blew down the field, shaking the thick heads of rye.

"There! Moving, coming through the grain. It won't get me. It mustn't get me!"

Grindle released Quadroped and grabbed Malker by the shoulder. "Malker, there's nothing there," he said. "It's only the wind. What's wrong with you?"

"Yellow tusks . . . red eyes . . . horrible!" Malker flung Grindle away and ran, plunging blindly through the rye as though some terrible monster were after him.

Gregin and Grindle watched him go in alarm. "Malker was right," said pudgy Gregin. "It's the pig, Grindle. The pig is evil. It's going to kill us all."

Grindle looked at Quadroped and shook his head. "That's just a piglet."

"But it talks, and the eel . . . it flies."

"They can't kill us," said Grindle firmly. "Didn't we tie them up? Malker's sick, hallucinating. Some sort of fever is what it is, fever-dreaming. Maybe the eel's bite had poison. We'd better get after him, see he doesn't hurt himself."

"What about them?" asked Gregin, indicating the struggling forms of Morrag and Quadroped.

"Leave them," said Grindle. "They'll keep. We'll deal with them later, after we've seen to Malker."

Quadroped lay on the ground and watched the farmers walk away. He began to shake.

I'm alive, he thought numbly. And then, *I hurt.*

His neck stung where the sharp blade of the knife had lightly passed. The ropes bit tightly into his tender flesh and the skin around them was red, swollen and throbbing.

A cold snout tickled at Quadroped's ear and he twisted his head to see what it was. Fairfax had returned and was snuffling at him.

"Are you two all right?" asked Fairfax.

"It's about time you showed up," said Morrag. "Untie us and let's get out of here."

"If," said Fairfax sharply, "I had shown up any sooner I would be tied up too."

He climbed up onto Quadroped's stomach and began to gnaw at the heavy ropes. "Stop twitching," he said.

"I can't help it," said Quadroped. "You tickle."

"Stop or I'll *bite* you," said Fairfax.

Quadroped tried, without noticeable success, to lie still. After what seemed like an unconscionably long time, Fairfax managed to part the ropes and clambered down. With a grateful snort Quadroped rolled over and sat up. The blood rushed back into his feet and that hurt worse than ever.

Fairfax scurried over to Morrag and began on his ropes. The eel had been intricately and elaborately bound. Fairfax had a difficult time freeing him. When the ropes had all been removed it was still necessary to help Morrag twist out of the knot into which Gregin and Grindle had tied him.

Quadroped listened to his friends arguing and snapping at each other as they undid the farmer's handiwork. Morrag was thrashing about trying to restore his circulation.

Fairfax was dodging about trying to remove the last bits of rope.

Then Quadroped's eye fell upon a small cloth bag that one of the men had dropped and left behind. Circulation restored, he rose cautiously to his hooves and ambled over to investigate.

Quadroped undid the leather drawstring with an ease born of practice and stuck his nose inside. His sensitive nostrils informed him that there was food in the bag. Hunger, forgotten in his fear of the farmers, returned with a vengeance. Without further ado he tipped the bag on end and let the contents roll onto the ground. Among the odd farm implements—small knives, nails, bits of string, and other oddments—lay half a loaf of rye bread.

"Morrag, Fairfax," said Quadroped. "Look. I've found some food." He bit off a small piece of the bread.

"Quadro, stop!" Morrag came whipping forward and smacked Quadroped on the nose with his tail, dashing the bread from his mouth. "Don't eat that!" he hissed.

"What's wrong with it?" asked Quadroped, rubbing his injured snout.

"I'm not sure, but . . . ." Morrag took the loaf and examined it carefully. "What do you think, Fairfax?"

Fairfax sniffed at the bread and frowned. "Not nutritious," said he. He scuffled in the dirt, looking closely at the broken heads of rye that lay crushed on the ground. "Aha!" he said.

"What is it?" asked Quadroped nervously.

"Ergot," said Fairfax grimly.

"What's that?"

"Fungus," said Fairfax. "And very, very dangerous."

Quadroped continued to look bewildered.

"Ergot is a tiny fungus that grows between the grains of rye," said Fairfax. "Cooking the grain does not destroy the poison. If eaten, ergot of rye causes hallucinations and slow, painful death. This whole field is infected, and the bread will be as well."

"Did ergot make Malker want to kill me?" Quadroped asked.

"Possibly," said Fairfax. "It would certainly explain why he ran off like that and left you two alone."

Morrag looked thoughtful. "And yet Gregin and Grindle seemed to have heard of this Demon Pig before," he said. "I don't think their behavior was entirely due to ergot."

Quadroped suddenly remembered the sounds of Malker's agony as he crumpled to the ground. "It's horrible," he said. He flung the bread as far away as he could and dropped his head to the ground, feeling sick.

"It's the rain," said Fairfax. "The grain's too damp to store. If it continues the whole harvest will rot in the barns. There will be famine this winter."

"We should get going," said Morrag. "Those men will be back."

They returned to the road and began to walk. It began to rain again. The road was wet and muddy. Toward noon a heavily laden wagon, drawn by a sinewy plow horse, came rumbling up beside them and stopped.

"Need a ride?" asked the horse in a doleful voice.

Quadroped looked at the horse in surprise. "You can talk," he said. "I didn't think horses could."

"Some can, some can't," replied the horse. "Hop up or be splashed with mud as we pass. My farmer will lend you a hand."

Morrag eyed the farmer with evident suspicion. Farmers were low on his list of safe companions at the moment. Fairfax, however, agreed. The farmer smiled and picked him up, depositing him on the seat beside him. Quadroped followed suit and Morrag was forced to follow.

The wagon lurched on its way again. "I'm Gant," said the plow horse. "My farmer is Madoc. He doesn't talk much."

"I'm Quadro," said Quadroped. "And these are Fairfax and Morrag."

Madoc and Gant both nodded. "There are sweet potatoes packed in the straw in the back if you're hungry," said Gant. "My farmer grew them himself." He sounded proud of this achievement.

Quadroped and Fairfax both availed themselves of this kind offer. Morrag looked faintly revolted.

"Where you are headed?" asked Morrag.

"To Adelchis," said Gant. "And you?"

"North," said Morrag.

Gant nodded. "That's all right then. We'll drop you off on the other side of river."

"When will we get there?" asked Quadroped. He was comfortable and dreaded a return to walking.

"Four or five hours," said Gant. "This weather makes traveling slow. I've never seen a fall this wet. It's lucky this road has a gravel bed, most roads are impassable these days."

Gant shook his heavy head and Madoc ceased to grin. Conversation lapsed as each contemplated the depressing state of the weather. Quadroped leaned back and tried to relax. The soft hollow sound of Gant's hooves in the mud was soothing, as was the rocking and bumping motion of the wagon. Gant plodded on, his head hanging wearily. It was hard work pulling a wagon all day. His sides steamed in the chilly air.

The rain stopped and the wind began to dry Quadroped's skin. He shivered and pressed closer to Fairfax. After a while he slept.

It was darker when Quadroped awoke. The wind blew in fitful gusts and leaves skittered across the road. They had come to the edge of a high plateau. Beyond them lay a long sinuous river, shining in the cold pale light.

"That is the Great Cenanda," said Morrag. "It forms the border between the Kingdoms of Akariel and Lyskerys."

"Ah," said Quadroped wisely. After a moment he asked, "Which Kingdom are we in now?"

"Such ignorance," said Morrag.

Quadroped shrugged, undisturbed by his lack of knowledge. "How can you tell where the borders are when it looks the same on either side?" he asked. "There aren't any fences or signs."

"True," said Morrag. "Well, we're in Akariel. Across the water lies Lyskerys, where Fairfax comes from."

"There's trouble on the road ahead," said Gant suddenly. "It looks like a border patrol."

"It can't be," said Fairfax. "It's illegal to stop traffic on the Northwest Way."

"See for yourself," said Gant, pointing his ears ahead.

Quadroped looked. He could just make out a group of horsemen standing at the far end of a long stone bridge. There was a flash of silver. The party was armed. In front of the bridge a great crowd of people seemed to be milling about. A long line of wagons stretched back up the road.

Fairfax peered at the company of warriors. "It *does* look like a border patrol," he said at last. "From Lyskerys, by their standards."

Morrag shook his head. A worried frown creased his scaly brow. "But why?" he asked. "There's never been any trouble between Akariel and Lyskerys."

Gant twitched his tail. "I've been past this patrol before," he said. "Other Kingdoms are watching their borders as well. Too many people are on the move."

"Where are they all going?" asked Quadroped.

"Someplace where the rain doesn't fall and there's food in the barns," said Gant. "But there is no such place and the patrols turn them back. We will be allowed to pass. They won't stop a wagon that's carrying food."

They proceeded down the hill and joined the long line of wagons waiting to cross over the bridge. They crept forward slowly and after a while Gant sent his farmer off to listen for news. Madoc returned looking highly disturbed.

"I think you had better all hide in the back," said Gant when he had heard Madoc's news. "It seems pigs aren't too popular here. The patrol won't let Quadro across."

"Why not?" asked Quadroped.

"They fear the Demon Pig."

Quadroped shuddered. The ergot-mad farmers had mentioned such a beast. Perhaps it was real after all. "What does it look like?" he asked.

"It's a huge white boar of ghastly aspect," said Gant. "It has glaring red eyes and horribly long yellow tusks.

If you see it, you die. It's been sent by the Black Unicorn to kill us all.''

Quadroped stared at the horse in horrified amazement. It had occurred to him that *he* was the Demon Pig.

"I don't believe it," said Gant. "But it's got people scared. They're saying," Gant lowered his voice to a dramatic whisper, "that the rain is Ravenor's revenge!"

"*Who* says?" hissed Morrag. As a creature of Ravenor he was quick to resent this slight.

Fairfax poked Morrag sharply in the ribs. Morrag subsided into grim silence.

"Rumors," said Fairfax, "are unreliable. I expect this one has people frightened."

"Frightened and angry," agreed Gant. "If you want to hear more you should come with us to Adelchis. The magician will be there tomorrow."

"What magician?" asked Fairfax.

Gant shrugged in his harness. "I don't know his name," he said. "You really should hide now."

"I think I will just stay here," said Fairfax. "It's only Quadro who needs to hide." Fairfax did not approve of straw; it made him sneeze.

"We shall *all* hide," said Morrag. "Quadro, you and Fairfax go first. I'll make sure you're covered, then slide in after. Be quick about it."

Quadroped dived into the straw and burrowed down, ignoring the way the stalks tickled and the lumpy potatoes poked at him. Fairfax grumbled softly under his breath but came after and nestled against Quadroped's flank.

"Can you both breathe?" asked Morrag.

"Yes," said Quadroped.

"No," said Fairfax.

Morrag ignored the hedgehog and quickly hid all signs of disturbance. Then he slid smoothly in after them. Moments later the line began to move forward. The wagon jolted on down the road.

Conversation was difficult beneath the sweet potatoes and muffling straw, nevertheless they managed it.

"These rumors about Ravenor are most disturbing," said Morrag. "Something terrible is happening to the

Kingdoms. This border patrol is a symptom of imminent sociopolitical upheaval. Fear of famine is causing dissension and increased factionalism manifesting itself as a renewed sense of national identity and separatism. The border patrols are only the start. In the coming fight for survival it's going to be every land for itself.''

"Oh," said Quadroped. He was not entirely sure he understood what Morrag was talking about but it sounded quite dreadful.

"We must go to Adelchis," Morrag continued. "I want to see this magician."

"Politics," said Fairfax, "are for princes. Adelchis lies west. It's out of our way."

"We have to get to Essylt," said Quadroped. "It's taking too long already. My parents have to be rescued *soon*."

"There is more at stake here than a handful of pigs," said Morrag. "We must find out what this magician is up to. If he's fomenting rebellion Reander must be told."

"But if it's that serious don't you think Reander knows about it already?" asked Quadroped. He was firmly of the belief that Prince Reander of Essylt was omniscient and omnipotent.

"No," said Morrag. "The Council is in session. Reander will have his hands full." The Kingdoms were jointly governed by the Council of Rulers who met quarterly in the great Council Keep of Essylt to pass legislation and make various administrative decisions.

"The Council will be considering Reander's treaty with Ravenor," Morrag continued. "This magician is probably only a local phenomenon but the last thing anyone needs right now is a mob screaming for war with Ravenor. The peace is a fragile thing and the Black Unicorn will attack if he's provoked."

"Adelchis will be dangerous," said Fairfax. "People are angry. Quadro could be hurt."

"We'll stay out of sight," said Morrag. "Quadroped is already so dirty he looks gray. If worse comes to worse we'll just paint him with mud, then no one will know that he's white."

Morrag prevailed. They crossed over the bridge without being detected and early the next morning they reached the outskirts of Adelchis. Madoc leaned over and poked them awake.

Quadroped started to roll over and was nipped sharply in the flank by Fairfax, who had no desire to be flattened and crushed so early in the day. A brief altercation occurred but at length both animals managed to get their feet under them and sat up, pushing the potatoes aside.

It was still dark and cold but the birds were up and quarreling with a will. The sun had risen over an hour ago but the clouds were so thick that only the most feeble white light could escape to illuminate the earth.

"Good morning," said Gant. "We're almost there. Get ready to jump when we stop."

Fifteen minutes later they pulled into the courtyard of a large hostelry. Gant stopped in the shadow of a large stable.

"Go now," Gant whispered. "The coast is clear. Good luck, and don't let the townspeople see you."

Quadroped and Fairfax hopped to the ground and scampered under the shadow of the great wagon wheels. Then Morrag led them at a run out of the door and around the back of the building. They found themselves on a small cobble-paved alleyway between two-story wooden buildings that leaned together at awkward, unbalanced angles. Their lower windows were cracked and almost opaque with dirt.

The alley led at one end to a wide boulevard lined with stately trees and at the other end to another, meaner alleyway. Morrag chose to avoid the larger streets, and so they soon found themselves wandering through all the more noisome ways of the town.

"We," said Fairfax, "are lost."

He stopped and attempted to brush the straw from his back without much success. The straw had firmly attached itself to the hedgehog's stubby spines, transforming him into an unkempt little haystack.

"Yes," agreed Morrag. He looked around the alleyway. It looked identical to the one in which they had started.

"By the time we reach the market the magician will have come and gone. Unless . . ."

He stopped and stared at Quadroped. Quadroped shifted nervously from hoof to hoof, misliking Morrag's suddenly speculative look.

"Quadro, could you find the way to the market by scent?" asked Morrag.

Quadroped shuddered. The town smelled of old garbage and mud. After his first whiff of the unpleasantly robust aroma he had assiduously practiced breathing through his mouth.

"Well?" demanded Morrag.

"I suppose so," said Quadroped gloomily.

He sniffed and recoiled at the overly ripe scent of decaying matter. Bravely he sniffed again. After a while his snout became accustomed to the noxious smell and he was able to distinguish individual scents from the odoriferous cacophony around him. A faint, pleasantly spicy smell wove through the pungent bouquet. Quadroped concentrated on it and distinguished cinnamon, cloves, nutmeg, and ginger. These rare commodities, he reasoned, were most likely to be found in the market. He began, unerringly, to home in on them.

Morrag and Fairfax followed Quadroped through the twisting maze of streets, straight up to the back door of a small bakery exuding a powerful smell of fresh gingerbread. Quadroped stopped and stared at the shop in dismay. Morrag and Fairfax were glowering at him, as though they suspected that he had led them there deliberately. A small basket of broken cookies, left by the door for beggars and dogs, did nothing to allay their suspicions.

"I thought spices would be found in the market," said Quadroped.

"Mmmmm," said Fairfax darkly. He dipped his snout into the basket and extracted a cookie. He devoured the gingerbread torso, head first.

"You'll have to home in on something else," said Morrag. "How about truffles? They won't be found in abundance outside the market."

"I'll try," said Quadroped.

He consumed the basket of cookies and then concentrated once more on his nose. After a long while he detected the faint and wonderful smell of fresh, ripe truffles. Following his nose he led them through the town, straight to the market at its center.

"Oh, well done, Quadro!" said Morrag, as the bright awnings of the market stalls appeared at the end of their current grubby alleyway. Quadroped blushed and waggled his ears with pleasure.

The market was a piglet's dream. Though goods were scarce by normal standards, it seemed to Quadroped that wonderful foods were heaped upon every counter. He paid no heed to the wilted condition of the vegetables for sale, or the mildewed state of the cheeses. Nor did he notice that flour was scarce and bread almost nonexistent. He saw only that slightly battered delicacies of all descriptions had fallen to the ground and lay, unnoticed, beneath the colored cloths that covered the base of every stall.

As they made their way toward the center of the market, sneaking along beneath the trestles, Quadroped feasted to his heart's content. By the time Morrag had found a place to watch the magician, Quadroped was quite delightfully full. It was a happy and contented pig that sat down beneath the scarlet fringe of a confectioner's stall to watch the magician perform.

The center of the marketplace had been left free of stalls. Toward noon this area filled with a crowd of excited, jostling people all chattering about the magician and the horrible season of rain.

"We'll never be able to see or hear him," said Quadroped. "All those people are in the way."

"Yes, we will," said Morrag. He had witnessed many such speeches in his seven hundred years. "He'll stand up on something so he's over their heads. And they'll quiet down to listen."

Morrag, as usual, was right. A few hours later a great hush fell upon the crowd. In the sudden silence Quadroped dropped a piece of fallen fudge and looked up. A slender figure, clothed in a rainbow of colors, stood above the crowd, arms outstretched and a familiar smile curving his pale, thin lips.

Morrag saw Quadroped's ears go flat against his head and the short bristles on his neck rise. The piglet's purple eyes were dark and scared.

"Quadro," he hissed, "what's wrong?"

"The magician," said Quadroped, pointing a shaky hoof. "That's Avice."

"It figures," said Fairfax.

"Hush," said Morrag. "He's starting to speak."

"People of Lyskerys," said Avice. "The rain has destroyed your crops. Winter is coming. Hunger is coming. How many of you will be alive in the spring? And for those who survive, where will you find the seed to plant? The spring seed sprouts and rots in the barns."

A general growl of agreement and dismay rose from the crowd. "Tell us something we don't know already," cried a man's deep voice.

"What can *you* do about it?" cried a woman.

Avice raised a hand for silence and got it. "I will tell you something you do not know," said Avice. "And I will tell you what you, not I, can do about this threat." He paused and the crowd shuffled expectantly.

"You have all heard of Ravenor," said Avice in a low voice. "You have heard how its terrible King, the Black Unicorn, waged war on this land for thousands of years. You have also heard how he was imprisoned in Chaos by the sorcerer Rhiogan, Prince of Essylt, and how, since that time the Princes of Essylt have defended this land lest the Black Unicorn escape and those Wars begin again."

The crowd murmured. People whispered among themselves of the legends they had all learned from childhood. Avice let them talk, a small smile on his lips. Then suddenly he raised his voice so that it boomed out over the crowd, shocking them into instant silence.

"People of Lyskerys," said Avice. "You have been betrayed! Reander of Essylt has set the Black Unicorn free!"

Shouts of amazement and a few of denial rose from

the crowd. Then, over and over, people began to ask, "Why?"

"Why?" said Avice. "For *power*. The Black Unicorn lusts to possess these fertile lands and the Princes of Essylt have joined him. Essylt is a cold, dark land of ice and Ravenor a place of deserts. They want the green fields, the pastures, the rich hospitable lands that all the other Kingdoms possess.

"You may ask," Avice continued smoothly, "what evidence I have of this." And indeed several voices had been raised in such a demand. "I shall tell you. Who will say that this unending rain is natural? The rain is Ravenor's Revenge. It weakens the land and the people, so that they cannot resist the armies of Essylt and Ravenor. It does not rain in Ravenor . . . and it does not rain in Essylt."

"It's too cold to rain in Essylt," said someone.

"Essylt would never ally itself to Ravenor," said someone else. "There's too much blood between them."

"Do you think so?" asked Avice. "You have all heard, no doubt, of the wedding between Glasgerion of Essylt and the witch named Morragwen?" The crowd had indeed heard. "Well, I shall tell you what you do *not* know. The witch is a Warlord of Ravenor. That marriage binds the House of Essylt to Ravenor and will forge a link of common blood between them."

The crowd murmured angrily. Several people demanded what the magician thought he could do about it.

"Ravenor is not invincible," said Avice. "The Great Wars, the immortal Black Unicorn, the dreadful powers of Ravenor, all these are illusions. They have been created over the ages by the Princes of Essylt to justify their leadership of the Council and their supremacy over all the other larger, richer Kingdoms."

"The rain," said Avice, "can be driven away. The crops can be restored. Even my humble powers can effect some cure. Behold!"

Avice raised his face to the heavens, his long neck arched back, his blond hair falling free in a silken banner down his back. He stretched out his arms to the side, waist high, elbows slightly bent, palms up as though he beseeched the clouds. Before the astonished eyes of the crowd the thunder clouds began to melt away, layer after layer, until a deep blue sky appeared and the sun shone warm and bright. A great cheer arose from the crowd.

"As the sun can be restored, so can the crops be revived," said Avice. "Many have brought their damaged crops and livestock here to the market, hoping that someone will buy. I can restore them." He stepped down, entered the crowd, and disappeared from sight.

"What is he doing?" asked Quadroped.

He stuck his head out but could only see a mass of jostling humans. The sun felt warm and good and so he moved slightly farther out. No one paid him any attention. They were all looking up, craning their necks for a sight of Avice.

Fairfax left the stall and scuttled out into the crowd. Hedgehogs were not uncommon and he attracted no particular attention. After a brief sortie he rejoined his companions. "He's restoring dead fruits and vegetables to life," said Fairfax.

"He's *what*?" asked Morrag.

"He passes his hand over a counter or cartload of withered fruits and they all plump up and start to look edible," said Fairafax. "I couldn't tell if it was real or illusion. People are very excited about it though."

"I should think so," said Morrag. People around them suddenly started yelling and cheering. Avice was approaching the stall. "Get back," said Morrag. "He mustn't see us."

Quadroped meant to comply but he was suddenly overwhelmed by a desire to stay put. The sun was so warm, the sky so blue. He felt happy and comfortable and safe. Avice approached. With a hiss, Morrag snaked around Quadroped's neck and yanked him back under the fringe, but not before Quadroped had stared for a long moment straight into Avice's sea-green eyes.

Avice passed on without a second glance and Morrag let out a sigh of relief. "He didn't see you," he said. "Quadro, what's wrong with you? Why didn't you hide?"

"I don't know," said Quadroped. He was trembling

now and all the peace he had felt a moment ago had evaporated. Once more his fear of Avice rose up, accelerating his heartbeat and making it difficult to breath. Avice *had* seen him, he was certain of it.

"Let's get out of here," he pleaded. "We've heard enough."

"Wait," said Morrag. "Look, he's going to speak again."

Avice had mounted to the platform once more. "Friends," he said, "what you have seen is a small cure, a *temporary* cure. I cannot dispel the rain forever or save more than a fraction of your crops. If you are to survive this dreadful affliction *you* must take action."

"What? What can we do? Tell us!" cried the crowd.

"What can you do?" asked Avice. "You can rise up against Ravenor and Essylt! You can end their power by defeating them in battle. You can crush their diabolical union and ensure that never again can they rise up to trouble the Kingdoms of the World. People of Lyskerys, you can *annihilate* them!"

The crowd roared, screamed, pushed, and waved its fists. Avice smiled at them.

"You are not alone," he said. "Already your Rulers are in Essylt attempting to bring its Princes down. But the Council alone cannot do it. The Kings must have their armies. Soon you will hear their summons to war. When the Council is broken the cry will go out and *you must answer it*. If you do not, if you remain here in your homes, you will die."

The crowd went wild. There was no doubt that they believed Avice implicitly.

"This," said Fairfax, "is not just a local problem. These people will fight."

"If the summons comes," said Morrag.

"If Avice has spoken to the high Lords of the land, that summons will come," said Fairfax.

"It must not," said Morrag. "Reander must stop these fools. If they set foot in Ravenor the treaty will be broken. Ravenor will lay this land to waste if ever it is raised to arms. Too many still thirst for blood."

Quadroped had a sudden image of the Warlord Man-slayer, his grisly kilt of human skins slick with blood, wading through the carnage of a great battlefield.

"Listen," said Fairfax. "Avice is speaking again."

"Enemies," said Avice, "are all around you. The eyes of Essylt are here, hidden in your very midst, waiting to work your downfall."

"Uh-oh," said Quadroped.

"Let's go," said Morrag. He led them quickly out from under the stall.

"You have all heard," Avice said as the three animals snuck through the crowd toward the edge of the market, "about the evil creature who set the Black Unicorn free, the demonic beast summoned up by Prince Reander to complete his fell designs."

The animals picked up speed but the crowd was tightly packed and its edge seemed very far away.

"You have heard that it is a great boar of ghastly aspect, of grisly mien, who brings famine and pestilence in its wake," said Avice.

Quadroped and his friends neared the edge of the crowd. They were almost out of the marketplace.

"That is not true. The traitor pig is none other than a small white piglet named Quadroped."

Quadroped could see the empty alleyways of Adelchis ahead.

"And he is right here," shouted Avice. "With his evil companions, about to make good his escape at the edge of the marketplace." Avice pointed directly at the three fleeing animals. "Catch them!" he cried.

"Here we go again," said Fairfax.

They burst out of the marketplace and ran up the nearest alleyway at a dead run. The crowd gave a great howl as it spotted them and lurched into pursuit. Stones and now-ripe vegetables began to pelt through the air.

"Ouch," cried Morrag as a fish head struck him. "Quadroped, try to smell earth and clean water. They'll lead us out of town to the fields."

Quadroped tried to calm his fears and think. He concentrated on his nose. "I've got it," he cried and ran ahead as fast as he could, Morrag and Fairfax racing after him.

Quadroped led them directly down a wide, tree-lined street and out into the countryside. The mob surged after them, yelling and screaming at the top of its lungs.

"Off the road," said Morrag. "They'll slow down in the fields."

Quadroped groaned. He was getting very tired of being chased across fields by maniacal human beings.

They ran and stumbled over the fields, ducking through hedgerows where the humans could not pass. By the time they had reached the woods at the far end of the fields they were exhausted, but the humans were far behind. They collapsed in the shelter of a dense bush and tried to catch their breaths.

"Are we safe?" asked Quadroped when he could speak.

"I don't think so," said Morrag. "They had dogs, they'll track us here. And Avice may have other means of finding us. We'll have to keep moving as fast as we can. Fairfax, this is your territory, do you have any idea where we are?"

Fairfax got up and began to snuffle around in various directions. He returned with an almost cheerful expression on his face.

"We're in Eunoe's woods," he said. "We've run due west."

"Can you find her house?" asked Morrag.

"Yes," said Fairfax. He scuttled swiftly ahead down some invisible path, leading them into the dark green heart of the forest.

Evening fell. Far away they could hear the barks of dogs. The townspeople were still some distance behind but they were clearly on the trail. *If we don't find Eunoe's house soon*, thought Quadroped, *they'll catch us*.

The sounds of the pursuit came closer. The cries of the people could be heard urging the dogs, and each other, on. Fairfax broke into a run. Quadroped and Morrag pelted after him. Minutes later they broke through a screen of bushes into a grassy clearing. In front of them stood a small white cottage complete with flower boxes and smoke pouring in friendly curls from its little brick chimney.

Morrag swam to the knocker and grabbed it in his teeth, beating a brisk tattoo on the wooden door. "Let us in," he cried.

The door flew open with considerable violence, flinging Morrag to the ground and knocking Quadroped off his hooves. Eunoe stood in her doorway, hands on hips, a dark frown joining dark eyebrows over flashing brown eyes.

"What *is* the meaning of this?" she demanded icily, surveying the three animals on the grass. "Go away, you unmannerly beasts, and be glad I don't turn you into frogs." She moved as if to shut the door in their faces.

Quadroped scrambled to his hooves in dismay. "Oh, please don't send us away," he said. "There are people after us and if they catch us we'll be *killed*."

Eunoe stepped out of the door and bent to examine her visitors more closely. They were liberally covered in mud and leaves, their features quite disguised.

"Quadroped!" she said in disgusted accents when she had identified him. "I should have known it was you." She straightened and cocked her head, listening to the unmistakable sounds of the pursuing mob.

"I suppose you'll have to come in," she said grudgingly. She stood away from the door and allowed them to enter, making sure that each wiped his feet on the doormat. "Visitors," Quadroped heard her mutter as he passed. "I hate visitors."

Eunoe ushered her unwelcome guests into a small sitting room. "You may *not* sit down," she said. "Mud on the carpets is bad enough. I will not tolerate dirty upholstery. What are you doing here? And who are those people?"

"They're from Adelchis," said Quadroped. Briefly he summarized their experiences in the marketplace. "They think I'm a demon pig," he concluded.

"Well," said Eunoe, "you really are a bundle of jolly surprises, aren't you? What fun to have an enraged mob heading toward my house. And a powerful magician to deal with as well!"

"I'm sorry," said Quadroped, looking doletul. "I didn't mean to."

"You never do," said Eunoe nastily.

A moment later shouts and yells told them that the mob and its hounds had reached the clearing and were descending on the house. Heavy blows fell on the door.

"Open up! Open up in there," shouted a man.

"Stay here," said Eunoe sharply. She went out into the hall and opened the door, inward this time so that the large man who had been thumping on it fell sprawling at her feet.

Eunoe looked at the crowd and raised one eyebrow over an icy eye. "Be silent," she said.

The people gaped at the tall, auburn-haired woman surveying them so calmly and with such obvious disdain. Feeling suddenly foolish they quieted down, standing rather sheepishly in front of her.

"You, get up," said Eunoe, prodding the man at her feet with a silk-shod toe. "What do you mean by coming here? What do you want?"

The man got up and stepped back a pace. "We're looking for a pig and a couple of other beasts," he said.

"Well, they're not in *here*," said Eunoe in offended accents. "Livestock belong in the barn, not the house."

"Oh, um, sorry, ma'am," said the man, backing away still further.

"Go away, you lout," said Eunoe. The man turned crimson, hung his head, and began to walk away. The rest of the crowd turned to follow him.

"Stop."

A cold voice halted the man in his tracks. Avice appeared, walking calmly through the crowd, which parted to let him pass. "I regret this disturbance, Lady," he said with a small smile. "But the pig is most certainly in your house."

Eunoe tilted her chin and looked down her nose at him. "Are you calling me a liar, sir?" she demanded.

"Are you not one, Lady?" said Avice. "I rather think Quadroped is in your sitting room just now."

Eunoe's eyes became suddenly very alert and her jaw tightened. "You are very sure of yourself," she said.

"Give me the piglet, Lady," said Avice. "If you do not, I promise I shall take him. I have no wish to harm a woman as lovely as you."

"Do you think you could?" asked Eunoe.

"I take my promises very seriously, I assure you," said Avice. Inside the house Quadroped shuddered.

Eunoe sighed and suddenly relaxed her stance. "Oh very well," she said. "Come in."

She ushered him into the house and slammed the door behind him. Then she led him straight into the sitting room to where Quadroped crouched. Quadroped gazed at Eunoe in dismay. He had known that Eunoe was an unfriendly person, but he had really thought that she liked him.

"There he is," said Eunoe. Avice smiled and stepped toward Quadroped.

"Oh, no, you don't," said Morrag. He sprang forward only to be frozen in midair by a pass from Avice's hand. Fairfax was similarly dealt with.

Avice stooped and plucked Quadroped off the rug and into his arms. Quadroped was still too stunned to resist.

"Now, little hoggling," crooned Avice, "I believe we have an appointment in the Fleshless Land."

"Take him and get out," said Eunoe, moving to stand before a table whereon reposed a large vase. "I have better things to do than deal with you all evening."

"Certainly, Lady," said Avice. He stepped forward and Eunoe extended a limp hand. Avice took it and bowed, bringing her hand to his lips in a courtly gesture. No sooner had his lips touched her skin than she grabbed up the vase in her free hand and brought it crashing down on the base of his skull. Avice went limp and crumpled to the floor.

Eunoe brushed her hands on the skirt of her dress and smiled faintly. Then she rolled Avice slightly on his side and extracted a breathless Quadroped. With a wave of her hand she freed Morrag and Fairfax.

"Quick now," she said. "Gather round me and grab hold of my legs. We must get out of here. He'll be awake soon and I don't think I'm powerful enough to deal with him."

"You dealt splendidly," said Morrag. He twined about her shoulders. Fairfax came up and sat on her foot.

"I took him by surprise," said Eunoe. "Sometimes a physical blow is more effective than magic. Now, where shall we go?"

"Someplace safe," said Quadroped.

"Essylt," said Eunoe. With a soft *pop* she blinked out of sight, carrying Quadroped, Fairfax, and Morrag with her.

Chapter Five

An awkward silence, tense with unvoiced fears, suffused the small round room in the Western Tower of the Palace of Essylt, where the Princes Reander and Glasgerion had gathered in solemn consultation with the rulers of three Kingdoms: portly Aumbry of Akariel; Aodh of Seamourn, stern and pale; and from Isfandiar, the skeletal form of Ghola, clothed in black. The meeting was not going well.

Glasgerion studied the three rulers in silence. Aumbry looked scared, Aodh and Ghola tense and watchful. These men were not friends, and they distrusted the Princes of Essylt. *I've been gone too long,* Glasgerion thought. Ten years ago he had left Essylt to search for the lost Key to Chaos. The Council had changed. Old friends had died to be replaced by strangers.

Glasgerion shivered and drew his gray wool cloak tightly around his lean frame. The light of the setting sun shone golden orange through translucent walls that could never melt. The room was cold despite all attempts to warm it, another testimony to the idiocy of building a

palace out of ice. With a sigh he returned his attention
to the matter at hand. The new Prince of Akariel was
speaking:

"The rain has almost certainly destroyed the beet harvest," Aumbry said mournfully, tucking fat bejeweled
fingers more deeply into his furry muff.

"The rain," said Reander, "has nothing to do with it.
My Lords, the treaty must be signed."

"My dear boy," said spidery Ghola of Isfandiar, waving a long finger in Reander's face, "the rain has *everything* to do with it. When the rain stops, then we can
discuss peace treaties."

Reander's eyes narrowed into unpleasant little slits.
Glasgerion took one look at his nephew and deemed it
wisest to reply in his stead. These men would not take
kindly to insults.

"Ravenor is not responsible for the weather," said
Glasgerion. He hoped fervently that that was the truth.

"The rain gets worse the closer one comes to Ravenor,"
said Aumbry, his fat face puckered in distress. "It isn't a
natural phenomenon, nothing stops it."

Aodh, King of Seamourn, frowned. "The mollusk beds
have silted up," he said. "The seaweeds grow stunted
and pale." The silvery layer of water that surrounded the
Sea King blurred his features but could not disguise the
anger in his voice. "Reander, we cannot sit still while
Ravenor casts its spells and our people starve. By spring
we will be too weak to defend ourselves against invasion."

"If you sign the treaty there will be no invasion," said
Glasgerion reasonably.

"So you say," said Ghola.

"The Black Unicorn has given his word that he will do
us no harm," said Glasgerion.

Ghola stared at Glasgerion for a long moment. "Your
faith in the Black Unicorn is really quite touching," he
said. "If a trifle naïve. No doubt your pretty new wife
has allayed your suspicions."

He turned to Reander. "Dear boy, this treaty of
yours . . ." He shook his head sorrowfully. Reander grit-
ted his teeth. "Most ill-advised, quite rash. I understand

that Ravenor's plight had engaged your sympathies, how could it not? A whole land on the brink of starvation and death! You should have brought the matter to the Council's attention. We would have taken appropriate action. But to go ahead and set the Black Unicorn free. To arrange a treaty with him on your own, without the benefit of wiser heads . . . most imprudent. You've overstepped your authority, dear boy."

"You swore you would lock the Gate, Reander," said Aodh. "You have betrayed our trust." Aodh was almost smiling. It was good to see the autocratic Prince of Essylt brought low.

Reander controlled his anger with some difficulty but managed to reply calmly enough. "I did not release the Black Unicorn," he said. "But I will not argue it with you for I can see you will not believe me. For whatever reason, the Black Unicorn is free and must be dealt with. You cannot intimidate him with force. If you try you will only succeed in unleashing his fury upon us all. He has no love for the Kingdoms, it will take little to provoke him."

"So you advise us to do nothing? To make peace at any cost?" Aodh's blue skin purpled in wrath. Fat Aumbry stepped hastily away from him. "Are the Kingdoms to be held hostage by this animal? Shall the rains fall and our people die while their rulers cower and do nothing for fear of Ravenor's wrath?"

"There is nothing cowardly about accepting this peace," said Glasgerion. It was clear these men would not believe Ravenor innocent of the rain. He tried another approach.

"The rain has done much damage and the winter will be hard but we can stave off famine. Jansiar, Essylt, and Ungartok have fish, Kervanathel's forests hold game. Together we can feed the Kingdoms until spring. War will bring greater suffering than a famine ever would."

"War is an expensive proposition," said Aumbry tentatively. "Perhaps we should do as they say, wait until spring."

Aodh looked disgusted. "And what if the rain does not stop?" he asked. "The food chain is being affected at its

base. The sunlight is diminished, the phytoplankton die.
By next winter there will be no more fish!''

"Why so eager for war, Aodh?" asked Reander.

Glasgerion winced and tried to silence his hotheaded
nephew. Reander smiled, his temper well and truly lost.
It was no secret that Aodh feared to lose his throne to his
exiled elder twin, Aedh. Aedh who had been exiled for
setting the Warlord Manslayer free and trying to kill Quadroped before he could lock the Gate. Aedh who was still
more than Aodh would ever be.

"Your army is dwindling, Aodh," said Reander. "By
fall they will all be in Ravenor with your brother."

"Aedh is a murderer and a traitor," said Ghola coldly.
"He is no longer welcome in the Council or the Kingdoms. Peace will not free him from exile. Aodh is right,
the rain may not stop. Ravenor must be dealt with this
winter."

Reander turned upon Ghola. "You would welcome war,
would you not?" he said. "Isfandiar's borders have been
creeping east. Ravenorian mines have made you rich. If
you break my treaty with Ravenor you will lose far more
than minerals. You will start a war you cannot end. There
will be slaughter such as the world has not known for a
thousand years. The Kingdoms will be destroyed. You
will doom your descendants to lives of unceasing strife
and the world shall be drowned in their blood."

"Spare us your histrionics!" An expression of faintest
disgust distorted Ghola's pallid features as he gazed upon
Reander. "We are not children to be frightened by such
wild tales."

"What is this talk of defeat?" asked Aodh. "You were
not wont to be such a coward, Reander. Last spring you
were eager enough for war."

Last spring war had seemed inevitable. Reander could
not very well have told his army the truth. It just wasn't
good for morale. Glasgerion wondered if there was any
point explaining this to Aodh. The Sea King seemed determined to believe the worst of Reander. And yet, the treaty
had to be signed. In a patient voice Glasgerion tried once
more to explain that war was not a bright option.

What effect Glasgerion's reasoned discourse might have had upon his obdurate audience was never known for his words were drowned out by a sudden crash of thunder. In an explosion of pure light Eunoe appeared, bedecked in eel and pig and hedgehog.

For a moment no one spoke. Then Aumbry's watery eye fell upon the bedraggled form of Quadroped, where he nestled in Eunoe's arms.

Aumbry paled, his mouth fell open, and his hands flapped at his sides. He gurgled incoherently. With a wild cry he leaped toward the door and twisted frantically at the knob. But the door, as was usual during important meetings, was locked. Trembling, Aumbry turned to face the startled company.

"Alas!" wailed Aumbry, pointing at the bewildered Quadroped. "The Demon Pig has come among us. We're *doomed,* all doomed to die of plague!" In the sudden, shocked silence all eyes turned to Quadroped.

"*What* did you call him?" demanded Reander.

Aumbry swallowed. His eyes slid nervously around the room, avoiding Quadroped. "The Demon Pig," he said. "Of Es, um . . . of the North."

Quadroped looked around at the hostile faces above him and tried not to cower. Avice's lies had spread further than he had ever imagined.

Eunoe smiled at Aumbry. "It's only Quadroped," she said. "He's really quite harmless."

Aumbry gave a weak chuckle but refused to move away from the door. "Silly mistake," he said without much conviction. "It was just its color. I'm sure it's quite a nice pig." He was still quite pale and his hands were shaking.

Glasgerion looked quickly around the room. Aodh was also alarmed, though he hid it well. Ghola was surreptitiously tucking something away in his sleeve . . . a knife! Glasgerion frowned. Ghola had been expecting some treachery.

"The Demon Pig," said Reander. "The Demon Pig of the *North.*" He stared at Aumbry. "An interesting sobriquet. Would you care to elaborate?"

"No!" said Aumbry. "I mean . . . it's just . . ."

"It's nothing," said Ghola. "A story to frighten children."

"Children and Aumbry," said Reander. "If it frightens the Prince of Akariel I think we should discuss it."

"It's late," said Ghola. "There is little to be gained by further discussion, and your guests appear tired."

He produced a key from his pocket and unlocked the door. "Aumbry? Aodh?" Aumbry bowed and hurried out, Aodh followed him. On the threshold Ghola turned and held up a skeletal hand in farewell.

"We shall speak together in Council tomorrow, Reander, Glasgerion," said Ghola. His serpentine gaze flickered over Eunoe and the assorted beasts. "It has been a most interesting meeting. Good night." He went out, closing the door softly behind him.

When Ghola had left, Reander turned upon Eunoe, the light of battle in his eyes. "Madam, how dare you break in on us like that? That meeting was crucial."

"It was ill done," agreed Glasgerion. "Those men were badly frightened. Aumbry looked as if the Black Unicorn himself had appeared."

"Aumbry is a fool," said Eunoe. "Imagine taking Quadro for a demon!"

"Ghola and Aodh were frightened as well," said Glasgerion. "They won't forgive this easily and we need their support in Council."

"Well, I'm sorry," said Eunoe. "We were in considerable danger. There wasn't time to check our coordinates."

Glasgerion studied Quadroped's gaunt figure and scratched and muddy hide with growing concern. "What sort of trouble have you gotten into now, Quadro?" he asked.

Quadroped gulped and looked nervously around. Reander eyed him sharply. "It has something to do with this Demon Pig nonsense, doesn't it?" he asked. "Out with it! What mischief have you been up to?"

"I . . ."

Quadroped looked into Reander's furious face and found he could not go on. It seemed like the wrong time to tell him about Avice. Reander was not going to like hearing that half the countryside thought he was in league with Ravenor.

Eunoe came to Quadroped's rescue. "Reander, it's freezing in here," she said. "Can we not discuss this someplace warmer?"

Reander frowned and looked around the tiny room with distaste. "It is cold in here," he said. "Let us adjourn to my chambers. Glasgerion, you might as well ask Morragwen to join us. No doubt she will wish to greet her eel."

Half an hour later saw the company standing about a dreary, cathedral-sized sitting room situated somewhere in the private northern wing of the Palace. Glasgerion's wife, the Warlord Morragwen, had joined them. She was a tall woman, fair of form and changeable. That night her skin was a rich golden hue to offset her glowing red eyes.

After a joyous reunion between Morrag and his witch, an equally happy reunion between the witch and the pig, a more restrained and dignified greeting between Morragwen and Eunoe, the formal introduction of Fairfax to Morragwen, and a general session of all-around hugging and hand shaking, the company sat down in the fiendish devices that passed for chairs in Reander's suite.

"Speak to us, Quadro," said Reander in accents of doom, "of Demon Pigs. Why did the sight of you frighten Aumbry so badly?"

"What is a Demon Pig?" asked Morragwen.

"It's a me," said Quadroped.

In faltering accents he proceeded to tell Reander about Avice and the meeting they had overheard in the marketplace that morning. When he had finished, Reander was looking exceedingly angry and Glasgerion was looking troubled.

"Avice," said Glasgerion. "An unusual name. I wonder . . ."

"What?" demanded Reander.

"It's probably nothing," said Glasgerion. "But there *are* stories about a character called Avice. He's supposed to be a trickster, a Lord of Misrule. I had thought he was only a folklore motif, but perhaps he exists after all. These rumors would be in character. He's a troublemaker, always showing up where he's least wanted."

"He's not the only one," said Reander with a dark look at Eunoe. "Why is he interested in Quadroped? How powerful is he?"

"Very, if half the stories told about him are true," said Glasgerion. "If he is active and bent on mischief, we may have a problem. There's been no sign of him in recorded history. I wonder where he's come from."

"These rumors are playing right into Ravenor's hands," Reander said. He looked at Morragwen. "Could Goriel have summoned this trickster to provoke the Kingdoms into war?"

Morragwen looked thoughtful. "Goriel still wants revenge," she said at length. "But I do not think he would break the truce. He swore to take no hostile actions against the Kingdoms. Releasing Avice would certainly be regarded as such."

"The Manslayer then?" suggested Eunoe. "His sense of honor is not so fine."

Morragwen shook her head. "Goriel holds him in check and he has not the mind for such a subtle plot."

Throughout this conversation Quadroped had been uncomfortably aware that Morrag and Fairfax were looking very stern indeed. The time had come to confess. Quadroped took a deep breath and, looking fixedly at the ceiling, said: "IsetAvicefree."

"You did what?"

Quadroped tried to meet Reander's eyes and failed; he stared at the floor instead. The designs on the rug were colorful, really quite fascinating when viewed up close. There was a lion, and a bear, and an intricate tree and . . .

"Well?"

"I only gave him some water," Quadroped said. "He looked so miserable. He was all chained up in the dark. I didn't know it would free him."

"Aumbry was right," said Reander bitterly. "You do bring about disasters. First the Black Unicorn and now this. I shudder to think what horror you'll think up next. You're worse than a plague."

"Reander!" said Glasgerion sharply.

"He's right," said Quadroped miserably. "It's all my fault." His snout crumpled up and tears, long suppressed, began to course down his cheeks. "There'll be a war, and Reander hates me, and I'll *never* see my parents again."

"For goodness' sake," said Eunoe, "now look what you've done. Although he is a menace to civilization and ought not to be wandering around the Kingdoms on his own. I've smashed one of my favorite vases for him, a mob has torn up my garden, and the wretched beast has covered me in mud."

Glasgerion looked at the dirt stains on her costume and grinned. "He is a trifle unkempt," he said. "I thought Morrag could keep him out of trouble; I see I was wrong."

"You'd better tell us everything, Quadro," said Reander. "What has happened to your parents? And how did you manage to set Avice free?"

So Quadroped tearfully related the story of his adventures since entering Whislewood Forest. While he was speaking, a servant came in with chocolate cookies and milk, which did much to restore his composure.

"So my parents are in the Fleshless Land," he concluded. "And I need you to set them free. You will, won't you?"

"No," said Reander.

Quadroped looked at him in dismay. After all his desperate struggles he had never expected refusal. Another tear formed and rolled slowly down his quivering snout.

"I fail to see," Reander continued, "how one small piglet can cause so much trouble. As if the rain wasn't enough, now we have a mysterious mischief maker and a malevolent Queen of the Dead to deal with." He looked at Quadroped's woeful countenance and relented. "We'll find your parents as soon as the treaty is ratified," he said.

"But that could take ages and *ages,*" said Quadroped.

"I profoundly hope not," said Reander. "Quadro, try to understand, Nieve is too formidable a foe for me to tackle right now."

"But they could be *dying*." said Quadroped.

"We may all be dying this time next month if those fools in the Council don't ratify the treaty," said Reander. "I can't help you, Quadro, my hands are full."

"Cheer up, Quadro," said Fairfax unforgivably. "If your parents are still alive a delay won't harm them, if they're dead it's already too late."

"What shall we do about these rumors?" Glasgerion asked, skillfully moving the conversation back into its original channels.

"Perhaps Quadro should come to the Ball tonight," said Morragwen. "No one who sees him will believe he is a demon. All the Council will be there and many others besides. If we can calm their fears perhaps they will begin to trust you again."

"One look at Quadro and even our closest allies will believe that we helped him open the Gate," said Glasgerion.

"They already do," said Reander. "No one believes I opposed him. The most we can hope for is that they will believe that I hoped to ameliorate Ravenor's sufferings and to promote peace. Quadro shall go to the Ball. And Quadro, wear your finest."

Quadroped groaned aloud at this command, for his "finest" was a horrible silken sort of saddlecloth heavily encrusted with gold embroidery and precious gems. It was heavy, uncomfortable, and rather silly looking. It had been lovingly embroidered for him by the high-ranking Ladies of Essylt for the occasion of Glasgerion's marriage to Morragwen last winter.

Still, three hours later when Morrag came to collect him and lead him to the Ball, Quadroped was glad of the valet who had scrubbed him thoroughly until his white coat shone in the lamplight and who had draped him in the hated cloth.

Morrag had outdone himself; small fiery opals adhered to the tip of every gleaming scale and a sheen of silver dust coated his entire body. As he rippled through the lighted halls he shone iridescent as the rainbow itself.

"I'm representing Ravenor tonight," said Morrag when

Quadroped complimented him on his exquisite appearance. "I probably shouldn't but Reander hasn't told me *not* to."

He inspected Quadroped critically before pronouncing his opinion that Quadroped would "do." "Although," he added, "one could wish that the dear ladies had not insisted on cramming *every* scene from your trip to the Gate onto such a small tapestry." Quadroped could only agree. The design left much to be desired.

Quadroped could hear and scent the party long before they ever reached it. Sounds of music, barely audible over voices raised in light laughter and idle chatter, and the smell of a thousand spicy perfumes filled the corridors of the central, public, wing of the Palace.

Looking out of a window into the courtyard below Quadroped saw a long line of notables waiting to enter the Palace. Fortunately the ballroom was also accessible from a small antechamber in the private wing of the Palace and they were able to enter without attracting too much attention.

The noise, lights, and splendid attire of the guests all combined to make Quadroped feel unaccountably shy and awkward. A waiter, clad in sober black and white, passed by with a huge platter of food.

"Ah, *rollmops*," sighed Morrag. He drifted off after the waiter and was soon lost from sight, leaving Quadroped quite alone.

Although Quadroped had been in the Great Hall on previous occasions, tonight it took his breath away. From the ceiling hung banners emblazoned with the devices of all the noble houses present. Huge crystal chandeliers spilled their diamond light across walls shining with mirrors or covered with brilliant tapestries. No less than three separate orchestras sat in the galleries, all perfectly in time with one another so that the room was immersed in sound. So noisy was it, in fact, that it was some time before Quadroped realized that a large red-and-white fox vixen had approached him and was staring insolently at his costume.

"Hello," said Quadroped timidly.

"What a horrible coat," said the vixen. "Aren't you

ashamed to be seen wearing it? I always think it is *so* demeaning for a beast to allow humans to dress him up.''

"Oh," said Quadroped. He looked at the vixen and wondered what he could say that would not be quite rude. After all, he felt much the same way about the ghastly garment.

"Of course," said the vixen, her yellow eyes glinting, "pigs are so *domesticated*."

Quadroped considered turning his back on this unpleasant new acquaintance but was stopped by the consideration that she might be somebody very important. If he insulted her perhaps she could make things worse for Glasgerion and Reander in the Council.

"*I* think the coat is quite charming, Ilketsni," said a deep, croaking voice. A large black cormorant sporting a red muffler around his long thin neck stepped toward them. "Costumes are merely a form of decoration, there is no reason why humans should have a monopoly on them. Why don't you run off and antagonize someone else? This piglet is not up to your weight."

With a disdainful twitch of her tail the vixen turned and trotted gracefully off, her sharp black nose in the air.

"Thank you," said Quadroped. "I'm Quadroped."

"And I am Briavel," said the cormorant solemnly. "Regent of Jansiar. You must be the little Key Bearer. I had hoped to make your acquaintance; there are too many humans and too few beasts or birds in positions of power these days."

Quadroped blushed slightly. He was not used to being treated with respect. He did not consider himself an important or influential pig at all, despite his powerful friends. "Who was that?" he said.

"Ilketsni," said Briavel. Then, seeing that Quadroped still looked confused, "One of the Councilors of Ungartok. She and that grande dame Angriska are old enemies of Essylt. Watch out for them, they'll cause you trouble if they can. Who are you with anyway?"

"I'm not," said Quadroped. He explained that Morrag had gone off in pursuit of a herring and was probably still floating around the hall in the wake of the platter of fish.

"Well, stick close to me then," said Briavel. "This is no place for any but seasoned politicians, too much is going on." He turned and led Quadroped into the crowd.

"I'm surprised that you were allowed in here at all," he continued as he forged ahead between the legs of the humans that crowded the floor. "You're rather young for such affairs."

"Reander wanted people to see me," said Quadroped. "He thought it would help dispel the Demon Pig story."

"He could be right," said Briavel. "But it may be dangerous. People aren't behaving rationally around pigs these days. There are many here who would like to see you dead."

Quadroped gulped nervously and looked around at the sea of legs above him. The vixen Ilketsni was staring at him from across the room. She licked her white teeth when he met her eyes.

Quadroped followed Briavel through the crowd, trying hard to remember all the names and faces and failing dismally. He did, however, manage to remember the names and faces of the rulers of each of the Nine Kingdoms.

Essylt lay in the north. From the east beside Ravencr came Ghola of Isfandiar and his southern neighbor, Mircea of Imchadiz. Aumbry of Akariel and Sioned of Lyskerys came from the center of the Kingdoms. From Jansiar in the southwest came the coromorant Briavel. From the Southern Sea came King Aodh. Kervanathel, away to the west, was ruled by bearlike Jehan. From Ungartok in the cold northwest came Ilketsni and withered Angriska.

It occurred to Quadroped, as he studied this list of dignitaries, that the Kingdoms were largely without Kings. Of all the Rulers, only Aodh held that high title. When he pointed this out to Briavel, the cormorant shook his head.

"There are no Kings because there is one," he said. "Or there was in the terrestrial Kingdoms. They got rid of him long ago."

"How?" asked Quadroped. Briavel's answer, he reflected, had been predictable. The Kingdoms, it seemed, had a distressing propensity for ridding themselves of unwanted immortals by throwing them into unpleasant realms.

Quadroped soon grew weary of the Ball. It was noisy and crowded and confusing. To make things worse, people behaved oddly whenever they caught sight of him. Conversations stopped when he and Briavel passed by. Aumbry of Akariel spilled his drink when Quadroped brushed against his leg and Ghola of Isfandiar fingered a knife.

"It's not working," said Quadroped dismally. His feet hurt and the saddlecloth on his back felt unbearably heavy. "People are still afraid of me."

"Idiots," said Briavel. He led Quadroped over to a large buffet table by the wall and surveyed the spread. After a moment he selected a large bowl of pudding and with an imperious flap of his wings instructed a footman to place it on the floor just under the table.

"You'll be safe enough here," he told Quadroped. "There are people I must talk to, and I can see that you would prefer to rest."

So Quadroped curled up under the table, where the white tablecloth would hide him from unfriendly eyes, and began to inhale his pudding. After a while he began to listen to the conversations around him.

What Quadroped learned as he sat beneath the table was disturbing indeed. Many people, it seemed, were truly afraid of him.

"Have you seen the pig?" a lady of Seamourn asked as she sampled the pâté en croute.

"Yes." Her gentleman companion shuddered and let fall his canapé upon the parquet floor. "There's something eerie about him. Did you see his eyes?"

"Horrible . . ."

The couple moved on.

Then there were those who saw Quadroped only for what he was, a baby pig. This did not seem to reassure them either.

"Did you see the pig?" said a man from Seamourn to his equally aqueous companion.

"Indeed. Does Reander still claim it opened the Gate without his consent?"

"He does."

"He's lying of course."

"Yes. I wonder why?"

The question of why Reander had chosen to open the Gate, and why he had lied about the circumstances of its opening also formed the subject of intense speculation. Was Reander really in league with Ravenor? Or did he truly hope for peace? Why *had* he married his uncle off to a Warlord? Over plates of food Princess Sioned of Lyskerys and the Cormorant of Jansiar discussed the matter.

"I can't believe it's simply a bid for power," said Briavel, selecting a shrimp. "Essylt's controlled the Council for years. Reander's hatred for Ravenor was real enough. He doesn't even like his new aunt."

"Then why did he open the Gate?" asked Sioned of Lyskerys.

Briavel shrugged and swallowed the shrimp. "To rescue Ravenor?"

"It's quixotic enough," agreed Sioned. "But it doesn't ring true. Why tell that story about the pig?"

Aodh of Seamourn strode up and joined them. "Maybe the Warlords defeated Reander," said Aodh, "and he was ashamed to admit it."

"And couldn't think up a better story than that?" asked Briavel. "Reander's no idiot and neither is Glasgerion. Their story's so implausible I'm inclined to believe it."

"If the Warlords had defeated him they would have killed him," said Sioned.

"If he had killed the Warlords, Morragwen wouldn't be dancing with Glasgerion right now," said Aodh, glancing over the heads of the crowd. He eyed the lissome witch with a leer. "Does she look dead to you?"

"Reander says the Black Unicorn brought her back to life."

Aodh laughed. "I think Ravenor wanted to avoid a fight," he said. "Our army was ready and waiting. The Black Unicorn needed this treaty to recover his strength. That tale of Ravenor's condition was true enough. Even Ghola doesn't deny it. He's been there since and seen the changes. Ravenor is green again."

"Then you think Ravenor means to attack?" asked Sioned.

"Undoubtedly," said Jehan.

"I disagree," said Briavel. "I think we should sign this treaty."

"You, my friend, have nothing to lose," said Aodh. "Jansiar is far from Ravenor and doesn't depend on plants for food. It's expensive, raising armies to fight other Kingdoms' wars."

Briavel's beak snapped shut in indignation. Princess Sioned changed the subject, and the three Rulers drifted away.

The Ball ended early, no one was having a very good time, and Glasgerion came and fetched Quadroped away to Reander's rooms, where Morragwen, Eunoe, Morrag, Fairfax, and Reander were gathered. Quadroped was feeling rather ill from a surfeit of pudding. The sight of Reander looking uncharacteristically miserable did nothing to soothe his already unsettled condition.

"It's all my fault," said Reander, running a hand through his hair. "If I hadn't bullied them so last spring . . . I took their scattered little war bands and turned them into something that could withstand Ravenor. They wouldn't be capable of starting a war if I hadn't trained their armies myself." Eunoe rather surprisingly sat down beside him and began to massage his neck.

"You did what you had to," said Glasgerion. "I should have stayed in Essylt."

"You had to find the Key."

"I shouldn't have freed the Black Unicorn," said Quadroped, anxious to share the blame.

"No," said Reander nastily. "And you shouldn't have set Avice free either." Quadroped subsided into tearful silence. Eunoe stopped rubbing Reander's neck and gave him a vicious poke instead.

"Morragwen must go back to Ravenor as soon as possible," said Reander. "And Morrag and Quadroped must go with her. The sooner our supposed Ravenorian allies are out of sight, the better. Your presence here only aggravates the Council.''

Glasgerion looked ready to protest this decree but Morragwen laid a gentle hand on his arm to silence him. ''He's right,'' she said.

''Perhaps the Black Unicorn can help you rescue your parents, Quadro,'' said Morrag.

Quadroped brightened a bit at this suggestion. The Black Unicorn was far more powerful than Reander and he knew something about bringing people back from the dead. Surely he would know how to deal with Nieve. Quadroped's hopes were soon dashed.

''Don't be a fool, Reander,'' said Eunoe. ''You can't let Quadro go. You need him.''

Reander stared at Eunoe. Eunoe frowned back. ''Don't look at me as if I've gone mad,'' she snapped. ''Who else can talk to the Black Unicorn if it comes to war? Thanks to Avice the people are angry and frightened. Some idiot may decide to attack Ravenor even without the Council's support.''

''Goriel won't let any incursion into Ravenor go unrevenged,'' said Glasgerion. ''A frontier skirmish could easily become a full-scale war. That was how the Great War first started.''

''Quadro is the only creature in the Kingdoms to whom the Black Unicorn owes a debt,'' said Eunoe. ''Ravenor owes its life to him. The Black Unicorn might overlook even a major *contretemps* if Quadroped asked him to.''

Reander looked faintly revolted at the idea of Quadroped as savior but he nodded reluctantly. He well knew the hatred with which the Warlords of Ravenor regarded him; it was a mutual feeling. Furthermore, he had added insult to injury by actually slaying all four of them.

''The pig stays,'' he said, then added: ''We have trouble enough without him roaming the countryside inflicting eels and hedgehogs and things like Avice on our unsuspecting peasantry.''

Fairfax regarded Reander steadily. His beady black eyes glittered. ''Hedgehogs,'' he said obliquely, ''brood long upon revenge.''

Morragwen turned to Reander. "I will tell the Black Unicorn what is happening here," she said. "Perhaps he knows of a way to stop the rain."

My parents might know one, Quadroped thought resentfully, *if Reander would only help free them.* He considered announcing this idea but decided it was wisest to remain silent. Pigs were unpopular enough already. Reander might think that the missing sounder had *caused* the rain. Which was silly, for had not the turtle assured him that his parents had been stolen only a few weeks before he came home? The rains had started long before then.

Shortly thereafter a depressed Glasgerion and his equally unhappy wife carried Fairfax and Quadroped to a small bedchamber in Glasgerion's suite, Morrag trailing dolefully along behind them.

By mutual consent, Fairfax and Quadroped ignored the full washbasin, placed so conspicuously in the middle of the floor, and crawled straight into bed. After a brief altercation concerning the disposition of the single pillow, both animals drifted soundly to sleep. Morrag brushed his teeth in a halfhearted way and then twined himself around the bedpost. Within moments he too was asleep.

At three or four in the morning Quadroped woke up, opened his eyes, and stared up at the ceiling. *What,* he thought, *if the turtle was lying?*

This terrible, horrible, awful thought refused to be ignored. The turtle had said his parents had been missing for a few weeks, but what if it had really been *months*? Did the turtle know the difference between weeks and months? The life of a turtle must be fairly monotonous. Did turtles have any sense of time at all? If his parents had been kidnapped just after he had locked the Gate then the pigs could be causing the rain.

Quadroped got out of bed and left his chamber, moving carefully so as not to disturb the slumbering Fairfax and Morrag. He needed sustenance, preferably in the form of a leftover chocolate cookie. As he trotted quietly down stairways and hallways toward the kitchens, whose location he had ascertained shortly after his first visit to the

Palace last winter, he tried to forget the possible meteorological misdemeanors of his sounder.

It occurred to him then that the threat of war was largely all his fault. After all, he *had* set the Black Unicorn free *and* he had freed Avice. The Black Unicorn wanted an excuse for war, Avice seemed bent on providing it. "I should have listened to the Sly Mold," Quadroped muttered aloud. "I should never have helped Avice."

"Uncharitable hoggling." Small bells chimed. Avice was suddenly standing on the step below Quadroped, regarding him with a melancholy eye. Quadroped recoiled and felt the smooth marble riser against his back. He could not retreat without turning completely around, for pigs cannot climb stairs backward.

Avice reached down and Quadroped squashed himself back into the corner between step and wall, but to no avail. The long, strong fingers closed around him and he was lifted high into the air to be held, suspended, snout to nose with Avice.

"Hello, Quadroped," said Avice. His smile was merry. His eyes danced and sparkled like emerald stars.

"Let me *down*," wailed Quadroped. "I don't *want* to go to the Fleshless Land. Let me *go!*"

"Such ingratitude," said Avice, shaking Quadroped slightly. "I really am quite angry with you, hoggling, after the chase you've led me. That blow to the head your witch friend gave me hurt. Don't you want your parents freed?"

"Yes," said Quadroped. "But . . ." Quadroped gulped. It seemed dangerously rude to inform Avice that he just did not want *his* help. Instead he said: "I have to stay and help Reander or the Black Unicorn will destroy the Kingdoms. They need me to negotiate for peace."

Avice chuckled. The chuckle swelled into a full laugh. The idea of Quadroped as ambassador plenipotentiary to Ravenor clearly tickled the trickster's senses. He opened his hands and let Quadroped fall, with a painful *thunk*, onto the cold stone floor.

"Ouch," said Quadroped. Briefly he wondered why it was that no one ever took the time to put him down properly. He glared at Avice, resentment and a sense of ill use largely replacing his fear.

"Very well, hoggling," said Avice. "You can stay awhile longer." He reached down and patted the shrinking pig on the head. "It would be a shame to end this game too soon. I'll fetch you when I've tired of your antics." He straightened and stepped back. For a moment his form wavered. He was there, then he was not.

Quadroped gulped and looked anxiously around, wondering if Avice was really gone or if he had just become invisible. Then he resolutely clambered to his hooves. He was not going to be dragged into the Fleshless Land just yet; Avice had given him a reprieve. Now he must forget about his parents and concentrate upon the imminent war with Ravenor, which was trouble enough. Firmly setting aside fears of the future, Quadroped set off again in search of the chocolate dessert.

When Quadroped awoke the next morning the Palace was in a bustle. The Council was about to enter the fourth day of its two-week session and servants scurried to and fro carrying messages, trays of food, clean clothes and shoes to their various masters and mistresses. No one had time to direct a pig toward breakfast. It was only his prior knowledge of the Palace, combined with a keen sense of smell, that allowed Quadroped to locate the small parlor where Glasgerion, Eunoe, and Morrag were dining on cereal, pancakes, and fresh raw squid. The squid, Morrag informed him, was wonderful and just the thing to wake up to.

Eunoe looked serene and calm in a robe of celestial blue. Glasgerion was stately in gray. Morrag had fastened small gems to his body and they shimmered and sparkled as he moved. With a sigh Quadroped recalled that beings dressed up in the Palace and reflected that at least his ears were clean.

"Hullo, lazy," said Morrag. "Have you seen Fairfax anywhere?"

"No," said Quadroped, clambering with difficulty onto a tall chair and surveying the breakfast possibilities. "He wasn't in bed when I woke up. Is he missing?"

"Yes," said Morrag. "But I'm sure he'll turn up. He's probably exploring the Palace."

"Morragwen's gone," said Glasgerion in a voice of doom.

"But I've decided to stay," said Morrag. "This Council is too exciting to miss. Ravenor will be positively boring."

Quadroped carefully buttered a stack of pancakes and wondered how best to tell his friends that he had met Avice again and that the trickster was in the Palace. As luck would have it he announced this news just as Reander, looking tired and harassed, entered the room.

"He's *here*?" Reander demanded.

"Yes," said Quadroped, feeling unaccountably guilty.

"Where did you see him?" asked Glasgerion. "What time was it?"

"Late," said Quadroped. "I was on my way to the kitchens."

Reander immediately turned and began calling out orders to various servants and courtiers lurking obsequiously about the hallways. In moments the word went out that a thorough search should begin for anyone answering to Avice's description.

"You won't catch him," said Eunoe helpfully. "He's playing hide-and-seek."

"Yes," said Glasgerion. "He's a wild card."

"Just what I needed," murmured Reander. His eyes lighted upon Morrag and he scowled. "Haven't you gone yet?" Morrag responded with a toothy grin. "Well, stay out of my sight," said Reander. "And try to keep Quadro out of trouble. Tempers are running high around here. He could get hurt." Quadroped gulped and wondered nervously where Fairfax was. The hedgehog was fierce but he *was* rather small and spines were not always an adequate protection.

The atmosphere in the Palace grew steadily worse in the next few days. The rain was still falling throughout the Kingdoms and Morragwen sent word that the Black Unicorn could not stop it. The harvest was now certainly

lost and there were reports of increasing unrest in the
countryside.

Much to Quadroped's dismay, Fairfax did not reappear.
Quadroped and Morrag disobeyed Reander's specific orders
and bravely ventured out of the private wings of the Palace
to search for their missing companion. But no one had
seen the missing hedgehog and a thorough search of the
Palace revealed no sign of him.

"Maybe Avice got him," said Quadroped at last.

"What would Avice want with a hedgehog?" asked
Morrag. "Let's go search the gardens."

That night events took a turn for the worse. Since the
night of the Ball, Quadroped and Morrag had taken to
sleeping at the foot of Glasgerion's bed. Glasgerion was
so busy that this was the only way they could talk to him
to find out what was going on.

"There's been a riot in Nasfir," Glasgerion announced
when he returned to his rooms around teatime.

"The capital of Isfandiar," Morrag informed the bewildered Quadroped. "How bad is it?"

"Bad," said Glasgerion. "The people are up in arms.
Ghola claims he can't hold them. He's called for war.
They're to vote on it tomorrow."

"But surely the Council will vote for peace?" said Morrag. "You've managed to win Sioned, Aumbry, Briavel,
and Jehan over, haven't you? That gives you a majority."

"It should," said Glasgerion. "But if fighting breaks
out the Black Unicorn will almost certainly use it as an
excuse to invade. Only a united army would keep the
Kingdoms from destruction. Nasfir has forced our hand.
We may have to fight for survival."

"What will you and Morragwen do if fighting breaks
out?" asked Quadroped timidly.

"I don't know," said Glasgerion. "I don't think she
does, either."

Quadroped sighed. Morragwen owed fealty to the Black
Unicorn. Glasgerion was a Prince of Essylt. There was a
long history of hatred between their lands. The recent
détente had encouraged Glasgerion and Morragwen to forget their political differences and give in to the love they

held for each other. Now it seemed as though they must part again unless one of them were willing to abandon both country and kin and bear the resultant guilt.

The next morning Quadroped watched as Glasgerion got dressed in the most elaborate costume he had yet donned. Then Glasgerion and Quadroped went out into the hall and joined Reander on a short, silent trip to the Chamber of Dress, where all the state vestments were kept. For the momentous decision, and perhaps to lend them courage for whatever would now transpire, both men would wear their finest.

The Groom of the Chamber strode proudly forward, head high and nose in the air. Boldly he threw open the great carved doors of the mighty wardrobe that dominated the room. His white gloved hands took hold of the sliding shelf whereon Reander's robes reposed. He pulled it forth, and uttered a mighty cry.

"Yaaah!"

Glasgerion and Reander looked at the Groom in alarm.

"It *bit* me!" cried the Groom.

As the Groom raised his injured finger to his mouth Glasgerion and Reander stepped forward and peered into the shelf. There, nestled among the heavy folds of silk and velvet, lay a furious Fairfax.

"Remove yourself, hedgehog," said Reander coldly. "Before I do you grave harm."

"Go *away*," said Fairfax. "Or I'll bite *you* too."

"What are you doing there?" asked Quadroped.

"Hibernating," said Fairfax. "Or trying to." His voice took on a plaintive note. "This palace is impossible. There are people everywhere."

"Well, you can't hibernate here," said Reander. "Come on out of there."

"But it's *cold*," said Fairfax. "Hedgehogs don't *like* cold."

"Out, or I'll drop you in the moat," said Reander.

Fairfax eyed him and then hastily complied. Reander was just nasty enough to do it, and the ornamental moat of Essylt was frozen year-round.

"Place him in the Spring Linens closet," Glasgerion instructed the Groom. "It's never opened until May."

Fairfax unrolled and grumpily allowed the Groom to pick him up and carry him from the room. Meanwhile Reander and Glasgerion drew forth the state vestments and put them on. Reander wore a floor-length robe of deep crimson cloth with a mantle worked with gold. The colors suited him and his hair seemed to glimmer like fire. Glasgerion's robe was of his favorite blue and gray, the blue an indigo velvet and the gray a shimmering silk. His white hair gleamed silver in contrast with Reander's reddish gold. Above these robes each man wore a heavy golden chain. On his brow Glasgerion wore a slender golden circlet. Reander wore a crown.

Quadroped watched the proceedings with awe. He had never seen either man look quite so splendid or so grim. Silently he followed them from the room and watched as they descended the great staircase that led to the central wing of the Palace and the chamber in Council Keep.

Morrag and Quadroped spent the day in the Palace Library, Morrag studying maps of the Ravenorian border and Quadroped trying to lose himself in picture books. Neither discussed the ongoing meeting. At four in the afternoon they returned to their rooms. At five o'clock Morrag stationed himself at the head of the stairs to wait for Glasgerion's return. From this post not even the promise of dinner could lure him and so Quadroped asked a servant to bring them both food on a tray. Together they sat and waited.

It was almost midnight before they heard footsteps coming up the stairs. Then Glasgerion and Reander came into sight, the weary droop of their shoulders revealing their message before they could speak. Reander passed silently by toward his own chambers but Glasgerion stopped and sat down on the top step. After a while he picked Quadroped up and hugged him tightly against his chest.

"The Council voted for war," he said.

Chapter Six

War! News of the Council's decision spread rapidly through the Palace and out into High Essylt itself. Not for a thousand years had the Kingdoms seen more than the occasional border skirmish or local feud. Messengers, brilliant in the livery of all lands and many houses, staggered breathless up Palace stairs, only to come hurtling down again on yet another errand. Experts in matters military: strategists, engineers, cartographers arrived daily, riding hard in answer to urgent summonses.

In the Council Keep committees and subcomittees met twenty-four hours a day to discuss the ramifications of war. Plans were made and changed and made again. And constantly, through the streets and corridors of that great city, the question was asked: "What will Prince Reander do?"

For the position of the Principality of Essylt in these matters was unclear. Essylt had the largest, finest army in all the Kingdoms. Should Reander hold his forces back the chances of victory would be greatly reduced. Reander, tight-lipped and angry, refused to commit himself to the

war. Glasgerion, urbane and charming as ever, would only
shrug and say quite honestly that he did not know what
Reander would do.

In vain did Princess Sioned of Lyskerys plead for some
definite promise of support. "We *will* fight," she said one
evening. "You cannot prevent this war, Reander. If the
Black Unicorn is as powerful as you claim, then it is best
that Essylt join its strength with ours. If you hold back
now, our defeat, and the inevitable slaughter that would
result, is all the more likely."

"If you can't win this war without Essylt," Reander
had replied, "then perhaps you should not start it at all."
He would say no more, and if the more generous thought
he would simply hold his armies back, others believed he
would join his forces with Ravenor's and block the invasion by force.

For the constabulary of Essylt, the last days of the
Council were particularly trying. They found it increasingly difficult to keep the peace. The foreign minions and
minor Lordlings who frequented the taverns showed a distressing propensity for repeating the rumors current in the
Palace. The loyal citizenry inevitably took umbrage at
these slurs upon their Princes' honor and usually demon-
strated this displeasure with force. Fervently, and to a
man, the constabulary wished that the Council would end
or that Reander would publicly make up his mind.

Quadroped, quite sensibly, spent these turbulent days in
the Palace Kitchens, comfortably ensconced in an ingle-
nook beside a smallish secondary hearth. There he was
able to forget about his manifold woes for whole minutes
at a time while a sympathetic staff presented him with
tasty tokens of their affection.

Quadroped had come to the conclusion that Essylt was
doomed, his parents were dead, and the Kingdoms were
falling to pieces. Avice and an angry Queen of the Dead
both wanted to grab him and all in all the future looked
dismal indeed. He was trying very hard *not* to consider
that future. In this he was thwarted by Morrag, who felt
it his duty to keep Quadroped informed of the current
political situation.

Quadroped and Morrag had both been forbidden to enter the Council Keep. However, while Quadroped was content to retire to the Kitchens, Morrag was not. It was not long before the intrepid eel had discovered that he could creep through the ventilation system and thus overhear any and all discussions occurring in the Palace.

The last day of the Council arrived to find Quadroped still lurking in the Kitchens, and it was here that Morrag eventually found him.

"*You*," said Morrag, "are a disgrace to pigdom." It was a bitterly chill day and Morrag was cross because a layer of ice on the river had robbed him of his midafternoon snack. "Don't you *care* what Reander said to the Council? How can you sit here eating all day long? You're getting all round again."

It was true. Quadroped, who had begun to look rather lean after weeks of arduous travel and infrequent meals, was once again an almost perfectly spherical ball of white. He looked the picture of a healthy pig if one ignored the rings under his eyes or the shadows that lurked in their purple depths.

"It's warm down here," said Quadroped. Then, "What happened?"

"Well," said Morrag, curling up comfortably before the fire, "they've all decided to assemble their armies at the ford on the Lost Skeggs, which is the river that forms the border between Ravenor and Isfandiar, fifty days from now. Everyone was swearing that they would bring their armies to the ford or die trying, and very noble they sounded too. Then Aodh of Seamourn stood up and asked Reander, straight out, whether he would join them there or not. And Reander said—" Morrag paused dramatically.

"That he would assemble his army and meet with them at the great ford of the Lost Skeggs at the appointed time."

"He's going to fight Ravenor?" Quadroped looked at Morrag in dismay. Somehow he had secretly believed that Reander would find a solution to this mess.

"Not necessarily," said Morrag. "You didn't listen to

me. All Reander said was that he would meet them there, but whether as friend or foe is anyone's guess."

Reander's meaning did not remain ambiguous for long. That evening, after the last of the Kings and Councillors had departed for their own lands, Glasgerion confronted his nephew over dinner and demanded to know what he intended to do.

Reander sighed. He looked pale, exhausted, and vulnerable. "Fight," he said.

"I know that," said Glasgerion crossly; he too looked tired and rumpled. "*Who* are you going to fight?"

"The Kingdoms," said Reander. "I am going to stop this invasion by placing my army between them and the Lost Skeggs."

"Reander, you've gone utterly mad," said Eunoe. "Essylt's army may be stronger than any one of theirs but it's too small to face the combination. You'll be slaughtered."

"How nice to know you care," said Reander.

"It's crazy," said Glasgerion slowly. "But it might work. If we could bluff them into reconsidering the treaty . . ."

"It's postively deranged," said Eunoe

"It should win us some more time," said Reander. "When they find they cannot dislodge us easily they may give up and go home. Who knows? If we stall them long enough maybe the rain will stop."

"It would have been a lot simpler if you had simply locked them all up in the dungeon when you had a chance," said Eunoe. "You could have kept them all in Essylt easily enough."

"The Council," said Reander, "is the only forum where the Kingdoms can meet and work out their problems without fear of violence or bloodshed. Council Keep is sacrosanct and will remain so as long as there are Princes of Essylt to guard it."

"Which won't be much longer, by the sound of it," said Eunoe. Her eyes held an unaccustomed sympathy as they rested upon Reander's careworn face. "If they do not give up, what then?"

"We fight on," said Reander. "To the death, if necessary."

"Now, that *is* madness," said Glasgerion. "What will it gain us? Essylt will be decimated and Ravenor will still be invaded."

"Reander," said Eunoe, "I know you swore you would keep the peace with Ravenor, but surely your word of honor is not worth so many people's lives?"

Reander smiled faintly. "I am not *that* proud," he said. He sat down and tried to explain. "Morragwen has told us that the Black Unicorn is off in the far east repairing his lands; that removes him from the picture for a while. The Warlords Goriel and the Manslayer have been left in charge of the west. Of the two, Goriel is the more deadly and the one with whom we will have to contend."

"Morragwen," Reander continued, "estimates that Goriel's forces are an even match for the Kingdoms', after we've taken our own little toll."

"The Kingdoms will find themselves in a stalemate," said Glasgerion. "They won't be able to pass far into Ravenor, and Goriel will be unable to carry the battle back over the border."

Reander nodded. "That's my prediction, assuming Morragwen has told us the truth." Given Reander's antipathy for all things Ravenorian, and his abiding distrust of his aunt, this was no minor admission.

"When the Kingdoms discover that they cannot win," Reander continued, "they will sue for peace."

"Which Goriel will refuse," said Glasgerion. "The Warlords *want* another Great War and the Kingdoms will have handed them an excuse. Goriel is not one to forgive and forget."

"That is where Essylt comes in," said Reander. "Goriel will have to summon the Black Unicorn if he is to carry the invasion back over our border. If Essylt sacrifices herself in Ravenor's defense, the Black Unicorn may be persuaded to temper his wrath and permit the Kingdoms to withdraw."

"You are placing a great deal of faith in the Black Unicorn's ability to see reason," said Glasgerion. "If the Kingdoms violate his borders and slay his people, he may forget that Essylt sacrificed herself to stop them."

"He may choose to forget," said Reander. "His enmity runs deep."

"He might listen to Quadroped," said Eunoe.

Reander shuddered. "I hope we may stop the Kingdoms ourselves. I have no wish to see my people slaughtered by friends and kinsmen but it's a chance we have to take. I can see no other way out of the situation. A Great War must be averted at any cost lest future generations be born and bred to war as they were in the past."

"Well," said Glasgerion, "if worse comes to worse we always have Quadro."

"Indeed," said Reander. "With Quadro on our side what could possibly go wrong?"

Reander's comment somehow reached the ears of the troops and was duly misinterpreted. When the army marched out from Essylt at the end of the week many a soldier had a white pig insignia blazoned on shoulder or breast, and small clay pig-pendants hung from saddles, bridles, belts, and throats. If any thought it slightly ridiculous that tried warriors should make a talisman of so unlikely a creature as Quadroped they wisely did not voice their opinions aloud.

Had Quadroped known with what faith and affection the common soldiery regarded him, it would have cheered him considerably; but Quadroped was largely unaware of his sudden popularity. He rode with Glasgerion and Reander, and the warriors who traveled with them were too hardened and far too grim to see aught in a baby pig.

Quadroped was discovering that traveling with an army in midwinter was not fun. He had always been a little afraid of horses, they bore an uncanny resemblance to the dreaded Black Unicorn, and he had a positive aversion for his saddle box. This pillow-lined contraption hung at the side of Glasgerion's saddle and had a sickening tendency to sway and jolt with the horse's every step.

The journey became worse. A week after leaving the city of Essylt, the army entered the rain-drenched lands of Isfandiar, Essylt's eastern neighbor. Glasgerion immediately succumbed to an allergy and his conversation became interspersed with sneezing and plaintive cries of "Mold spores!"

Glasgerion was not the only person in the party to be affected by airborne molds. Eunoe was similarly affected. The witch had, rather surprisingly, chosen to accompany the army in the role of Quartermaster. She had cast off her lovely silken gowns and was sensibly, and most charmingly, attired in breeches, fleece-lined vest, and high leather boots. A hooded fur-lined cloak completed this ensemble. Unfortunately, her temper did not match her pleasant appearance. Eunoe had never suffered a head cold before and her tongue, already sharp, became more acerbic than ever.

Neither Quadroped nor Reander had been affected by the dismal weather. Reander was looking brighter and more energetic than he had in weeks, red eyes and an itching nose not withstanding.

"He's glad to be out and doing something," Glasgerion said. "He never could take all the waiting."

As for Quadroped, he was sincerely sorry that his nose was no victim of the much maligned molds. Reander had, in a moment of compassion, requisitioned a piece of oiled canvas to shelter Quadroped from the wind and rain. This he had fastened to the top of the saddle box, nailing it firmly down on three sides. The air in the box had become hot and clammy, and it *smelled*.

I shall be quite ill, thought Quadroped miserably. He poked his head out from under the canvas and looked around for something to distract him. Tall grasses, occasional glimpses of distant bovine herds, a white beach, and a chilly green sea were all that met his eye. The bleak splendor of the Northern Steppe stirred his soul for quite ten minutes.

"I'm bored," said Quadroped to Morrag, who was swimming along beside him. "How long before we get to the border?"

"Months," said Morrag cheerfully.

"Months!" Quadroped shuddered. Even a week in his saddle-box with nothing to eat except salted fish and unbuttered oatcakes was too much for a pig to endure.

"Perhaps a bit less," said Morrag. "We're moving very fast, Quadro. Reander wants to be at the border before anyone else gets there. We should arrive well ahead of the rest."

Quadroped looked back at the line of horses and wagons that stretched down the road for miles. "The rest?" he asked.

Morrag condescended to enlighten Quadroped in matters military. "Reander has some one hundred lords," he explained. "Each of whom has a private force of ten to twenty men. That gives him a cavalry about one thousand five hundred horses strong, which can be summoned and moved relatively easily. Each of those lords is also responsible for a district and can muster perhaps fifty fighters, some of whom may have their own horses but most of whom will have to march on foot."

Morrag paused and did some rapid calculations while Quadroped gazed into space and wished he had never expressed any curiosity about armies. The forces Morrag was so blithely discussing seemed impossibly huge. Quadroped had difficulty imagining how many people five hundred were. The thought of thousands of warriors all bristling with weapons and trying their best to kill one another made him feel quite ill.

"So," said Morrag, "Essylt has about two thousand cavalry and four thousand infantry. It also has about three thousand extra people like blacksmiths, armorers, cooks, surgeons, heralds, pages, wagoners, and grooms. There are probably four thousand horses, and easily twice that many mules, donkeys, and oxen. Most of those are pulling wagons or are heavily laden with food, fodder, tents, weapons, and all the other supplies you need to support so many beings for a couple of months.

"Now, if the army all marched together you would have something like twenty thousand creatures all walking at a moderate pace on a road where five men or three horses can travel abreast. Why, the first part of the army would be on the road for hours before the last part of the column even began to walk. And just think how long it would take the army to get over a bridge, or through a pass where they had to march single file.''

"Months," said Quadroped gloomily.

Morrag nodded. "Reander has divided his army up and sent each section to the border by a separate route. That way they can travel faster and the Kingdoms can't tell how many men he's got. We should all be at the Lost Skeggs well before anyone in the Kingdoms gets there. That should give Reander the advantage.''

Winter came, freezing the rain into hail and icing the roads, killing many a horse that traveled too fast. Snow fell in drifts, melted into brown slush, and the wagons got stuck axle-deep in mud. Little rivers ran down the road. The mold spores died off to be replaced by flu and fever.

The colder and more exhausted the army became, the slower they traveled and the more they ate. Food and medicinal supplies began to dwindle with distressing rapidity. Reander and Eunoe began to use magic to keep the army moving. Eunoe became crosser. Reander looked tired and worried once more.

Toward the end of the month the army reached the border and turned south on the last leg of the journey. The frontier was a wild and desolate land of high windswept moors etched with deep gullies and steeper ravines. When the cloud cover lifted, the soaring peaks of the Crystalline Mountains could be seen, their summits crowned in ice. Snow and furious winds roared down from those forbidding heights, gifts no doubt from the Warlord Goriel, the wintry guardian of Ravenor's mountain chain border.

Reander had positioned small war-bands all along the mountainous border as soon as the prospect of war had arisen. Reports from these units began to come in. The news they brought was alarming.

The truce had been broken. The belligerent marcher lords of Isfandiar had not been content to await the Council's decision but had taken matters into their own hands. Reander's patrols had successfully routed several small war-bands bent on crossing the border. But the border was long, the paths across the mountains too numerous for any force to guard completely. It was certain that some of the marauders had slipped through Essylt's grasp. But if any had entered Ravenor, none had returned. That land was by no means defenseless and could take care of its own.

"At least Ravenor hasn't retaliated," said Glasgerion cheerfully.

"Not yet," said Reander. "But they will."

Three days later they came across their first sight of an Isfandi raiding party. Their path wound along the top of a steep hogback ridge. In the canyon below, Reander's keen eyes spotted the flash of sunlight on armor. With a gesture he halted the line and dismounted.

Reander bid his people be silent, lead their horses out of sight, and stay with them until they should be summoned. Then he began to make his cautious way down the steep side of the gorge.

"I'm going after him," said Eunoe. She slipped off her horse and began to sneak down the hill. Morrag swam silently after her.

"Me too," said Quadroped, as Glasgerion dismounted and prepared to follow as well. He was anxious to get out of his saddle-box and any excuse would do. Besides, it could not be all that dangerous. He had Reander, Glasgerion, Morrag, Eunoe, and a whole army to protect him.

"All right," said Glasgerion. "But keep quiet and don't lag behind." He lifted Quadroped out of the box and placed him on the ground. Then he hurried off without even waiting for Quadroped to stretch his sore muscles or gain his footing on the gravelly ground.

Quadroped could tell the exact moment when Reander became aware that he was being followed for he stilled and his hand went straight to his sword hilt. When he saw who it was he released the weapon but looked most displeased. Ignoring his impromptu entourage, Reander continued to make his way stealthily toward the warriors below.

It was quickly apparent that some disaster had befallen these Isfandi raiders for they went on foot and were covered with dirt and blood. Many were limping or dragging along, supported by their abler comrades. More than one head was bared of its helm and a keen eye could discern empty scabbards swinging lightly at their owners' sides. Furthermore, the raiders feared some pursuit for many were the anxious glances they cast over their shoulders and the pace they had set themselves was grueling, surely too fast for their injured.

Reander leaped up upon a convenient boulder. "Halt!" he cried. It was most gratifying to see that the party below did just as he asked. Fifteen frightened faces, bloodstained and weary, peered up at him in dismay.

"Who are you?" demanded a tall dark-skinned woman who, judging from her costly accouterments and slightly less timid stance, was their leader.

"Reander of Essylt."

"Oh, thank God!"

The commander's cry was so heartfelt that Reander visibly began to relax. He jumped off the boulder and ran quickly down the scree slope until he stood just above the commander. Glasgerion, Eunoe, Quadroped, and Morrag followed close behind, dislodging an avalanche of loose stones as they went.

"Help us, I beg you," said the commander, falling to her knees at Reander's feet. "They're not far behind us. They'll be here soon."

"Who will?" Reander had tensed again; his sword came, unsheathed, into his right hand. "Identify yourself. What are you doing in these mountains? And what has brought you to this pass?"

"I am Ariseid of Avallen," said the woman with a slight lift of her chin. "A week ago I set out with my men under orders from my Lord Ghola to make a foray into Ravenor. We were a reconnaissance party, charged to spy out the enemy's movements."

Ariseid paused and caught her breath. "They're massing for war. And we didn't find them, they found *us*. Two-thirds of my men are dead, tortured to death. We managed to escape but they were on our trail before dawn. We'll not live long or pleasantly if they catch us.''

"You are already dead.''

The chilling voice came from high on the hill behind Ariseid and her men. There, tall upon a dark red horse, rode the antler-horned Warlord called Manslayer.

No flicker of alarm disturbed Reander's face. Arms crossed, legs slightly apart, he gazed up at the Manslayer, unmoved. Eunoe stood firmly at Reander's side, matching his calm. Of the three only Glasgerion betrayed any sign of perturbation; he moved and grabbed Quadroped up into the safety of his arms.

Quadroped cowered in Glasgerion's arms, ears flat against his head, eyes wide and frightened. The Manslayer was coming closer, his horse half walking, half slipping, down the steep hill. Flayed human skins, given life by the breeze, girdled his hips and flowed from his back. War paints of rusty red and black colored his powerful torso and masked his face. The jewels at his neck were set in human teeth. Close up, his cat-eyes burned yellow madness. Five feet from where Reander stood he drew to a halt and dismounted.

"Well met, Prince,'' said the Manslayer.

Reander stepped forward, away from his friends, and acknowledged this greeting with a brief nod. "Manslayer.''

"I see you've caught the game I've been hunting,'' said the Manslayer. "Give it to me, for our peace.''

"Do not surrender us, Prince,'' cried Ariseid, once more flinging herself at Reander's feet. "Let us at least die fighting. Do not give us to him alive.''

"Get up,'' said Reander, his eyes never straying from the Manslayer's face. "A strange hunt, Warlord, that has humans as its quarry. I cannot approve your choice of sport.''

"These mortals have violated our treaty, Prince,'' said the Manslayer. "They entered Ravenor in arms. They are mine by right, to do with as I will.'' As he said this he smiled and his eyes glowed with horrid anticipation. Behind him fifty warriors came over the hill and began to ride down into the canyon.

"He's right," said Glasgerion softly. "But if he gets them he'll torture them to death." ·

Quadroped looked at Reander and shivered. The Prince looked grimmer than he had ever seen him. Clearly he was struggling with a decision. A decision that *should* not be so difficult unless . . . Quadroped was uneasily aware that Reander was fully prepared to kill his own people in battle to prevent the invasion of Ravenor. Would he not be willing to sacrifice these warriors for peace as well?

Eunoe clearly had similar misgivings for she shot Reander a darkling look and whispered: "Don't you *dare*."

"We are in Isfandiar," said Glasgerion softly. "Reander, the Manslayer has no jurisdiction here. It is *our* right and responsibility to punish these warriors."

With a wave of his arm Reander brought his men down from the heights. His commanders came thundering down the path and spread out over the hillside behind him. Several dismounted and came to stand at their Prince's side. The Manslayer observed the arrival of these reinforcements without comment. Only a slight narrowing of his yellow eyes betrayed his annoyance at being outnumbered by Reander's men.

Reander gestured curtly toward Ariseid and her men. "Get them back," he said.

Ariseid's band hastened to comply with this command, scrambling up the hill to where Essylt's warriors could form a protective ring around them. Ariseid herself moved back behind Reander but refused to retreat further without learning what the fate of her people would be.

Reander lifted his chin and squared his shoulders a trifle. "You trespass here, Warlord. You have no rights in Isfandiar."

"Does peace mean so little to you then, Prince?" said the Manslayer. "Your protection of these criminals sanctions their crimes."

"Neither I, nor Essylt, sanctions what these warriors have done, and well you know it," Reander replied. "Had you caught them on your own soil you might have punished them as you pleased. But these people have crossed the border and have placed themselves in my hands. This is a Kingdom affair and I will not tolerate your interference.''

For a moment Quadroped thought that the Manslayer might leap for Reander's throat, so angry did he seem. Then he relaxed slightly and an evil smile lit his features.

''And what punishment shall you mete out to them then, Prince?'' asked the Manslayer. ''Execute them as they deserve and I shall go with no ill feelings.''

''That is one solution,'' Reander agreed.

A commotion broke out at Reander's back as Ariseid attempted to break free of her guards. ''Traitor,'' she cried. ''Would you slay us at the command of this vile Ravenorian *thing*?''

''Be quiet,'' said Reander.

Ariseid glared at him. ''If you must have blood,'' she said, ''kill me, but spare my men.'' Despite her brave words, Quadroped noticed that she trembled and her eyes flickered nervously between Reander and the Manslayer.

''I am not going to execute you,'' Reander told her coldly.

''Torture, then?'' suggested the Manslayer hopefully.

''Nor will I torture her.''

''Then what *will* you do?'' Manslayer and Ariseid both asked, albeit in slightly different tones of voice.

''I think,'' said Reander thoughtfully, ''that I shall just keep her.''

He addressed the Manslayer. ''As you are no doubt aware, Warlord, I have placed several war-bands along the border to prevent just such an occurrence as this. I am presently on my way to meet the rest of my forces at the ford of the Lost Skeggs and there attempt to hold back the Kingdoms' intended invasion of Ravenor until such a time as they come to their senses.''

''So?'' asked the Manslayer.

''So I shall draft Ariseid into my army,'' said Reander. ''She and her fellow Isfandis may pay for their invasion of Ravenor by defending it against any further transgressors.''

The Manslayer did not look particularly mollified by this sentence. Ariseid looked furious. ''I do not have sufficient forces to take these mortals from you, Reander," said the Manslayer, "but Ravenor will not tolerate these aggressions much longer. Unless these incursions cease we shall retaliate and exact what punishment *we* think just."

"The Black Unicorn's treaty was with me, Manslayer. I have not broken faith with your sovereign yet. Do not break his word by further transgressions of the border. Go back to your own lands, or help me to hold back the Kingdoms if you will."

"I will go," said the Manslayer. "And I will keep to my own land until Goriel bids me to do otherwise. But if you fail to stop the Kingdoms we shall summon the Black Unicorn. Once he has tasted blood you shall not easily turn him back. Fight well, Prince, we shall be watching you."

With that the Manslayer turned and forced his steed up the steep hillside, his men riding quickly behind him. In a moment they had crested the hill and were lost from sight and hearing.

"You were lucky," said Morrag, swimming forward to Reander's side. "You obtained his promise not to act without first consulting Goriel. That should buy you some time and possibly some common sense."

"True," said Glasgerion, "But for how long? Both of those Warlords are eager for battle."

"They'll wait and watch awhile before they take any major action," said Reander. "Why should they waste their forces fighting the Kingdoms when we're here to do their work for them? If the Kingdoms defeat us, then they'll move in. And the Kingdoms will be an easier match for them, having been weakened by the previous battle."

"I don't understand." Ariseid was looking at Reander with confusion. "You do not side with Ravenor, I have seen that. Yet you would weaken our army and make it an easy victim for their swords. Why?"

"It's a gamble," said Glasgerion. "We hope that peace can be restored before it comes to that final conflict."

"It sounds a noble cause, but hopeless," said Ariseid after a moment of thoughtful silence. "Would it not be better to join your strength to that of the Kingdoms? The battlefield is an odd place to seek a lasting truce. If you fail you will have died to no good purpose.''

"Purpose enough if by our sacrifice we can persuade Ravenor not to take the war further than the defense of the realm," said Glasgerion.

"Perhaps," said Ariseid, unconvinced. "I shall espouse your cause since you say I must. I owe you my life and cannot in honor do other than give you my service." She bowed deeply and went back to join her men.

Glasgerion replaced Quadroped in his saddle-box and the army resumed its march south. Ariseid and her warriors fell in and in the following days showed themselves willing to obey orders and stay out of trouble. Indeed they proved themselves useful by guiding the army through the hills by paths that only people familiar with the area would have known. With their help the army finally reached the ford of the Lost Skeggs, five weeks after it had set out from Essylt and some three weeks before the Kingdoms' armies were due to assemble at the ford.

Quadroped caught his first sight of the Lost Skeggs at sunset as the army rode along the high palisades that rimmed the valley. The Lost Skeggs was a mountain river, flowing fast and foaming over sharp stone teeth. Some great tectonic disturbance in eons past had sheared the mountain chain in half, forming a wide rift valley. Here the Lost Skeggs became broader and quieter. The stone it had carved from the mountains was deposited as soft banks of gold sand and slightly coarser gravel beds. In winter, when much of the water was trapped on the peaks in snow and ice, the river ran shallow in places.

Quadroped eyed the valley that was to host the forthcoming battle with mixed feelings. Dry grass, dotted with bushes and low scraggly trees, covered the valley and rose halfway up the hills to be replaced by dark stands of whispering, red-trunked pines. Through the center of this plain ran the river.

Here the Lost Skeggs was gentle, half shadowed, half bathed in light, meandering around long spits of golden sand. Quadroped's keen ears could hear it murmuring as it rippled along, filling the valley with song.

In the middle of the broad alluvial plain stood a cluster of tents, perhaps thirty or more, with their colorful banners snapping in the wind. Smoke rose up from outdoor hearths. Horses stamped and tossed their heads. People bustled between the tents, their shouts and laughter carried faintly upon the wind.

"Who are they?" Reander demanded, as he rode up beside Glasgerion.

"Not ours," said Glasgerion. He squinted, shielding his eyes with one hand as he tried to identify the pennants. "Isfandi, I think. The breeze makes it difficult to see their devices."

"Bring Ariseid up here," Reander ordered one of his ubiquitous aides. "We'll see if she can identify her countrymen for us."

The aide wheeled away and returned ten minutes later with Ariseid. Ariseid studied the camp at length before turning puzzled black eyes up to Reander.

"They're from Isfandiar," she said. "I recognize several of the pennants. But they shouldn't be here. We had orders to rejoin Lord Ghola and the main army before coming to the ford. Still . . ." She returned to her study of the camp. "I see Broras's colors down there. He's a marcher Lord, ambitious and not overly bright. He *might* try to challenge you alone in hopes of winning favor in Lord Ghola's eyes."

"Hmmm," said Reander. He waved two fighters forward and gave them orders to escort Ariseid back to her men.

"A guard is not necessary," said Ariseid. "I gave you my word that I would not seek to escape."

"You will find it easier to keep your word if you do not have the option of escape," said Reander mildly. "It is not an easy thing to watch your own people set upon and attacked. I would not think less of you if you tried to warn them."

Ariseid nodded and went off under guard without further

protest. Reander returned his attention to the camp below. "We have to dislodge them," he said. "Tonight."

Glasgerion raised an eyebrow. Nighttime attacks, while effective, were not strictly honorable.

Reander frowned. "The sooner we disperse them the better," he said. "I want to be in control of the ford before the Kingdoms' army begins to assemble. If we wait until morning anything could happen. This may be the vanguard of Ghola's main army."

"I don't like it," said Eunoe, studying the encampment intently. "The formation is all wrong. They have only minimal defenses. They must know that we're on the way. They should have scouts out. Our position should have been spotted by now. They should be taking defensive action."

"We'll scout out the rest of the valley before we attack," said Reander. "If they have reinforcements lying out of sight, we'll find them." He turned and, ignoring Glasgerion's protests, went to give his commanders their orders.

Night fell. It began to rain. Reander's army made camp in the shelter of the pines, out of sight of the Isfandi encampment, and settled down to wait.

In Glasgerion's leaky tent Quadroped tried his best to fall asleep. Glasgerion was writing a letter to Morragwen and the room was bathed in golden light and the unpleasant odor of kerosene. Morrag was curled up beside him. The eel's scales felt slippery and cold.

"Stop hogging the blanket," said Morrag as Quadroped tried to snuggle deeper into its frayed warmth.

Quadroped shivered as icy drops of rain leaked down onto his head. "Piglets are highly susceptible to colds," he said, clutching the blanket to him.

"Nonsense," said Morrag.

"Give Morrag the blanket," said Glasgerion absently. His pen scratched irritatingly as it scrabbled across the paper.

Quadroped relinquished a fraction of the blanket and watched as Morrag rolled its warm folds around him.

"There are advantages," said Morrag, "To sharing a blanket with a radiant butterball."

"You're taking too much," said the radiant butterball in offended accents. "Give it back."

Word came an hour after midnight. A scout came gliding silently into the camp and flung herself on one knee where Reander stood with his generals around him.

"We have circled around the Isfandi camp," she said. "We found only a few guards, whom we have silenced. The valley and the hills are otherwise uninhabited. The way is clear for the attack."

"Good." Reander dismissed the scout and turned to his lurking commanders. "My Lords, prepare your men."

Within moments the camp sprang to life. Fires burned brighter. Warriors moved quietly and quickly to don their armor, saddle their horses, and ready their murderous weapons.

While these momentous events occurred Quadroped slept peacefully on, dreaming of bowls full of acorns. His first intimation of trouble came when a heavy mailed finger prodded him ungently in the stomach. Quadroped squealed, and opened his eyes to the sight of Glasgerion, unfamiliar and menacing in helmet and armor, bending over him.

"Shhh," hissed Glasgerion, patting Quadroped soothingly on the head with rather more force than necessary due to the weight of his gauntlets. "It's only me."

"What time is it?" asked Quadroped grumpily.

"It lacks several hours 'til dawn," said Glasgerion. "We're about to attack the Isfandi camp."

Quadroped sat up, fully awake now and considerably alarmed. He stared at Glasgerion's armor. "Are you going to attack it too?" he asked.

Glasgerion was not particularly adept at fighting, as Quadroped had cause to know. He was a bard, a politician, a scholar, but not a warrior. Quadroped had somehow assumed that when it came to actual combat Glasgerion would stay somewhere safely on the sidelines, issuing orders.

Glasgerion correctly interpreted Quadroped's remark and smiled. "Morale," he said. "I'm not much good at swordplay but I'm good at leading the troops. It makes them feel better when they see both of their Princes are in the field fighting with them. I suspect the fact that I can't defend myself very well makes them fight all the harder."

"Oh," said Quadroped in a small voice.

"Now listen," Glasgerion continued, "I want you to stay right here until I come back. *Don't* leave the tent, no matter what you hear going on outside. This first skirmish won't take very long. Reander expects they'll retreat and wait for the rest of the army as soon as they see the size of our force. Try to go back to sleep." Glasgerion rose and walked briskly from the tent before Quadroped had a chance to protest or even to wish him good-bye.

I'll never get back to sleep, Quadroped thought. Vivid images of Glasgerion lying dead or wounded on the battlefield, his blood trickling down in slow rivulets to eddy away in the shallows of the ford, began to chase through his brain.

"Quadro."

Quadroped looked up and saw the familiar form of Morrag waving slowly in the doorway. "Quadro, get up. You're going to miss the whole thing."

"Oh, but . . ." Quadroped was quite comfortable and warm and sleepy. The night outside was cold and dark. "Glasgerion told me to stay here," he said. "I don't *want* to watch."

"Up or I'll bite you," said Morrag. He bared his teeth and advanced on the reluctant piglet.

The familiar threat produced the desired effect and soon Quadroped found himself clambering down a steep hillside that seemed to be covered with prickly bushes and sharp stones. "I can't see anything," he complained.

"Shhh," said Morrag. "They'll hear us."

Quadroped shuddered and peered around. How close to the enemy were they? he wondered. Close, he decided as his keen ears began to pick up the stealthy sounds of men creeping around below. Morrag, no doubt, would not be satisfied with anything less than a front-row seat.

At last Morrag called a halt and permitted Quadroped to sit down. The enemy camp was visible a few hundred yards away as a ring of orange lights where the embers of their campfires glowed.

For a long while everything was still. From the Isfandi camp came a watchman's cry announcing the hour. From below came ragged breathing and the occasional curse as someone crawled blindly into a nettle. Then the silence was shattered by the thin clear sound of a horn calling the army to battle.

With whoops and yells the warriors rose from concealment and raced in upon the sleeping camp. The banked fires suddenly flared as men, startled out of sleep, stumbled to stir them up. The sight of sword blades flashing in the firelight as they came chopping down into some unfortunate's flesh was to haunt Quadroped for a long time after.

The sounds of the battle were ghastly as well. The steady ringing of metal on metal, similar to the sounds made in a blacksmith's shop, was only the background for a steady chorus of screams and choking cries. Agony pierced the night, reverberating redly in Quadroped's ears until tears ran from his eyes and he had to hold his ears flat with his hooves to block out the terrible noise.

"Quadro, Quadro, wake up!" Morrag's urgent whisper jolted Quadroped back to an awareness of the night. "Something's wrong. Reander's *losing*!"

"What?" Quadroped looked down at the battlefield. He could mark no difference in the seething mass. "How can you tell?"

Morrag hissed in exasperation. "If you look you'll see that our people are getting split up into little knots. They're losing coherency. That means the fight is out of Reander's control. What I don't understand is, why? The Isfandi party is smaller and they *ought* to be poorer fighters. Reander should have had no trouble routing them."

Morrag glided farther into the night, the better to see the battle. Quadroped stayed where he was, unwilling to watch the defeat and death of his friends. A flash of brilliant white light split the night followed by a thunderous crash. An odor of burned flesh came wafting gently on the breeze.

"What was *that*?" asked Quadroped, trying to breathe through his mouth.

"Bad news," said Morrag. A series of smaller flashes lit the sky. "Reander's using magic. Magic," he added darkly, "is not very good for dealing with enemies en masse. It's only really effective in single combat." He peered downward through the gloom. "Eunoe has little blue flames dancing all over her, I wonder . . . Oh, *no*!"

"What?" demanded Quadroped. He had buried his face in his hooves and was no longer watching the battle.

"Glasgerion's down," Morrag reported. "Not dead, but his sword arm's taken a blow. Not surprising really, the way he was waving it around. What does he think a shield's for anyway? Reander's over him but faltering. The men are drawing around Reander, defending him. Good thing he's wearing that gold dragon-helm, bit gaudy but it's easy for the men to spot. Eunoe's down on her knees trying to bandage Glasgerion's arm. I don't think they'll last much longer, although—"

"Don't tell me," said Quadroped. "I don't want to hear."

"If they decide to fight to the death they could hold out another hour or two. Essylt's warriors don't die easily as Ravenor has learned to her cost. *Wait!* There's another group riding up . . . sixty of them, or more. Oh, whatever am I going to say to Morragwen? She was so *fond* of Glasgerion."

Quadroped, unable to bear the suspense any longer, uncovered his eyes and came out of the bush just as another tremendous flash of lightning lit the sky. A cloud of glowing smoke rose up and began to take strange form. Over the heads of the battling hosts appeared the terrible form of a vast, incandescent white pig.

Chapter Seven

The great luminous pig glared down upon the cowering Isfandi host. Night stars twinkled gruesomely in its empty black eyes. Beneath this frightful apparition rode sixty mounted warriors. Flames shot forth from their gleaming spears. They brandished their swords in righteous wrath.

The enemy faltered, and fell beneath their onslaught. Terrified cries of: "Ahhhh . . . the Demon Pig!" rose into the night. From Reander's beleaguered forces a ragged cheer broke out. With cries of: "The Pig! The White Pig!" the warriors of Essylt threw themselves forward and began to drive the enemy away from their fallen Prince. In minutes the tide of the battle had shifted. The Isfandis began to fall back.

"Who *are* they?" asked Quadroped.

Morrag coiled and uncoiled with suppressed excitement. "It's Morragwen," he said. "It has to be. No one else has such pyrotechnical flair. Oh, how I'd like to go down there and sink my teeth into a neck or two!"

Quadroped looked at Morrag in some alarm. He did not relish the thought of being abandoned on the hillside in the middle of the night. Wounded Isfandi soldiers were beginning to stumble toward them in their retreat.

"Don't worry," said Morrag, correctly interpreting Quadroped's silence. "I won't leave you alone. I wonder whom Morragwen's brought with her? They're blue skinned. They look like sea people but they're dressed in black. Standard's black too. No, wait . . . it has a golden scallop shell on it."

"Aedh," said Quadroped. "It's Aedh."

Quadroped recalled the exiled Prince of Seamourn with mixed feelings. He remembered Aedh as a stern man, but one who had been kind to Quadroped until he had discovered that Quadroped had the Key. Then Aedh had become a monster, attempting to deliver Quadroped and Glasgerion into the hostile hands of Ravenor. The attempt had failed but Aedh's uncle, King Angmar, and the cheerful Court Jester, Caelbad, had both been killed in the encounter.

Quadroped watched as Aedh's men efficiently slaughtered the remaining opposition. He felt ill. The revolting sounds of the battle, forgotten in his fear for his friends' lives, now sounded twice as loudly in his ears. Once again he covered them with his hooves and tried not to hear the shrieks.

"Come on," said Morrag, an infinity of misery later. "It's over, we've won. Let's get back to the tent before anyone misses us."

Numbly Quadroped uncovered his ears and looked up. Dead warriors lay sprawled around the campfires, their forms dissolving into anonymous dark lumps away from the flickering light. People were walking, or shuffling, around the field, bending over the fallen and occasionally calling for aid.

In the midst of it all was Reander, moving briskly among his weary men. His voice, calling orders, could be heard clearly from where Quadroped sat. He sounded calm, controlled, commanding. The light of a fire fell briefly across his face, lighting his hair and glinting in his eyes. Quadroped saw that he was smiling.

Quadroped lowered his eyes and looked away. Glasgerion was kneeling beside a moaning man, presumably serving as doctor. Morragwen and Eunoe, he supposed, would be doing the same. He took some comfort from the thought that they would aid the enemy's wounded with the same care and skill they lavished on their own.

Quadroped followed Morrag back to camp in a daze. The eel was humming slightly. "Did you see the way Reander parried that giant's ax?" Morrag asked.

"No," said Quadroped. He was shivering and shuddering inside. How could Morrag be so unmoved by the scene they had just witnessed?

"I've seen seven hundred and one years of this sort of thing," Morrag said in answer to Quadroped's unspoken query. "You have to learn to detach yourself a little. I find concentrating on fighting techniques helps."

"I suppose," said Quadroped. He hoped that he would never live that long nor see that many horrors.

"Go to sleep," said Morrag. He made Quadroped lie down beside the smoldering hearth and wrapped the contested blanket tightly around him.

Glasgerion and Morragwen returned to the tent several hours later. Glasgerion began to rummage around the tent trying noisily to be silent. Eventually he located his harp. After checking to see that Quadroped was safely tucked in he and Morragwen went back outside.

Quadroped, staring sleeplessly into the dark, heard Glasgerion's harp mourning softly to the night. The music was obscurely comforting. As the sound of Glasgerion's songs for the dead soothed away the memories of pain and bloodshed, Quadroped fell asleep.

The next morning Quadroped opened his eyes onto a nightmare. The camp was filled with the wounded. Dead littered the valley below. Mist hung in shreds above the field, half hiding the shadowy forms of the wolves as they slunk from corpse to corpse. Raucous ravens fought over the feast. Great eagles shrieked. The carrion eaters wheeled overhead, dark shapes in the bright morning air.

Quadroped turned resolutely away from the grim view and went in search of Glasgerion and Morrag. He passed

the cook tent without a backward look. Today food had
no power to make him feel better or to set the world to
rights.

As Quadroped approached Reander's large tent he could
hear Reander's voice lowered in quiet but bitter argument
with Glasgerion, Morragwen, and Eunoe.

"I hate to say I told you so," Eunoe was saying, "but
I did. If it hadn't been for Aedh . . ." She faltered. Quadroped surmised that for once Reander's glare had been
baleful enough to still even Eunoe's sharp tongue. Or perhaps she was becoming more sensitive to his moods. They
had spent a lot of time together recently, considering that
they did nothing but bicker.

"He saved your life, Reander," said Glasgerion.

"He murdered Angmar. He would have killed you if
Morragwen hadn't interfered," said Reander. "He's a traitor. Let him go back to Ravenor, I have no use for such
as he."

"The more fool you," said Morragwen. Her skin and
hair had turned deep red, to match her eyes and temper.
"Aedh sacrificed his uncle for the good of his people. He
believed, as we all did, that the Gate would open and the
Great War begin again. By aiding Ravenor he thought to
win peace for his people. He bargained for neutrality. He
would not have taken up arms against the Kingdoms."

"You defend him because your loyalties are as mixed
up as his," said Reander. "How many warriors from the
Kingdoms have you killed?"

"Many," said Morragwen. "I admit it. War is not a
black-and-white issue. We take what actions we think right
at the time. Sometimes the future proves us wrong."

"You are not blameless yourself, nephew," said Glasgerion. "Last night you slew citizens of the Kingdoms,
people whom you, as a Prince of Essylt, ought to have
protected."

"What choice had I?" said Reander. "Do you think I
enjoyed it?"

"Of course not," said Glasgerion, a trifle too quickly.
Reander was one who knew too well the dark exhilaration
of killing.

"We're not accusing you, Reander," said Eunoe gently. "We've all agreed that there's no other way to avert a Great War. But do you think Aedh enjoyed killing his uncle?"

"Aedh's crime," said Glasgerion, "stemmed only from a shallowness of vision. You seek to save all the Kingdoms from the Black Unicorn's wrath. Aedh only sought to save Seamourn."

Morragwen had faded from red to pale pink. "I have spoken with Aedh," she said. "Reander, he knows well what he has done and it haunts him. He has sacrificed two of the men he held most dear, and he has lost the land for which that sacrifice was made. He is punished."

"Reander, let it rest," said Glasgerion. "Aedh needs to help us, do not begrudge him this."

"Very well," said Reander at length. "He may stay. And you, Quadro, may stop lurking outside the door and come in."

Quadroped jumped guiltily and entered. It was not fair, he decided. No human had a right to have such an acute sense of hearing.

"Hello," he said to Morragwen. Then, "Why are you here?" The question was a trifle rude, but he couldn't think of a polite way of asking and he really did want to know.

"The Black Unicorn sent us."

Quadroped turned around. Aedh stood in the doorway, Morrag hovering at his shoulder. Condensation had formed droplets all over the silvery layer of water that enshrouded him. The ground under his feet was visibly damp.

"Another eavesdropper," said Reander, rising from his seat. "But a more skillful one than Quadroped here, for I never heard you approach. Well met, Aedh. Your arrival last night was most timely."

Aedh smiled rather quizzically. "You are gracious," he said. "I had not looked for a warm welcome from you."

Reander looked slightly uncomfortable but said only, "I believe that we owe you our lives. Come in and be seated."

Aedh pulled up a chair beside Glasgerion, and Quadroped managed to clamber, with some assistance, onto Glasgerion's lap. Morrag draped himself decoratively around the back of Morragwen's chair.

While they were resettling themselves Quadroped heard a small piping voice call his name. With a twitch of his ears, Quadroped located the sound and peered surreptitiously at Aedh's shoulder. There was a pink object there, half-hidden by the fringe of the Sea Prince's hair. It was tubular, and a delicate ring of tentacles encircled its crown. It looked like a little sea anemone.

"Pseudo-Polyp!" Quadroped cried. "How did *you* get here?"

"Hello, Quadro," said this unique and intelligent coelenterate. The small anemonelike creature waved its tentacles in friendly fashion. "Aedh brought me. Aodh was being perfectly horrible, and Adjurel had the whole palace redecorated in puce, so I left. One of the warriors gave me a lift when he left Aodh's service for exile."

Pseudo-Polyp was duly introduced to all at the table. Then Reander took charge of the conversation once more. "I am eager to hear how it is you have come to my aid," he said.

"My men and I have been somewhat at loose ends in Ravenor," Aedh began. "We are no small force and the Black Unicorn has little need of warriors at present."

"It is a tribute to your leadership that so many men have followed you into exile," said Reander.

"More likely my brother's lack of it," said Aedh. "In any case, when the Lady Morragwen told me what was happening in the Kingdoms I asked to be allowed to aid you. The Black Unicorn has released me from my oath of allegiance to him. I come here as a masterless man."

Reander looked at Morragwen. "It would appear that you have been hard at work," he said. "Our thanks."

Morragwen blushed and turned a deep rose. "I did little enough," she said. "The Black Unicorn is not eager to embark on another war just now."

"He's off in the far east trying to set the land in order," Aedh confirmed. "From what the fire-giant Toridon has told me the situation there is very bad."

"Which is not entirely good news," continued Morragwen. "With the Black Unicorn busy in the east, Goriel is the supreme authority in the west. He will not help you avert this war."

"He has already tried to promote it," said Reander. "Last night we fought Ravenorians."

"Hah," said Morrag. "I knew no mortals could fight so well."

"They *were* rather hard to kill," said Eunoe.

"But they ran when they saw the Demon Pig," said Morragwen. "Only an Isfandi would do that. That trick would not frighten a Ravenorian child."

"I had Ariseid check the bodies at first light," said Reander. "She identified about half of them as Isfandis. As for the others, their armor was familiar but not their faces." There was a moment of silence as everyone tried *not* to imagine how Ravenorian warriors had obtained Isfandi armor.

"It was a trap," said Reander. "But not of Isfandi design. Ariseid's Lord Broras probably had no idea that half of his men weren't human. It is easy to steal across the border dressed in stolen gear. I doubt that Broras examined his new recruits too closely. He was just a convenient fool, eager to challenge me with his small band of men."

"Goriel would not stoop to such a trick," said Morragwen.

"But the Manslayer would," said Reander. "And Goriel would turn a blind eye and let him."

"Really quite a cunning trap," said Eunoe. "I wouldn't have thought the Manslayer had it in him. He always seemed rather dim."

"Never underestimate him," said Morragwen seriously. "The Manslayer is malignant, bestial, and depraved. He is also quite brilliant at getting what he wants. He wants blood, lots of it."

Reander looked slowly around the room. "If the trap had succeeded," he said, "both Glasgerion and I would be dead. There would be no one left to halt the invasion of Ravenor. The Warlords would have their excuse for war. We can no longer trust Goriel to play fairly with us. From now on, we watch our backs.''

Morrag sighed. "Looks like Ravenor is back in the black books again," he said to Quadroped. "I wonder if Reander will make Morragwen go home."

"Over my dead body," said Glasgerion. Under the table he gave Morragwen's hand a comforting squeeze.

The meeting broke up shortly thereafter and all went about their separate tasks. Reander, surrounded by a flock of chattering tacticians, went to survey the alluvial plain. Glasgerion rode with him, as did a reluctant Quadroped. Glasgerion had forgotten to remove him from his saddle-box and so he perforce had to join them in their tour.

The water ran swift over shallow shoals where the Lost Skeggs gave access to Ravenor. At its deepest the river came only to a pony's belly but the current in these channels was dangerously strong. On the Kingdoms' side the plain was covered in tall grass and intermittent bushes. The Ravenorian side was distinguished by its sparser ground cover. Only a few hardy plants sprouted between the tumbled rocks. The barren Ravenorian floodplain was the more noticeable for its contrast with the dense woods of pine that covered the hills, without prejudice, on both sides of the valley.

A bridge of stone had once spanned the ford, and its ruined pilings still stood gathering weeds and refuse around their massive feet. Reander was of a mind to rebuild this bridge. It would take little effort and would offer a path of retreat into Ravenor. Should Essylt be defeated it was likely that her soldiers would fare better in the hands of Goriel than in the hands of their former confederates. Reander's suggestion was unanimously rejected, his commanders preferring death at the hands of their fellow humans to life among the inhumans they guarded.

Reander established his camp where the Lost Skeggs first foamed into the valley. The site was within walking distance of the ford yet far enough away to be out of the way of the coming confrontation. The steep flanks of the hills rose up behind, sheltering and guarding the huddle of tents, and the slight elevation ensured that the camp commanded a view of the field. This done, he set to work building defenses. By sunlight and torchlight the earth-works grew, great ramparts and ditches to defend the ford. The river itself was dredged deeper and mined with sub-merged stakes to hinder invaders should Reander lose the fight.

Days passed in organized chaos. The Kingdoms' armies began to arrive, and brought with them the rain. Warriors in their thousands rode down into the valley, trailing dark storm clouds behind them. On the far side of the plain a metropolis of tents and pavilions sprang up. By the river the ground became marshy.

Ravenor arrived. Across the river, in the dark stands of pine, they placed their tents. Manslayer's red mingled with Goriel's silver. Morrag and Morragwen crossed the river daily, trying to persuade Goriel to back Reander's force with his own. Goriel remained obdurate. He would wait and see. He sent neither aid nor encouraging word, and his hostile presence added immeasurably to the strain under which everyone labored.

Two weeks went by, the Kingdoms' army was almost complete. It was four times the size of Essylt's army and covered the plain and the hills beyond. Tension mounted. Faces became drawn, laughter strained. Weapons grew sharper and brighter as their masters labored over them by the hour. Messengers flew, like arrows, between the lines trying to negotiate peace.

The rain continued to patter down. Talks broke down, the Kingdoms called Reander's bluff. In private, where the army could not hear, Glasgerion counseled retreat. But Ravenor was watching and Reander would not back down. A date for the battle was set.

It was no part of Reander's strategy to carry a piglet into battle. Events conspired, however, to change his mind. Since coming to the valley, Quadroped had been left largely to his own devices. No one had time to play with a pig or to think of tasks that a pig could do. So Quadroped had taken to exploring.

Quadroped's activities were noted by those who wished him ill. On the day before the battle, Quadroped and Pseudo-Polyp went to play on the sandspits that lay by the ruined bridge.

Quadroped splashed out to the bar. The ruined pilings of the bridge had caught all manner of flotsam in their toes. Quadroped and Pseudo-Polyp were soon completely absorbed looking for riverine treasures. Neither one noticed that two sinister shapes had detached themselves from the shadows of the pilings and were sneaking toward them across the sands.

Quadroped held up the twisted fragment of a root. "It looks like a dragon," he said.

"*They* look like rats," said Pseudo-Polyp. "And I think they're out to get us!"

Quadroped turned around. Two strange women were creeping toward him. Their shoulders were hunched, their heads lowered, their hands curled clawlike in front of them. Pseudo-Polyp was right. They did look disturbingly like a pair of giant rodents.

Quadroped cast a frightened look toward the shore. There were three guards on top of Reander's earthworks but their backs were to the river.

"Help!" cried Quadroped at the top of his lungs. The guards paid no heed. The Lost Skeggs drowned out his cries. The rat-women scurried closer.

Quadroped retreated to the edge of the bar. Wet sand sucked at his hooves. The water was icy, the current frighteningly strong. With freezing hands the water pulled at Quadroped's legs, trying to roll him and carry him off.

"Go with the river," said Pseudo-Polyp. "You can swim ashore somewhere downstream."

Quadroped hesitated. He stepped back. One rat-woman pounced, grabbing him by the scruff of his neck and hauling him into the air.

"Got him!" she cried. She held him up for her comrade to see.

"Not very big, is he?" said her comrade, examining Quadroped with beady brown eyes. "What does Ghola want with him?"

"His head on a pike," said Quadroped's captor. "The 'Demon Pig,' dead for all to see."

"He doesn't look like a demon to me. Too cute."

"He'll look worse when he's goried up a bit," said Quadroped's captor. "Once the flies get to him no one will look too closely. Quickly, chop off his head. We'll just take that and his tail back. It's easier than carrying a whole pig."

"Right."

A knife whispered from its sheath at the rat-woman's waist. The curved blade swept back and up.

Here we go again, thought Quadroped, and choked down a hysterical laugh.

"Desist!" cried Pseudo-Polyp. With a mighty hop he leaped upon the rat-woman's hand and stung her with all of his might.

"Ouch!" cried the rat-woman. Her hand opened and Quadroped fell to the sand.

Pseudo-Polyp jumped bravely down and landed firmly on Quadroped's back. "Run!" he cried.

With a terrified snort Quadroped scrambled to his hooves and took off toward the shore as fast as his four feet could carry him. As he neared the earthworks his terrified squeals alerted the guards. With drawn swords they came racing down and fell upon his pursuers. Within minutes both women were dead.

The guards left the bodies on the bar and carefully carried the distraught piglet to Glasgerion. Glasgerion immediately swept Quadroped up in his arms and, after giving him a quick hug, raced off shouting for Reander.

Reander, Glasgerion, Quadroped, Pseudo-Polyp, and a bevy of anxious aides all trooped back to the river. The dead women lay there, their eyes reflecting the gray of the sky. The ends of their long brown hair fanned gently out in the water.

Reander knelt beside the corpses, examining them. His aides knelt also and began to whisper and shake their heads in a wearying, worrying, way.

Reander stood and took Quadroped from Glasgerion's

arms. "What happened?" he demanded. He shook Quadroped slightly, as if to ensure that he worked.

"They wanted to kill me," said Quadroped. "They wanted to put my head on a pike!"

Reander swore rather nastily and tossed Quadroped back to Glasgerion. His aides muttered and frowned. After the defeat of the Isfandis no one could deny that the 'Demon Pig' was a powerful mascot. The enemy troops feared him. For Reander's army the White Pig had become the source of all their luck. While he was alive they surely would come home safe to hearth.

"Quadro cannot stay alone in camp tomorrow," said Glasgerion. "The Kingdoms may send their assassins again."

Reander scowled. "Get him a coat of mail," he said. "He shall ride with you, Glasgerion."

"In the front lines?" said Glasgerion. "Reander, it's too dangerous. Let him stay back in the earthworks."

"If he goes with us he might as well be useful," said Reander. "The sight of their mascot will encourage our people. Besides, that way we can both keep an eye on him."

Glasgerion sighed but hesitated to point out that in the heat of battle Reander was unlikely to remember something so insignificant as a baby pig. They all waded back to the shore and Reander stalked away, his flock of assistants grumbling and arguing behind him. Glasgerion carried Quadroped back to his tent and put him to bed. Then he went out to consult with the armorers on the subject of chain mail and pigs.

All that night it rained, a sullen downpour that offered no dramatic lightnings but only a creeping cold. Reander took one look at the sky and cursed. The battlefield would be ruined, the ground slippery and treacherous under the horses' feet. The troops regarded the lowering skies with stoic complacency. Sunshine, said many, could only distract the commanders from their business and lend an unwanted air of cheer to an otherwise solemn occasion.

All that day and far into the night the armorers worked. Before dawn the coat was finished. It was a miracle of craftsmanship, a work of love. A coat of mail made up of thousands of tiny silver links that covered Quadroped from head to toe. Gold inlay embellished the garment's hem and swirled across the flat guards that sheltered his eyes and ears and even protected his tail.

Quadroped was not appreciative of this gift. It was heavy. The chain links scratched and rubbed at his soft hide and the metal was cold on his skin. He could not even remove the horrid thing, for the clips required human hands to undo them.

Dawn approached. Every horse that could be found was pressed into service. Those fighters who could obtain no mounts were stationed upon the earthworks. Infantry was of little use against the Kingdoms' cavalry and Reander had no wish to see the gallant common folk of Essylt slaughtered without good cause. His archers he placed higher up upon the earthen walls where they might slay any of the Kingdoms' fighters who managed to break through the lines.

Reander had forbidden Morragwen to fight. The presence of a Ravenorian Warlord in his army could potentially compromise his negotiating position. He still hoped that the Kingdoms would give up and go home after the battle had cooled their blood a bit.

An hour before sunrise, Reander gave the order to mount. Glasgerion carefully placed Quadroped in his saddle-box, now coated in steel and fastened with chain. Morrag and Morragwen came to wish them luck.

"Keep your head down, Quadro," Morrag said. "And stay with Glasgerion. If he's unhorsed, jump down. You'll be safer on the ground at his side than on the back of a frightened horse." Quadroped nodded. He was beginning to feel grateful for the layers of chain mail that enmeshed him.

Glasgerion kissed Morragwen farewell. Morrag hugged Quadroped. Then Glasgerion gave Quadroped's mail coat one last check, mounted, and rode off toward the standard at the front of the lines.

On both sides the armies assembled. Row upon row, watching each other. The eastern sky grew pale behind the massed ranks of darker thunderclouds. Watery light bathed the flat land and colored everything gray. Somewhere a raven croaked. After a silence another raven replied. All sounds seemed slow, subdued.

Then came the sound of a horn, low and vibrating on the damp air, to be joined a moment later by a higher, shriller cry. With a terrible rumbling of hooves the Kingdoms' army began to move.

From his position in the center of the foremost line Quadroped had an excellent view of the approaching foe. The army of the Kingdoms seemed without number, a vast sea of bobbing, moving, roiling humanity against which Reander's forces seemed pitiful as a dam of straw trying to hold back a river in flood. Behind him, across the gray waters of the Lost Skeggs, Ravenor sat waiting upon its revenge.

Essylt's army moved to meet the foe. Reander rode first, with him went Gladgerion and Eunoe. Furious gold, mild silver, and steadfast bronze, leading their people to battle. Quadroped sat and trembled in his box, feeling small and helpless.

The first wave struck. Blood was shed, washing away the oaths and the sacred pledges that bound the Kingdoms together. Steel rang like bells. The air was filled with the cries of men and the terrible shrieks of their horses.

Quadroped was shaken violently from side to side as Glasgerion's horse sidled, reared, plunged forward, and then retreated. Quadroped moaned and clung to the sides of his box, terrified that he might be shaken loose and dropped down into a sea of wounded men.

After the first rush, Quadroped's fear subsided enough to permit him to observe what was happening. Glasgerion, he saw, was never permitted to come within range of the enemy's swords. Though the conflict was fiercest around him his guard stood firm and kept the foe from their Prince's side.

Quadroped also observed that the command of the army had switched from Reander to Glasgerion. In the heat of the battle Glasgerion remained outwardly calm. He received reports, made decisions, and shouted out orders, which someone was presumably still rational enough to obey and relay. Off to one side Quadroped saw Reander hacking energetically away at the foe. That Prince would not permit his warriors to guard him.

The day dragged on. Glasgerion continued to call out his orders in a firm clear voice, urging the fighters on. The battle grew fiercer as warriors called up their last reserves of energy and pushed back exhaustion. Muscles, aching with fatigue, continued to ply the heavy swords, and if the force of the blows was dimmed well, they were lethal nonetheless.

The armies parted as the light left the field. At nightfall Reander was still in control of the ford. Against all odds his army had held the field. As he rode back to camp Quardoped gave thanks that it was winter and the days were short. He did not think that he could have borne the nightmare much longer. The thought that he would be back on that field at dawn filled him with sickening terror.

The next day the slaughter was renewed, and again Essylt's army stood firm against the foe. But their numbers were sorely depleted and the multitudes set against them seemed hardly to have dwindled at all.

On the third day the line broke and the Kingdoms, by sheer weight of numbers, forced Reander's forces back behind their earthwork barriers. There they dismounted and fought on foot beside the infantry, there being no room for the horses to maneuver. The horses they sent away to graze on the valley slopes.

Now Reander's archers came into play. Over the heads of the defenders came flights of arrows. They darkened the sky, whistling as they descended upon the foe, like hungry crows upon ripe grain.

Morrag and Morragwen came now to fight by Glasgerion's side. "I will stay back no longer," said Morragwen.

"I am a Warlord of Ravenor. I will not leave the defense of my homeland to you."

"Do as you wish," said Reander. He was weary of battle, of the blood of fellow humans on his sword. If Ravenor had not been watching his every move he would have spared his men this last day of slaughter and surrendered to the Kingdoms' army. But Ravenor *was* watching. Bitterly he wished that the other Warlords felt as Morragwen did. If Goriel had lent his aid the war might have had a different outcome.

Quadroped was glad that Morrag was again by his side. He felt very small and vulnerable now that he no longer had a saddle-box to protect him. On horseback the humans had not seemed quite so large. Morrag stayed close beside Quadroped, savagely biting any foot that crossed the earth barriers and threatened to step on his friend.

Now those who could work magic did. Puffs of colored smoke and playful lights danced between massed and struggling bodies. That day the fighting did not end with the passing of the light. By torchlight the Kingdoms pressed on. Before dawn the earthworks began to fall, the first ditches bridged with bodies, the outer walls breached. The Kingdoms stormed the barriers over stairways of the slain.

Quadroped had become tired of doing nothing but dodge enemy weapons and had made himself useful by carrying arrows to the archers. He was just fetching a particularly cumbersome bundle when a loud cry from Morrag halted him.

"That *lunatic*!"

Quadroped looked hastily around, and dropped his mouthful of arrows.

"What does he think he's going to accomplish by that? It's suicide." Morrag was balanced high upon his tail, swaying back and forth like a cobra.

Quadroped looked in the direction Morrag was glaring. Reander had broken free of the circling earth walls and was running forward onto the plain, closely followed by Eunoe, his standard-bearer, and his usual gaggle of officers. The enemy closed eagerly around them, hiding them from sight.

"Damn! Quadro, stay here." Glasgerion scrambled up out of the ditches and ran after his hotheaded nephew, hoping to reach his side before he could be cut down. Morragwen took off at Glasgerion's heels.

Morrag looked at Quadroped, clearly torn between his duty to guard the piglet and his desire to defend his mistress. Quadroped hesitated. The earthworks were comparatively safe and he was small enough to hide. He looked after Glasgerion, and chose. If his friends were all going to die he wanted to be with them at the end.

"Come on," he said. "Let's go."

Between the feet of the warriors he ran, too small and too fast to be noticed in the struggle. Morrag swam low to the ground, hovering just over Quadroped's head as they wove through the writhing combatants. Ahead they saw Glasgerion and Morragwen catch up and merge with Reander's guard, hacking their way through the ranks of enemy that stood between them. Panting and puffing, Quadroped joined them and followed, unnoticed, in Glasgerion's wake.

"Nephew, get back to the lines," Glasgerion ordered. Reander ignored him, recklessly throwing himself toward the hostile blades that surrounded him.

"He encountered Princess Sioned," said Eunoe, who had remained by Reander's side throughout. "They fought. I saw her fall."

Glasgerion bowed his head. A sword hissed down and Quadroped squealed. Glasgerion deflected the blow just in time. "What are you doing here?" he demanded, catching sight of Morragwen, Morrag, and Quadroped for the first time. "Get out of here. You'll be killed. Morragwen, take Quadro and get away."

"I'm staying with you," said Morragwen. She paused to incinerate a hostile warrior with a chartreuse energy bolt.

"Me, too," said Quadroped.

*   *   *

Reander's defenders moved into a protective clump, backs together and faces to the hostile hordes that pressed in upon all sides. Reander might be determined to die but so long as he lived his friends would fight to protect him. Quadroped crawled between their legs, until he reached the center of the human knot, and there he stayed.

Warriors fell by the dozen. A pile of dead grew around the beleaguered fighters. The enemy just pulled them aside and continued to attack. Reander's death meant victory, rest, and a good hot meal.

Sparks leaped up between steel and iron. Shields split and betrayed their owners. One by one the warriors of Essylt fell. The circle tightened. The fight went on.

It can't last much longer, Quadroped thought. *If their swords don't get us they'll just crush us to death.*

Reander would not stay put. Again and again he bolted forward. He was fighting three men when the defender to his right fell, leaving his side exposed.

"Reander, ware right!" Glasgerion shouted and tried to move to his nephew's side. A sword was raised high for the killing blow.

Fast as Glasgerion moved, Quadroped moved faster. Beneath Reander he ran, straight across the enemy's path. The warrior stumbled, heavy boots crashing into Quadroped's side and knocking him breathless into the dirt. The sword continued its descent, deflected but still deadly. Quadroped lay on the ground and watched. The blade sliced cleanly into Reander's side and a rill of blood flowed forth. Reander cried out, wavered, and fell, crushing the winded pig. Quadroped heard a great cheer arise from the Kingdoms. Above the tumult, over the sounds of the dying hosts, came the terrible words:

"The Prince of Essylt has fallen!"

Chapter Eight

A ghastly quiet fell over the field. In the eye of the battle all motion ceased. The warriors stood, transfixed, around the fallen Prince.

The silence was broken. Hooves thundered. Aodh, King of Seamourn, appeared on his bloodstained charger. His starfish-circled helm was off. Behind him rode his guard, muddied and grim. The sea of swords parted to let them pass.

Straight up to Glasgerion the Sea King rode. "Throw down your arms!" he cried. "The victory is ours."

"Obnoxious brat," hissed Morrag under his breath.

Reander's surviving guard raised their swords, prepared to die with their Prince. Aodh's horse sidled and stamped. The Sea King looked down at Glasgerion. A gloating smile twisted his lips. "Surrender, Glasgerion. Your nephew is dead. Ravens shall feast on his eyes."

"No, he's not," said Quadroped, still squashed in the mud under Reander. "He's breathing."

"Yield to me, Glasgerion," said Aodh. "Yield and your people shall live."

Glasgerion removed his helm and looked up at Aodh, his expression resigned. He sheathed his sword. "Lay down your swords," he said. "The battle is over. I surrender."

Aodh turned to the warrior at his side. "Dunir," he said. "Take these murderers away."

Quadroped squealed as angry warriors bore down upon him. Rough hands dragged Reander up and away. A huge hairy ruffian grabbed Quadroped up and carried him off of the field. He was taken into the enemy camp, fitted with a collar of iron, and chained up in a big dark tent. An icy draft whistled under the canvas sides. The floor was wretchedly damp.

For over an hour Quadroped huddled alone in the gloom. Outside the sounds of the battle were hushed. The cries of the wounded rose from the field, moaning and weeping for aid.

A shadow fell across the wall of the tent. Hands fumbled to untie the tent flap. Quadroped backed away from the door as far as his bonds would permit. The executioner had surely come to drag him before the Council.

The tent flap opened. Two prisoners were hurled inside, both bound in iron chains.

"Glasgerion, Eunoe! You're alive!" cried Quadroped.

"For a while," agreed Glasgerion. He groaned and sat up. Quadroped climbed into his lap.

"What a miserable place," said Eunoe. "I suppose chairs are too much to ask, but they might have provided a lamp." She stood up and moved restlessly around.

"Perhaps they feared we'd set ourselves alight," said Glasgerion.

"Idiots," said Eunoe.

"Can't you make a magical lamp?" asked Quadroped.

"No," said Eunoe. She shook the heavy manacles on her wrists. "The arthropods weren't taking any chances when they designed these things. They're spell-wrought. I'm almost as helpless as you are."

There was a silence. Quadroped snuffled tentatively. "What's happening?" he asked. "Where's Morrag? Are they going to kill us?"

"I don't know," said Glasgerion. "Morragwen has escaped into Ravenor, taking Morrag with her."

"It was a lovely explosion," said Eunoe with evident satisfaction. "She singed Aodh's horse when she left. It threw him into the mud."

"Is Reander . . . ?"

Eunoe shrugged. "Who knows? Those sea slugs carried him off."

She came over and sat by Glasgerion. "How badly was he hurt, Quadro? Where was he hit? What did the sword wound look like?"

Quadroped tried to remember. There had been so much blood. "He was cut on the right side," said Quadroped. "On the chest, from just under his arm to his waist."

"The ribs," said Eunoe. Her expression grew brighter. "Perhaps he yet lives. The bones may have deflected the blow."

"If a broken one hasn't punctured a lung," said Glasgerion. "There's no point worrying about it. If the sword didn't kill him the Council will."

Eunoe and Quadroped looked at him in surprise. Glasgerion was a habitual optimist. It was usually Eunoe who took the dimmer view.

Glasgerion unpinned his cloak and rolled it up into a pillow. He lay down, pulling Quadroped onto his stomach. "Get some sleep," he said. "We'll need strength for whatever's before us."

Night fell. Wolves slunk out of the woods to feed. In the camp the watch fires were lit. The wounded were tended, the dead sorted out from the living.

Quadroped was awakened after midnight by the sounds of approaching feet. He scrambled to his hooves and bounced on Glasgerion's chest.

"Wake up," he said. "Someone's coming."

Glasgerion sat up and shook Eunoe awake. In pitch blackness they sat and listened. The sounds were clearly audible now. Several people were drawing near, dragging something quite heavy behind them.

The tent flap was thrown back. Four hulking shapes entered, backlit by a flickering torch. Two limp bodies were heaved unceremoniously into the tent. The flap was closed, the light extinguished. Darkness descended once more.

Glasgerion groped his way toward the nearest body. "Who are they?" he asked. "Quadro, can you tell?"

Quadroped's nose twitched. "That's Reander," he said.

"And the other?" asked Eunoe, studying the face with her hands.

"It's Aedh," said Quadroped. "But something's different. He doesn't smell of the sea."

"The insects have stripped away his water layer," said Eunoe. "It's not fatal, but he will be in great pain when his skin begins to dry out. What's this?"

Eunoe paused as her fingers encountered something small and rubbery on Aedh's shoulder. She prodded blindly at it.

"Ouch," said the object. It stretched out a tentacle and stung Eunoe's hand.

"Hello, Pseudo-Polyp," said Eunoe. "What have they done to Aedh?"

"Aodh had him beaten," said Pseudo-Polyp. "He would have killed him but his officers wouldn't stand for it."

"Aodh was ever a horrid boy," Glasgerion muttered. His fingers encountered the gaping wound in Reander's side and he cursed. "Eunoe, come here."

Eunoe hobbled to Glasgerion's side as fast as her fetters allowed. "How bad is it?"

"Very," said Glasgerion.

Eunoe ran her hands over Reander's still form. At his wrists she touched iron and stopped. "They've chained him up as well," she explained. "Vindictive beasts!"

"They're afraid of him," said Glasgerion.

"In his condition?" Eunoe's questing fingers began to examine the sword wound. She drew her breath. "I don't like the feel of this," she said. "It's deep and it's still bleeding. I wish we had something to clean it with. It's bound to become infected. Help me remove his shirt, Glasgerion. This has to be bandaged before more blood is lost."

Reander's chains prevented the removal of his shirt but Glasgerion and Eunoe were able to tear most of it off his back. Eunoe tore the dirty cloth into strips.

"Lift him up," she instructed Glasgerion. With competence born of long practice she began to wrap the make-shift bandages tightly around Reander's chest.

"We must keep him warm," Eunoe said. She tied the last bandage in place. "Glasgerion, give me your cloak."

Glasgerion wrapped Reander's unconscious form in his mantle. He lifted him into his lap so that the damp earthen floor might not chill him. All through the long night he cradled his nephew in his arms, keeping him warm and still.

Morning came, turning the walls of the tent gold and sending dust motes sparkling down around the captives. Aedh was awake and able to sit. The return of warmth and light cheered everyone up until they saw the extent of Reander's injuries.

Reander's face was flushed, his body burning with fever. Blood had seeped through the bandages at his side. Eunoe undid them. Torn flesh, dirty and inflamed, bordered a jagged cut from which dark fluids flowed.

Eunoe shook her head as she studied the wound. "He will die," she said. "Without proper care he hasn't a chance."

"Do not grieve, Lady," said Aedh. "Reander did not deserve a criminal's death at the hands of a foolish Council."

"Fools, indeed," said a deep croaking voice. Briavel, Cormorant of Jansiar, entered the tent. "They intend to invade Ravenor this morning."

Briavel's bright eyes fell upon Reander's insensate form. He squawked. "Summon a doctor," he cried, sticking his long skinny neck out the door. "At once, immediately, *now*."

His long neck snaked back inside. *"Humans,"* he said in disgusted tones. "Had I known they would treat you like this . . ."

A doctor appeared, assistants in tow. Briavel fell silent

as he bent to examine Reander. "Nasty," he said at length. "But he'll do." Briavel nodded, well pleased.

Aedh fixed stern eyes upon the bobbing cormorant. "He will not thank you for this," he said. "You do him no kindness to save his life for a headsman's ax."

"You might be right," Briavel agreed. "But others will lose their heads if he is allowed to die. The Council want Reander alive for the pleasure of killing him themselves."

Glasgerion bowed his head. "I never thought Reander would be spared," he said. "How will our people fare? Do you know what the Council intends?"

"Ilketsni wanted to kill them all," said Briavel with a shake of his head. "I put a stop to that. Mass executions would only demoralize our troops. Too many of them have friends or kindred in Essylt."

"Your senior commanders will spend the war in prison. They'll escape with their lives, if not their lands. The others will be given a choice, join us or join their officers in chains."

"That *is* good news," said Glasgerion.

"I'm afraid it will go harder with you," said Briavel. "Many would have agreed to your exile, Glasgerion, had you not married a Warlord. As it is . . . The vixen Ilketsni cries for your death. Most of the Council support her."

"Ungartok has always hated Essylt," said Glasgerion. "What of Eunoe? And Quadro, surely he can be spared?"

Briavel ruffled his feathers. "It sickens me to admit this, but the piglet must die. The army believes him a Demon. They will not fight while such a creature remains in the camp alive."

"And Eunoe?"

Briavel studied a broadly webbed foot. "Ilketsni wants her dead as well," he said. "She wants no heir to inherit Reander's throne or avenge him when he is gone."

"What? Why the insinuating little—!"

Anger temporarily froze Eunoe's vocal cords. Her expression was murderous. Her brown eyes flashed literal sparks.

"Ungartok plans to annex Essylt," said Briavel.

"They would," said Glasgerion. "I'm glad my wife's got safely away. Tell Ilketsni that Morragwen bears no child to threaten her claim. I would not put it past her to follow Morragwen into Ravenor itself if she suspected otherwise."

The Regent of Jansiar nodded. A rather awkward silence fell upon the occupants of the tent.

The tension was broken by the arrival of several young pages loaded down with furniture, blankets, and food. Chairs and rugs and a bed for Reander were carted into the tent with much shouting. A huge barrel of water was rolled in along with a keg of ale. Several large baskets of fruit were brought in and set down as well. There were supplies enough to last the prisoners a month.

Glasgerion surveyed these offerings with raised brows. "My thanks," he said. "But somehow I doubt we'll be needing all this."

"Oh, you probably will," said Briavel cheerfully. "You won't be killed until this war is over. You took quite a toll and we need your people to swell our numbers. Your warriors will fight better if they know you're alive."

"You plan to start the attack today?"

Briavel nodded. "There's no point delaying. We haven't the doctors to heal the wounded nor the food to wait till they mend. Our scouts report that Goriel's force is much smaller than ours, even with all of our losses."

"It probably is," said Glasgerion. "But you will not find them easy prey. It doesn't take many Ravenorians to defend their border."

"You are all a bunch of idiots," said Eunoe. She looked up from wiping Reander's fevered brow. "You are committing suicide, and taking a lot of innocent people with you."

"Look on the bright side, Lady," Aedh supplied. "You're on Ravenor's side now. If the Black Unicorn wins we'll be freed."

Glasgerion frowned at that. He might be married to a Warlord but he was still a Prince of Essylt, and Ravenor was his hereditary foe.

The invasion of Ravenor commenced as promised. Only

Briavel had the inclination to speak with the prisoners, and he was far too busy. They could do nothing but sit and listen to the sounds of the battle, which came to them faintly from the far side of the river.

Reander regained consciousness. His companions quickly wished he had not. He was cross and uncooperative and news of the Kingdoms' activities did little to soothe his foul temper. Informed of Ungartok's plans for Essylt he practically gnawed on his chains.

"What's happening now?" became the sole topic of conversation. The suggested answers were occasionally imaginative, frequently accurate, and inevitably grim and depressing.

"At least we're all still alive," Glasgerion told Reander. "That's more than we thought would happen. If things turn out the way you planned, the Kingdoms will soon give up."

By the third day of battle the Kingdoms had begun to learn the true nature of the foe they had so rashly engaged.

"Nothing kills them!" a woman wailed as she was carried into camp on a stretcher.

"They don't die," another said. "They just pull the weapons out of their flesh. Their wounds don't even bleed."

"We are being driven back," Briavel told them on the fourth day of the war. "We cannot hold our position. Ravenor will soon cross the river."

"The invaders become the invaded," said Reander.

"Go, Goriel," said Eunoe spitefully.

Glasgerion stared at the cormorant. His eyes were sad. "If only you had listened."

Seven days after Essylt's defeat guards came and hustled the prisoners outside, leaving Aedh and Pseudo-Polyp alone in the tent. Reander went first, supported by Eunoe. Glasgerion followed, Quadroped tucked firmly in his arms. They were marched through the camp, past a thousand hostile eyes, and shoved into a large striped tent.

The Council was seated around an oaken table. Three seats were empty. Mircea of Imchadiz and Jehan of

Kervanathel had died fighting Ravenor. Sioned of Lyskerys had fallen at Reander's hands.

"I can stand," whispered Reander, pushing Eunoe's supporting arm away from his waist. "Glasgerion, put Quadroped down. You look silly holding him like that."

Quadroped wrapped his front legs tightly around Glasgerion's arm. He did not want to stand alone on the floor looking up at all these frightening humans. Glasgerion scowled at Reander and tucked Quadroped a bit closer against his chest. He was not the premier Prince of Essylt, he could afford to sacrifice his dignity for a friend.

Aumbry of Akariel rose slowly to his feet and cleared his throat. He glanced at Ghola, then waddled around the table and came toward them. A few feet from Reander he stopped. A strained smile appeared on his pudgy face.

"Well met, Reander, and welcome," said Aumbry. He embraced Reander tentatively, as if afraid he might bite.

Reander shook off the unwelcome hands and seemed suddenly to grow a bit taller. His chin came up, his shoulders went back. A decidedly supercilious look graced his aristocratic countenance. Chilly green eyes glared down on unfortunate Aumbry.

"From the warmth of your welcome I surmise that you're having some trouble."

"You surmise correctly, O Best of Princes," said Aumbry. He tried to look cheerful and failed.

Reander looked rather pointedly at the heavy iron chains that still bound him hand and foot.

Aumbry flushed. "Guards, unchain them. Here you, fetch wine for our guests."

"We'd prefer an offer of seats," said Eunoe.

Reander was tiring, though he hid it well. His legs trembled. A deep red patch was growing on his bandaged side. The wound was open and bleeding.

"Chairs! Chairs!" said Aumbry loudly. In a trice fine seats with silken pillows were brought and they all sat down.

"Let me guess," said Reander, leaning back in his chair, his weakness disguised as languid negligence. "You have realized that Ravenor is a dangerous foe. You are worried about what your unprovoked attack has started.''

Fat Aumbry bridled. ''Not unprovoked,'' he said. ''The rain . . .''

Aodh interrupted Aumbry's protestations. ''We outnumber the enemy twenty to one,'' he said. ''Yet we can make no headway.''

''They are most difficult too kill,'' said the vixen Ilketsni. ''As we have learned to our sorrow.''

''The tide of the battle is turning,'' said Aumbry. ''We shall be forced to admit defeat.''

''You will not escape so easily,'' said Eunoe with a vicious smile. ''Goriel will follow you home. The Black Unicorn will come to lay the Kingdoms to waste.''

''Dear Lady, I fear you are right,'' said Ghola of Isfandiar. ''We would have done better to have endured the rain than to have started this futile campaign.''

Reander stirred restlessly in his chair. His side ached. ''I fail to see,'' he said, ''how any of this concerns me. It's too late to say that you're sorry.''

''Reander, we need your help,'' said Briavel.

Reander looked uncomfortable. He had no desire to watch the proud cormorant plead. His eyes fell upon Sioned's empty seat and his expression hardened.

''Your faith in me is touching,'' said Reander. ''A thousand of my people died to protect you from your own folly. I have been wounded. I have seen my friends killed, some I have killed myself. What more would you have of me?''

''Dear boy, I should have thought that obvious,'' said Ghola with a wave of his spidery hand. ''Intercede for us, arrange a truce.''

''You would trust *me* to treat with Ravenor for you?'' asked Reander. His eyes gleamed. He was enjoying this. ''I'm glad I've regained some stature in your eyes. I'm sorry. I can't help you.''

''Can't or won't?'' snarled Ilketsni. ''This war is *your* doing. You never should have let the Black Unicorn go free.''

Briavel shook his dusky plumage and fixed Reander

with a beady eye. "You sacrificed your army to save the Kingdoms," he said. "Will you abandon us now? Go to Goriel, he will listen to you."

"No," said Reander. "He won't."

Reander sat straighter. His expression grew serious. "Goriel will never agree to a truce," he said. "He will not rest so long as any of us are left alive. A thousand years ago a Prince of Essylt turned Ravenor into a desert. Because of the Kingdoms, Goriel's wife and twin daughters died."

"But all that was long ago," said Aumbry. "It's not *our* fault that Ravenor's a wasteland."

"Warlords of Ravenor," said Reander, "are long-lived. Goriel makes no distinction between us and our ancestors. His hatred is very real."

"What shall we do, then?" asked Aumbry.

"We must contain the fighting at the ford," said Reander. "Goriel must be persuaded to content himself with slaughtering the invasion army. He must not summon his sovereign. If the Black Unicorn enters this fray we will have lost everything. He is a berserk. His blood lust will drive him to invade the Kingdoms in return. A conflict shall begin that shall last for generations."

The Council digested this unpalatable news in silence.

"I had hoped that Essylt's sacrifice would spare you this," said Reander. "We have a duty to the as-yet unborn. They must be saved from Ravenor. Only our deaths can achieve this." Reander's unexpected sympathy persuaded the Council that he spoke the truth.

Ghola straightened his shoulders. "No sacrifice is too great for the Kingdoms," he said. "We will do what we must. Reander, go to Goriel. If you can, persuade him to take the Council's lives and leave our warriors alone. If not, we shall stay here and fight until all are dead."

"I cannot go to Goriel," said Reander. "He will not treat with a Prince of Essylt."

"You dealt with him before," said Ilketsni. "When you unlocked the Gate . . ."

"I killed him," said Reander. "It has not endeared me to him."

Reander smiled a fiendish smile and waved a hand toward Quadroped. Quadroped waggled his ears. "My Lords, that is our only hope. We must send Quadroped to Goriel. It was he, and not I, that opened the Gate and set the Black Unicorn free."

"Then it *is* a Demon Pig," cried portly Aumbry, turning pale. "I knew such a guileless exterior could only harbor a spirit of boundless malevolence. He is responsible for all our ills."

Quadroped's ears drooped. "I'm sorry," he said. "But I thought it would be all right. The Black Unicorn promised not to destroy the Kingdoms. I didn't know," he added with a bit more spirit, "that you would go and invade Ravenor."

"No *animal* could have done such a thing," said Ghola.

Ilketsni's bright gaze swept over the spherical form of Quadroped. "Animals can do a great many things," she said. "But this piglet is so . . ."

"Silly?" supplied Reander. "Foolish looking? Round?"

"Edible," said Ilketsni with a snap of her jaws. "We can't send a pig. Why, it wouldn't know what to say."

"Then we can send someone else to go with him," said Reander. "My Lords, I am deadly serious. All Ravenor owes Quadroped a debt. He is the only creature in the Kingdoms who could possibly convince Goriel to see reason."

Ilketsni preened a thoughtful whisker. "Glasgerion . . . ?"

"Glasgerion's marriage will not influence Goriel," said Reander. "He is a Prince of Essylt. Nor can Morragwen help us. She is the youngest and least powerful of the Warlords. Her words will not weigh with Goriel."

It was agreed that Quadroped should go to Goriel. No one thought to ask Quadroped what he thought of this plan and he was too shy to say. They fell then to discussing who should accompany Quadroped. No one wished to leave such delicate negotiations to the sole discretion of a pig.

"Send Aedh," said Reander. "The Manslayer owes his freedom to him and Goriel bears him no malice."

Aodh leaped to his feet in fury. "Aedh is my prisoner," he said. "I will not let him escape again. He will return to Seamourn, to stand trial for his crimes."

"Who then?" asked Reander. "Goriel will not speak to Ghola, for Isfandiar holds Ravenorian mines. Aodh is incapable of diplomacy. Briavel and Ilketsni are both privileged to be beasts and Ghola refuses to send them. Aumbry . . ." Aumbry paled and gasped as Reander's eyes fell upon him. "Aumbry would not wish to go."

"Send me."

All heads turned to the doorway whence the soft voice had come. Princess Sioned of Lyskerys stood there, looking pale but otherwise unhurt.

Reander rose and went to her, taking her hands in his. "I thought I had killed you," he said.

"It was not so serious, as you may see," said Sioned with a smile. She took her seat at the table. "I awoke from a coma two days ago, refreshed as from a long sleep. Do not blame yourself, Reander. We met in battle, now we meet as friends. I would be glad to go with the pig."

"It is too dangerous," said Reander, hovering over her solicitously. "In your weakened condition . . ."

"She looks fine to me," said Eunoe. "I wish you would sit down, Reander. You *are* wounded."

"Reander, I am fully recovered," said Sioned. "I wish to go."

"Then you are a fool," said Reander.

Quadroped could not help but agree with this sentiment. He recalled his own meetings with Goriel and shuddered. The Lord of Snows was winter personified: cruel, dispassionate, deadly.

"Sioned would make an excellent envoy," said Briavel. "Her tact and diplomacy are legend."

"She does not know what she is getting herself into," said Reander. "None of you do."

"That may be true," said Ghola. "But there is no one else. The pig cannot go alone."

There was little left to say but they said it at length. Glasgerion and Eunoe escaped with Quadroped, leaving

Reander to deal with the Council. Quadroped was carried off to an elegant tent wherein stood a tub of warm water.

"Bath," said Glasgerion.

"No," said Quadroped.

"Yes," chorused Glasgerion and Eunoe.

Quadroped was unceremoniously dumped in, muddy mail shirt and all. Eunoe advanced upon the spluttering piglet, a large sponge clenched in her hands.

While Quadroped was being restored to pristine condition, Reander came in with Pseudo-Polyp riding on his shoulder. He deposited the small coelenterate on the rim of the tub.

"I came to say good-bye," said Pseudo-Polyp. "Aodh's agreed to let Aedh go free. Adjurel is pregnant. Reander pointed out that her child will be King Angmar's rightful heir. Aedh would never challenge the baby's claim to the throne. Even if he did, the people would never support him."

"What will Aedh do now?" asked Quadroped.

"I don't know," said Pesudo-Polyp. "He cannot remain in the Kingdoms. I suppose we'll go back to Ravenor."

Pseudo-Polyp sighed. His crown of tentacles drooped a bit. "I always thought we'd return to Seamourn someday," he said. "But now it looks like we'll be wandering around forever. I wish we could settle down. Aedh is a far better administrator than a mercenary. I miss life at court. Warriors are so boring. They have no polish and less conversation. Still"—the tentacles perked up a bit—"at least we're alive, thanks to Reander."

Pseudo-Polyp left. Quadroped was released from his bath and dried with a fluffy towel. His coat of mail was polished until it shone. His coat of small bristles was brushed. Throughout these proceedings Reander lectured him on how he should address Goriel and exactly what he should say.

"I'll never remember all that," Quadroped told Glasgerion when Reander had gone.

"Don't worry about it," said Glasgerion. "If all goes well, Sioned will handle the negotiatons. If Goriel won't recognize her, then do the best you can. All we want is a promise from Goriel to spare the civilian population. If he wants lives he can have the army's. But try to get him to settle for the Councillors. Don't hesitate to sacrifice us, Quadro. The Kingdoms can get new rulers.''

''All right,'' said Quadroped. He privately vowed that, come what may, he would not sacrifice his friends. The rest of the Council could pay for peace, Essylt had done enough.

Quadroped followed Glasgerion out into the night. There was a ring around the moon and frost in air. Across the cold waters of the Lost Skeggs, Ravenor's watch fires glowed. Between Quadroped and the river lay the battlefield, lumpy with shadowed cadavers.

Sioned stood by the riverbank, pale and dressed in ghostly white with silver around her waist. Ariseid was also there, standing at the stern of a flatboat, pole in hand, ready to ferry them to the other side. The Isfandi warrior had not been forgiven for fighting on Essylt's side.

Ariseid helped Quadroped board, seating him in the back of the boat. Sioned sat down beside him. She spoke not a word as Ariseid pushed them out into the currents. The Princess of Lyskerys sat, silent and calm, gazing ahead. Quadroped huddled beside her.

Water slapped against the hull in harmony with the rhythmic splash of Ariseid's pole. Quadroped abandoned his worries and pointed his nose into the wind, letting his ears blow back. He could smell pitch and canvas, old rope and the smoke from Ravenor's fires.

Quadroped was just beginning to enjoy the trip when the boat stopped and he was thrown rudely forward. ''What's happened?'' he asked, picking himself up off the bottom of the boat.

''A sandbank,'' said Sioned placidly.

''I don't think it's a sandbank,'' said Ariseid. ''Not here. Piglet, *get down*!''

Quadroped ducked just as a huge tentacle came whipping down, slapping into the boat with a terrible force. Ariseid switched the pole to her left hand and made to draw her knife; her sword she had left in the Kingdom's camp.

Sioned rose suddenly and grabbed Ariseid's arm. "No weapons," she said. "We are coming in peace."

"We'll be killed," said Ariseid.

"Be still," said Sioned.

A second tentacle wrapped around the boat, a trifle less enthusiastically this time. Several additional appendages appeared and attached themselves to the sides. A large head, complete with myriad eyes and dripping fangs, emerged and leered evilly down.

Sioned paid the beast no heed. Her tranquil reaction soothed Quadroped's fears. Sioned was right. The beast did not seem disposed to bite them, it simply cradled them in its arms and began to tow them to the farther shore. Quadroped decided charitably that the evil leer might just be a lopsided grin.

It was impossible to tell what color the watery monster was; in the moonlight it was black and silver. Quadroped colored it pink in his mind. He painted the tentacles blue.

When they reached the Ravenorian shore the riverine beast swam away. They disembarked and were quickly surrounded by a band of Ravenorian warriors, who scowled darkly at them and demanded to know their business.

"We come in peace," said Sioned. She stood amid the warriors with peculiar tranquility, her hands limp at her sides. "Our business is with Goriel. We are not at liberty to discuss it with anyone else."

Sioned would give no other reply to their questions. At length the warriors stopped badgering her and decided to let her have her way. They left Ariseid in the boat, weaponless and surrounded by guards, and escorted Sioned and Quadroped up into the hills, through the rustling trees, to Goriel's camp.

Goriel's tent was black. Silver pennants fluttered above it, reflecting the light of the moon. Black-clad warriors stood watch around it, Goriel's people pale of skin and blue of eye. They wore eternal mourning for their Warlord's wife and daughters.

Two great wolves came silently out from the shadows to bar the path, necks bristling, lips drawn back in silent snarls. Quadroped's guards stopped a respectful distance from the beasts.

"Two are come from the enemy," said the captain of the guards. His voice was quiet and low, calculated not to alarm or challenge the wolves. "They will not state their business save to Lord Goriel himself. We thought it best to bring them."

One wolf came forward then, leaving her mate to bar the way, and circled around Quadroped and Sioned. Sioned held out her hand. The wolf looked curiously at her but came forward to sniff at her fingers. To Quadroped's horror Sioned proceeded to pat the savage beast on the head.

The wolf bore Sioned's touch for a moment, then she continued to circle. She paused again before Quadroped, her cold wet muzzle inches from his face.

"I know you, pig," said the wolf.

Quadroped was reminded that Reander had killed several of Goriel's werewolves last year. He closed his eyes and thought of teeth. He hoped that his armor would save him.

The wolf forbore to crunch Quadroped in her jaws. Instead, she turned and led the visitors back toward the tent, the guards pushing them on behind. At the entrance of Goriel's tent both wolf and guards stopped and indicated that Quadroped and Sioned should enter alone.

The interior of Goriel's tent was cold and still. Icy ghosts of frozen air rose from Quadroped's nose as he breathed. A great empty space, lit by black candles, stretched away before him. The tent, Quadroped noticed gloomily, was larger inside than out. It also had a different shape. The tent had been round on the outside. Inside it was long and rectangular.

At the far end of the room several people stood, clustered around a long wooden table, their backs to the door. They were all hunched over something, arguing fiercely in whispers. Sioned moved slowly toward them, seeming almost to float. Quadroped trailed after her, ears down and far from oblivious to the threatening gloom of the tent.

When Sioned and Quadroped were halfway down the hall the people turned and stepped aside, revealing a long wooden table upon which a map of the Kingdoms was spread. Goriel sat at the table's head. His great wings were folded behind him, framing his face in silver. Obsidian eyes studied his guests without pleasure. In perfect stillness, without a word, Goriel watched them approach; he did not rise to greet them.

Sioned came to stand at the foot of the table. Quadroped stopped just behind her, in the comforting shelter of her robes, and looked nervously around. The Manslayer did not appear to be present. This cheered him slightly until he peeked at Goriel's face.

Sioned stared at Goriel as if she would memorize his every feature. Goriel returned her gaze in dreadful, implacable silence. Minutes passed. Quadroped began to fidget. It would be dawn soon and the fighting would be renewed.

Reander had warned Quadroped that he must, on no account, speak first. To do so would be a serious breach of etiquette. Quadroped suspected that Goriel was trying to force Sioned to break the rules. Few creatures could bear his inimical glare for long. But Sioned was not reacting as a normal human should. Her dreamy brown eyes met Goriel's without effort. Her lips were actually smiling.

For the first time it occurred to Quadroped that Sioned might be ill. She had just recovered from a terrible blow to the head. Quadroped twisted and gazed up into Sioned's face. Her eyes were wide and unfocused, the pupils unnaturally large.

Something had to be done. Goriel and Sioned seemed capable of staring at each other all night. It was clearly up to Quadroped to alter the situation. He took a calming breath.

"Hail, Warlord," said Quadroped loudly, and promptly forgot the rest of Reander's carefully prepared speech.

Goriel moved. He shifted slightly in his chair and turned his cold eyes upon Quadroped. Quadroped stared fixedly at the floor, pretending that he had not spoken. A slow smile curved Goriel's icy lips, then died in his brilliant eyes.

"Well met, Key Bearer that was," said Goriel. His voice was low, beautiful to the ears. "I did not look to find you in the company of my enemies. When last we met you spoke to me of peace."

Quadroped looked up, then looked away. It was impossible to think clearly while staring into that beguiling, frightening face.

"The Kingdoms *do* want peace," he said at last.

"Eternal peace," said Sioned.

Quadroped looked at Sioned in dismay. Her remark was macabre and provocative. Goriel's attendants shuffled nervously, their faces wary and strained.

Goriel continued to address Quadroped. "The Kingdoms have a strange way of showing their goodwill," he said. "War is a game seldom played among friends."

"They're very sorry they invaded you," said Quadroped. "They won't do it again."

"They are weary," said Sioned in a musing tone. "They seek rest in the arms of the soil."

Goriel raised his eyes from Quadroped and looked on Sioned again.

"Who is this Lady?" he asked. "Why does she speak so strangely?"

Sioned stared blankly into space. She looked neither healthy nor sane.

Quadroped sighed. Where, he wondered bitterly, was the legendary tact and diplomacy of which Briavel had spoken so highly? "This is Sioned, Princess of Lyskerys," he said at last. "Reander knocked her unconscious in his last battle. She's still a little confused. Maybe she should sit down."

"Very well," said Goriel.

Two attendants came forward and led Sioned to a seat. To Quadroped's intense relief she obeyed them and sat down quietly in the corner. Her eyes, however, remained unnervingly glued to Goriel.

"It does not raise my confidence in the Kingdoms that they send such a one to speak with me," said Goriel, regarding Sioned with a pitiless eye. "Are piglets and madwomen the best they can do? Or the best that this errand merits?"

"Sioned seemed perfectly healthy in camp," said Quadroped. "Reander and Glasgerion both wanted to come but they didn't think you would hear them."

"They were right," said Goriel.

"My name is not Sioned," said Sioned suddenly.

Goriel turned, his expression cold and forbidding. "The Kingdoms ask much of me, piglet. This war is of their making. They knew what the outcome would be."

"But they didn't," said Quadroped eagerly. "They thought Reander was lying when he told them how powerful Ravenor was."

Goriel looked faintly amused. "I see," he said. "And our lands are not so valuable now that they know they must buy them with blood."

Quadroped realized belatedly that he had not used a very convincing argument. He thought back on all Morrag had told him of the political situation in the Kingdoms. "Only Imchadiz and Isfandiar wanted your lands," he said. "The others just wanted to stop the rain."

"Ravenor is not causing the rain," said Goriel.

"Yes, but the Kingdoms think you are," said Quadroped. "They weren't fighting for land, or because they hated Ravenor. They were fighting to ward off a famine."

"Ravenor has only a harvest of souls to offer the winter," said Sioned suddenly. "It is a barren land."

She rose to her feet. A strange radiance filled her face as she looked upon Goriel. "We walked together under leaves of jade, in Indrasir," she said.

For a terrible moment Goriel's face reflected anger. Then that expression, like all others, died upon his face. "I trust she knows not whereof she speaks," he said. "Otherwise I would kill her."

Quadroped hurried on. "The Council believed that Reander had made a pact with you to free the Black Unicorn and invade the Kingdoms," he said. "They thought the rain was sent to weaken them, so that you could defeat them more easily in the spring."

"An excellent idea."

Quadroped jumped and looked over his shoulder. The Manslayer stood behind him. Quadroped wondered uneasily how the Warlord had moved so softly and how long he had been standing there.

"Hungry people make a pleasant prey," said the Manslayer.

Quadroped shivered. The Manslayer wanted to kill him. He could tell from the way that he smiled.

The tent flap lifted and Morragwen entered. Her skin was dark as the nighttime sky, her hair as pale as the moon: Goriel's colors, silver and black. Without a word she crossed to Goriel's side.

"Don't be scared."

Quadroped looked up. Morrag had flown in with his mistress. Now he hovered over Quadroped's head. "Be brave, Quadro," he said. "Goriel is listening to you." He swam off and rejoined Morragwen.

"Ravenor is not pleased to have been cast in the role of scapegoat," said Goriel. "I have lost many warriors in this conflict. Their lives were precious to me."

"Death is also precious," said Sioned. "You, of all men, should not hold its value so low."

Quadroped winced. He wished that she would stay quiet. "If the war continues more people will die," he said. "The Council says you can have their lives, and those of their army as well. They're willing to die to prevent another Great War."

Goriel remained unmoved. Quadroped racked his brains for some argument that could win this ruthless Warlord to his side.

"Reander tried to stop the Kingdoms," he said.

"True," said Goriel. His expression softened a little. "Essylt has lost much in this affair. Does Reander sue for this peace?"

"Yes," said Quadroped eagerly.

"What is this talk of peace?" asked the Manslayer. "The Kingdoms are at our mercy. We'll never have such a chance again."

"Vengeance is at hand," said Sioned. "The Kingdoms

themselves have opened the way. The slaughter shall be terrible. The Lost Skeggs shall run red with the blood of the slain.''

"Precisely," said the Manslayer, eyeing Sioned with considerable approval. "Go back to Glasgerion, piglet. Keep out of our way. If you're lucky you may be spared."

Morragwen could no longer hold her peace. "Goriel, don't listen to this psychopath."

"Be silent," said Goriel. "Neither of you has leave to speak. I, and not you, shall decide the outcome of this meeting and of this war."

"Remember Eltis," said Sioned. At the name Goriel stiffened and turned sharply toward her. "Arelis's ghost calls for blood. Avenge your daughters, Goriel."

Goriel came suddenly to his feet. Before Quadroped knew what was happening he had reached Sioned, striking her so hard that she collapsed, senseless, upon the floor. Goriel turned away from the fallen Princess and addressed Quadroped.

"Go back to Reander," said Goriel. "Tell him that if he will give Essylt to us, to hold as hostage, then we shall let the Kingdoms be and content ourselves with this army. Tell him also that our thirst for Essylt's blood has been appeased. Let him hold back his forces from the coming fray. They shall be spared our anger."

Quadroped gulped and nodded. He looked at Sioned. Her eyelids were beginning to flutter as consciousness returned. "The Lady shall stay," said Goriel. "There are questions I would have answered."

Quadroped shook his head. "I can't go without her," he said.

"Then stay," said Goriel. He turned to his attendants. "We require privacy. Leave us."

The attendants filed from the room, leaving Quadroped alone with Morrag, the three Warlords, and the insensate body of Sioned. Goriel bent and picked Sioned up in his arms. He laid her down upon the table, arms over her head.

"Hold her," he told the Manslayer. "Keep her still."

"With pleasure," said Manslayer. He took hold of

Sioned's arms, forcing her to lie back. Goriel blew out all of the candles save one. Then he approached the table. He raised his arms.

"Stop," cried Quadroped. He dashed forward and butted his head fiercely against Goriel's legs.

"Sit down and be quiet," said the Manslayer. "He hasn't done anything yet."

"Don't hurt her," pleaded Quadroped.

"I won't," said Goriel. "At least, not much."

He turned his attention back to Sioned's now struggling form. As Quadroped watched, an arc of blue light spread out from Goriel's hand. As the light touched her Sioned screamed.

"Morrag, *do* something," said Quadroped to the eel, who was floating beside him. "He's torturing her."

"There's nothing I *can* do," said Morrag. "Goriel could kill Morragwen and me in an instant."

The ghastly light crawled over Sioned's body, encasing her in a glimmering cocoon. She writhed, convulsed, and then her body once more went limp.

"Come forth," said Goriel.

From Sioned's body a wreath of smoke began to trail upward, as though a tiny fire had been lit in her abdomen. The smoke rose and spread out until it hung in a horizontal layer above Sioned's unconscious form.

"Take shape," said Goriel.

The smoke rose again, rolling and twisting on air until it had resolved itself into the spectral form of a young woman; a woman, Quadroped noted with surprise, who did not resemble Sioned in the slightest.

All traces of anger vanished from Goriel's face. An expression of tenderness, and of longing, softened his arctic features. "Glaissin?" he said.

At the sound of her name the phantom's eyes flew open. She stared into Goriel's eyes, and smiled. Wordlessly she opened her arms.

Chapter Nine

A smile of great beauty transfigured Goriel's face as he moved toward the arms of the phantom. The Manslayer snarled and seized him by his shoulders.

"Don't touch her," he said. "She means you harm. This is some trick of the Kingdoms'."

Morragwen laid a restraining hand upon Goriel's arm. "The Manslayer is right," she said. "This is not Glaissin. Your wife is lost forever. Even the Black Unicorn failed when he tried to raise her spirit."

Goriel shook off Morragwen's and the Manslayer's hands. He stepped back, his expression suddenly weary. "I know it cannot be Glaissin," he said. "And yet, the likeness is exact. Who in the Kingdoms would recall my wife? Or have the power to create this illusion?"

"Reander," said the Manslayer. He pointed an accusing finger at Morragwen. "She has told him about Glaissin."

"Nonsense," said Morragwen. "If I wanted to harm you, Goriel, I would not choose such a strange method."

"How else could you hope to harm him?" sneered the Manslayer. "You are too weak to hurt Goriel save by treachery."

"This is ridiculous," said Morragwen. "Reander is try-ing to make peace, not promote war. Why should he wish to kill Goriel? There would be no better way to ensure the Black Unicorn's presence."

"I do not think this is Reander's work," said Goriel. "He has never stooped to deceit. Let us see what this apparition is made of."

Quadroped felt Old Magic at work in the room. His head ached, his stomach hurt. A thousand insects buzzed distractingly in his ears. He smelled and tasted hot metal.

The sensations stopped. Glaissin still stood there, arms open and smiling. She laughed. It was not a chilling or a wicked laugh, just a happy gurgle of pleasure.

"Goriel," she said.

Glaissin stepped forward on air and began to look around. "What has happened?" she asked. "I was in the garden. I . . ." Her hands fluttered and clasped each other. "Goriel, where am I?"

"Do not speak to her," said the Manslayer. "Send her back."

"You are dead, Glaissin," said Goriel. Then, because his words had frightened her, he put an arm about her, holding it steady in the air that it might not pass through her intangible form.

Glaissin shuddered, "I cannot feel your arm," she said. She turned and placed her small hands upon Goriel's chest. "See, my hands pass right through you. Am I dead?"

"Yes," said Goriel. He took her transparent hands in his own.

Glaissin's expression grew thoughtful. "I remember now," she said. "The raiders came. There was pain, and then . . . another place. Goriel, why am I here?"

"I don't know," said Goriel. "But you cannot stay. You must go back, my love."

"Must I?" Glaissin looked sadly around.

"The dead have no place in this world," said Goriel. "If you stay here you will harm us all."

"I will go then," said Glaissin sadly. She floated through Goriel's arms and went to the table where

Sioned's body lay. "Who is she?" Glaissin asked. "Does she have no spirit?"

"It has already been claimed in battle," said Goriel. "A Prince of Essylt slew her. Her mind was the door through which you came and through which I must send you back."

"Kiss me once, then, before I go," said Glaissin.

"Goriel, no," said the Manslayer. Once more he grabbed Goriel's shoulders.

"Do not send me away so coldly," pleaded Glaissin, stretching forth her misty arms. "Kiss me and make the parting sweeter."

"Don't," said the Manslayer, tugging hard.

"Goriel, the Balance has shifted," said Morragwen. "It could be death to touch her now."

Goriel shook off the Manslayer's hands and held out his arms for his wife. Glaissin backed away.

"I would not hurt you," she said.

"You could not," said Goriel. His arms came around her.

Goriel bent forward until his lips met the earth-cold lips of his long-dead wife. They kissed. Then Glaissin's ghost evaporated into thin air. With a soft sigh Goriel drooped and crumpled to the floor.

"Treachery," cried the Manslayer. He knelt beside Goriel, searching for signs of life. He found none.

"Goriel is slain," said the Manslayer. "His spirit has been sucked away. The Kingdoms shall pay for this deed in blood!" He turned his yellow eyes upon the cowering Quadroped. The slit pupils widened.

"You," said the Manslayer. "You die."

Quadroped took one look at the Manslayer's face and fled. The Warlord leaped to catch him. Morragwen moved faster, grabbing Quadroped up in her arms and holding him over her head.

"Leave Quadro alone," said Morragwen.

"Never," said the Manslayer. "I've wanted to kill that sanctimonious little beast ever since I first laid eyes on him. Give him to me, *now*."

"I won't," said Morragwen.

The Manslayer sprang at her, grabbing her around the waist. She fell. The back of her head hit the table with a sickening crunch. Quadroped fell to the floor and rolled several feet toward the door.

The Manslayer turned to pursue his prey. Morragwen grabbed him around the throat. Fireworks began to explode through the tent as the combatants turned to magic.

"Quadro, get out of here," cried Morrag. He lashed through the air to his mistress's aid.

Quadroped took one last look at the scene in the tent, and fled. Under the feet of milling guards and leaping wolves Quadroped ran, past the watch fires, out into the forest that surrounded Goriel's camp. Behind him he heard the news of Goriel's death being relayed from tent to tent.

Quadroped scrambled through the dark, moving steadily uphill, away from the river. The Manslayer would not think to look for him in this direction. He would assume that Quadroped had run toward the river, and the safety that lay on its other side.

Quadroped was soon out of breath. He began to slow down and consider what best to do. Around him the woods were filled with normal nocturnal noises. Crickets sang, trees creaked and sighed, small creatures scurried on the pine needle floor.

Quadroped tipped his ears this way and that. There were no sounds of pursuit. He was safe. He was also trapped in Ravenor.

Quadroped could not return to the river, for the Manslayer's minions would be searching the shore. In the morning they would turn to the woods. Quadroped's only hope of escape was to move as far away from the Kingdoms as possible, into the heart of the forest.

Quadroped began to climb slowly uphill. The woods were dark and frightening. Branches clutched at him, trying to hold him back. Stones tripped him and bruised his feet.

Quadroped had not gone far when he saw a light glimmering through the trees. The pale radiance beckoned to

him, promising a moonlit clearing in the woods and easier
traveling for his tired hooves.

Quadroped hurried forward into the light, and stopped.
He had made a dreadful mistake. The glow came not from
the friendly full moon, but from phosphorescent fungi.
The clearing was filled with luminous toadstools, clustered
thickly upon the trunks of the trees. *Clitocybe illudens*,
the poisonous Jack-O'-Lantern of the Woods, surrounded
him on every side, its fat yellow stalks and orange caps
alight with the coldest of fires.

Quadroped stared at the toadstools. Cradle stories
returned to haunt him, tales of the Fearsome Fungus Folk.
When nights were black and branches tapped at the windows, Mushroom Men came to carry bad piglets away. In
the depths of the forest the Fungus Folk lurked, waiting
for wandering piglets.

The Jack-O'-Lanterns moved. All over the clearing the
flat caps tipped back, revealing wicked, wrinkled faces.
They crept down the rotten trunks of the trees, their red
eyes fixed on the pig.

Quadroped snorted in terror and began to back away.
Toadstools sprouted behind him, barring his way. Before
him a gaping hole appeared as the sandy soil gave way
beneath his hooves.

Quadroped scrabbled at the crumbling sides of the pit.
He began to slide, his heavy coat of mail pulling him
down. Tree roots, shaggy and coated with soil, hung out
into space. Quadroped grabbed one and clung to it. The
dirt clogged his mouth and trickled down his throat. His
jaws trembled and grew weak.

Quadroped hung on to the root and fearfully looked up.
The fungi were clustered thickly around the rim of the pit.
They began to advance down the root.

Jack-O'-Lantern perched above Quadroped's nose and
scowled dreadfully upon his captive. "You are making
things very difficult for yourself," he said. His minions
chittered in unpleasant chorus. "I really hate to do this,
but . . ."

The rufous toadstool released a burning cloud of spores.
With a mounting sense of horror Quadroped felt his nose

go all stuffy and ticklish. He sneezed. His mouth flew open. Down he fell, past all of the soil horizons, down, to a secret land beneath the roots.

Quadroped landed on the leaf-strewn floor of the pit with a thump that rendered him nearly insensible. The rings of his chain mail coat bit painfully into his sides. His head hurt. A crowd of coralline Fungus Folk surrounded him, bathing him in their bluish glow.

The many-branched fungoids looked delicate but Quadroped was too dazed to fight. With unpleasant threats and long, pointed sticks the fragile fungi prodded their captive to his hooves, forcing him to rise and begin the long walk through the labyrinthine heart of the Fungus World.

Down putrid, jellied corridors Quadroped's captors hustled him. On tired, aching hooves he traveled through the twisting passageway. At last his captors stopped poking him and left him to lie, in a shuddering heap, on the floor of the great Fungal Hall.

Quadroped slowly began to recover his scattered senses. Eventually he revived enough to sit up and look around. He found himself in the middle of a moistly dripping chamber of awe-inspiring proportions and tasteless hues. Mustard yellow and purple-reddish tones prevailed. The floor was slimy, porous, and of spongelike resilience. Strange, spiky growths grew in uneven intervals upon the walls, exuding unhealthy green light. The air in the hall smelled overpoweringly of hydrogen peroxide, damp, and rot.

The Fungus Folk began to arrive in great numbers, all hurrying into the room. For the first time Quadroped was able to study the appearance of his captors in all their varied detail. They were not a comforting sight.

The beings before him were odd and unlovely in appearance. They came in myriad sizes, shapes, and pallid hues. Their flesh had an unpleasantly moist appearance while their hair, if such it could be called, was coarse and fibrous. It rose from their heads to form horns, or stalks, the tops of which sported umbrellalike growths resembling huge mushroom caps. Their features were uniformly pinched and wizened. Their tiny hands and feet were elongated and of disturbingly clawlike aspect.

Each of the Fungus Folk resembled some earthly fungi in his or her general appearance. Quadroped's trained eye and wondrous nose identified the gibbous blue stalk of a dream-inducing *Inocybe* hand in hand with the anastomosed form of a False Morel. *Claviceps purpurea*, the Ergot-of-Rye and bringer of madness, was there. Trumpets of Death, Deceivers, and Bleeding *Mycena* clustered around him. The allantoid forms of Devil's Fingers stood about like slugs on end. Coconut-scented Sickeners with their rusty red caps leered at each other, and snickered. Hirsute Inky Cap, Chantarelle, amorphous False Amadou, and Weeping Widow dripping trails of dew, all formed a part of that saprophytic host.

Quadroped gazed around the increasingly crowded hall with feelings of dismay, not unmixed with the revulsion a healthy pig must feel upon suddenly being presented with an assembly of animate and hostile foodstuffs. The denizens of that noisome land glared back at their captive with reddened eyes, equally revolted by the vision of a well-fed pig.

The crowd fell silent. In the distance Quadroped could hear the sound of woodwinds, tweedling out a melancholy air. A sweetly musty scent invaded the chamber. Adrenaline shot through Quadroped's system. His heart began to pound. Down went his ears, flat against his head. The short bristles at his neck rose up in fear.

A stately procession of plain brown-and-white mushrooms came into view. The pleasant scent grew stronger. With a little groan, Quadroped recognized the Family of Deadly Amanita. In their midst he espied their lord and master, Ferethel the Fungus Lord, the dread Destroying Angel.

Death Cap minced up to Quadroped. He was brown and ordinary as any common mushroom. "May the Hyphae of the Great Mycelium be praised," he enthused. "With this pig in our power nothing shall stand in our way."

Ferethel examined Quadroped with eyes as white as a blinded man's. The Ruler of Toadstools was snowy of flesh with a ruffle of skin at his long slender neck that looked like a linen cravat. In languid tones he addressed the exuberant Death Cap beside him.

"So, *Phalloides*, this is the last of the fairy pigs?"

"Indeed it is," said Death Cap, bowing low. "*Clitocybe illudens* caught it in the woods tonight. Mushrooms and Mildews shall grow over all. You shall be Lord of the Earth."

"Excellent," said Ferethel.

The Panther, Ferethel's ivory brother, stepped forward. He examined Quadroped with a critical eye. "What is the nature of its powers?" he asked.

"I don't know," said Death Cap, "but it has escaped Nieve's grasp so they must be great indeed."

"Summon those that trapped it," said the Panther to his red white-warted cousin.

Amanita muscaria, the Fly Agaric, bowed and moved away. She returned trailed by a mushroom of fiery hue. *Clitocybe illudens*, the poisonous Jack-O'-Lantern of the Woods, groveled before his lord and master and tittered sycophantically.

"Enough," said the Panther. The tittering ceased. "Tell us what powers this piglet displayed upon capture."

Jack-O'-Lantern fluttered the gills decurrent upon his stalk. He looked upon Quadroped in wary confusion. "Powers?" he asked. "Why, none, most putrefied Prince. We trapped it quite easily. It ran straight into the trap and fell down the pit. *Xylaria hypoxylon* awaited it and escorted it here. It gave them no trouble at all."

Ferethel frowned. Around him his court gurgled nervously, and many oozed forth slime. A delicate dendritic mushroom scuttled forth and prostrated itself at Ferethel's feet. A bluish glow escaped and shone around it.

"Is this true?" demanded Ferethel of his quivering subject.

"Indeed it is, O Virulent One," said *Xylaria hypoxylon*, antlers all atremble. "It was dazed by its fall and made no effort to escape us. It still seems dazed, for see, it is passive even now."

"Hmmm," said Ferethel.

"I trust the fall has not damaged its brain," said the Panther. He stared thoughtfully at *Clitocybe illudens*. "It is of little use to us if it has lost its senses. Perhaps dropping it down a deep pit was not the wisest thing to do."

The orange Jack-O'-Lantern quivered pitifully. "It is not hurt," said *Clitocybe illudens* earnestly. "It merely holds its tongue, denoting wisdom rather than stupidity upon its part."

"I hope so," purred the Panther.

Clitocybe illudens gulped and crept back toward Quadroped. "Show us your powers, pig," he commanded.

"I can't," said Quadroped.

The Panther stalked forward. "Mushroom toxins can provide an almost bewildering array of physical sensations," he said. "Pleasure, pain, death . . . the choice is yours. Your fellows have learned to obey us."

"My fellows?" Quadroped looked at the Panther with a sense of foreboding. Could the fairy pigs be here, held captive in Ferethel's halls? If they were they had to be rescued. But how? Quadroped stared at the porous floor and thought harder than he had ever thought in his life.

The Fungus Folk let Quadroped alone, believing that he had obeyed their commands. Fairy pigs always stared blankly into space when invoking their mighty powers.

At length Quadroped was forced to admit that there was no way to rescue either his parents or himself. If the Ferethel was strong enough to imprison a fairy sounder then there was naught that a piglet could do. Unfortunately it also became apparent to the mushrooms that Quadroped was not cooperating. The Fungal Halls were free to any sign of condensation. Spies in the world above reported no change in the weather.

"You are unwise to displease us," said Ferethel in his softest voice.

"We have been patient with you, pig," said the Panther. "But you have exhausted our patience. I shall count to ten. If you do not demonstrate your powers to us by then . . ." He paused and began his count.

Quadroped stared miserably at the deadly Panther and wished yet again that he had some vestige of the magical abilities that were his birthright. He thought about rain, hoping that perhaps in these last moments some power might suddenly be awakened in him. Nothing happened. The Panther reached ten and frowned.

"You are brave but most foolish, pig," said the Panther. "We *can* force you to aid us. We shall start, I think, by giving you a severe stomachache. Excruciatingly painful, but not deadly."

The Panther clapped his hands and a small pudgy puffball rolled forward with a wedge of violaceous mushroom flesh. "We have no way of stopping or shortening the reaction," said the Panther. "Your pleas will not end the pain. But when it has passed I think you will be ready to help us, if only to avoid another dose."

"No," said Quadroped, backing away. "You don't understand. I don't *have* any magical powers."

"No powers?" The Panther looked at Quadroped in mild surprise. "*Clitocybe*, have you fetched the wrong pig?"

"No," wailed the Jack-O'-Lantern.

Ferethel spoke. "You are the pig who freed the Black Unicorn of Ravenor?"

"Yes," admitted Quadroped.

"And you have no magical powers?"

"None," said Quadroped.

"We think," said the Ruler of Toadstools, "that the pig is telling the truth. A pity, still, there may be some use for it yet."

Ferethel waved a languid, squamous hand in Quadroped's face. "Take it away," he said. "We will consider its disposal later, at our convenience."

Once again Quadroped was surrounded by spiky *Xylaria hypoxylon* and prodded to his hooves. Through the uliginose underworld his many branched captors marched him, and sang a little ditty as they went:

Old is the dark where no dew falls
Where fungal jellies coalesce
Where sightless salamanders crawl
And grotesque mushrooms phosphoresce

Where rotting chambers fall away
While death-watch beetles lay their eggs
In spongy halls that seep decay
While mindless slugs attack the dregs.

The last quavering notes of the mushrooms' song died away. They had reached the lowest, darkest regions of the maze. Through the noisome stench of rotting matter wafted a wondrous bouquet. Quadroped's snout twitched, his ears perked up, his eyes began to shine.

On eager hooves Quadroped approached his prison. The great doors creaked open and he flung himself inside. He was so happy he did not even notice the doors being slammed shut behind him. Quadroped's long journey had come to an end. He had finally found his parents.

Quadroped's nose led him straight to his mother's warm flank and, with a great sob of relief, he buried his head in her side. "Mother," he said. "I've found you. I thought you were dead, but I've *found* you." Quadroped's mother snorted soothingly and butted her damp snout against his downy ears.

Quadroped's happiness was short-lived. His parents did not seem particularly glad to see him. They snuffled at him, but they spoke not a word of welcome. Indeed, they said nothing at all. Happiness was replaced by worry and the knowledge that something was terribly wrong.

"Mother," said Quadroped. "What's the matter with you? Why won't you speak to me? What's happened?"

Mother pig grunted softly and nuzzled her youngest child. Her movements seemed slow, her scent was not quite right. Quadroped turned to his father and tried again. The boar shook his head and wandered off, no longer intrigued by the new arrival.

They're acting just like normal beastly pigs, thought Quadroped. *As if they had no minds at all. The mushrooms must have drugged them. At least, I hope they're drugged.* With a jolt of fear Quadroped recalled that some mushroom toxins could damage the brain forever.

Quadroped found himself a relatively clean pile of straw and sat down to consider this latest development. If his parents were drugged he might be able to restore them to some semblance of normality by withholding the food that the Mushrooms provided. His mother's side had not been as pleasantly soft as he remembered, her ribs had felt quite sharp. Quadroped surmised that the pigs were being partially starved. It might be a long while before the next meal arrived.

As the hours slowly passed, Quadroped had more than enough time to wonder what had become of his friends. Morrag and Morragwen would be in the Manslayer's power by now. The sadistic Warlord would not treat them gently, now that Goriel was no longer alive to forbid his colleague's grim sports.

Goriel's death would lead to a second Great War. The Manslayer would never agree to a truce. The Black Unicorn would be summoned, and would come to avenge his best-loved Warlord. The Kingdoms would be destroyed. All of Quadroped's friends would die. Glasgerion would never see Morragwen again. It was, all in all, a thoroughly depressing prospect.

The grating of a key in an iron lock roused Quadroped from his reveries. The Mushrooms were opening the door. It was too dark to see what they were doing but Quadroped's nose suggested that, at long last, it was feeding time.

Quadroped hastened to the door, anxious to prevent his parents from consuming whatever toxins the fungoids had provided. He was too late. The sounder had already gathered there and were crowded so thick about the food trough that he could not push through. Worst of all, his mother and father were up in the front, their snouts already buried in the disgusting, fetid muck.

"Mother, Father, *stop!*" Quadroped cried. "Don't eat that stuff. Please. I *need* you."

Quadroped's frantic cries alarmed the herd. The drug had worn partially off in the long interval between feedings. It was now starvation, rather than any toxin in their blood, which dimmed the minds of the fairy pigs. The pigs turned away from the trough.

"You mustn't eat that food," said Quadroped. "It's drugged. It's turned you all into beast-pigs."

"We are hungry," a sow said simply. Quadroped almost wept, he was so happy to hear another pig speak.

"The drug makes us forget where we are," said another. "It makes us forget that we must live out our lives here in the depths of the Fungus World."

"Quadro, is that you?" Quadroped's father pushed his way through the herd and came up to snuffle his son. His mother and brothers were right behind him.

"We thought that Nieve must have you," said Mother Pig tearfully.

"Yes, what happened to you?" asked Tannakin and Tantony, Quadroped's elder brothers. "How did Ferethel catch you? We thought the Black Unicorn would protect you."

"Yes, piglet," said the ancient Sanglier in a dry, unfriendly tone. "*Do* tell us what you have been doing while we rotted here below."

Quadroped turned toward the mighty boar, confused by his hostile tone. In a subdued voice he began to relate everything that had happened to him and all the terrible things that were occurring now in the upstairs world.

"What happened to you?" he asked when he had finished. "I didn't think Fungus Folk could harm full-grown pigs. How did you fall into Ferethel's hands?"

"That," said the Sanglier, "is your fault. Had you not broken our covenant with Nieve she would never have placed us here. You have doomed your Sounder to this ghastly fate. You have plunged the world into war."

"Me?" asked Quadroped in a very small voice. "What did I do?"

"You made peace with the Black Unicorn," said the Sanglier. "When Nieve commanded you not to."

"Nieve?" said Quadroped. "But she hasn't told me anything. I've never even met her. I didn't know she existed until Avice told me about her."

"You don't need to see Nieve to hear her," said the Sanglier. "Her voice is the wind. We all heard her calling out to you, telling you not to go to the Gate. She wanted the Great War to begin anew, but you, foolish piglet, disobeyed her. And don't tell me that you didn't know she was your Overlord. We may have conveniently strayed out of the Fleshless Land, and succeeded in losing ourselves for several millennia, but we have always tacitly acknowledged Nieve's rule, and her father's before her. Why, the renewal of vows is a basic part of the training."

"Oh," said Quadroped.

"Stop bullying my son," said Father Pig. "He never received the training. He has no powers to train."

"We never told Quadro about Nieve," said Mother Pig. "We only told him the usual story about our ascent from the Underworld. And he can't hear the wind speak, he's never been able to."

"Hrumph," said the Sanglier. "You should have watched him better. A piglet without powers should stay close to home. He should not be allowed to concern himself with weighty affairs of state."

"I came home as soon as I could," said Quadroped.

"Not soon enough," said the Sanglier. "Because of you we have been forced to make it rain, to create a damp and dripping world where the Fungus Folk, those vilest of creatures, may thrive."

"Then you *are* causing the rain," said Quadroped.

"Of course," said the Sanglier. He turned and walked stiffly away. The other pigs all followed him, leaving Quadroped alone with his parents. Quadroped hung his head.

"Don't cry, son," said Father Pig. "You couldn't know. I know you wouldn't have disobeyed Nieve if you had heard her commands."

"But I would have," said Quadroped. "The Sanglier said Nieve *wanted* the Great War to start again. I couldn't have let that happen."

"Honor," said Father Pig, "demands that you obey Nieve no matter what she commands. She is your liege. Your ancestors pledged her their allegiance in ages past. You must honor that bond, as must we all. We must stay here and do as Ferethel bids until Nieve herself sets us free."

"But she's *evil*," said Quadroped. "She's killing thousands of people. You have to stop making it rain. You're causing famine and madness and war."

"Quadro, try to understand," said Father Pig gently. "Oaths and promises bind our society together. Without such rules there would be no governance. Societies would fall apart, there would be anarchy. We cannot bend the rules to fit our own ideas of right and wrong. If Nieve has done evil it is not our place to correct her. She will be punished by those beings who, in their turn, hold power over her."

Quadroped turned from his father in dismay. How could his father *be* so wrong? He was still trying to understand his father's point of view when his keen ears detected a tiny voice.

"Piglet, Quadro . . . Over here."

Quadroped turned. His questing snout collided with some gelatinous substance and he recoiled.

"Ugh," he said. "Who is that?"

"It's me," said the voice. "The Sly Mold. I've come to help you escape."

"Why?" asked Quadroped. "Aren't you a fungus too?"

"You gave me a name," said the slime mold. "The other fungi never would. They all look down on me. They're not sure if I'm a fungus or a protist. 'We are fruiting bodies of the Great Spiritual Mycelium,' hah! They are none of them willing to practice what they preach. Just because I lack dividing cell walls . . . Why, I'm as multinucleate as the rest of them and a lot less sessile!"

"I'm sure you are," said Quadroped respectfully.

"Bah!" said the slime mold. It pointed an amorphous appendage toward the wall behind Quadroped's head.

"There's a hole in that wall over there," said the slime mold. "Ferethel doesn't know it exists and these foolish pigs won't use it. Now hurry."

"Stop," said Father Pig sternly. "My son must remain here and obey Nieve's commands like the rest of us."

"Listen to me," said Sly Mold. "If Quadro stays here

he'll be killed. Ferethel has decided to eat him. The Amanitas will devour his flesh. They'll toast one another with
your child's semiliquid remains."

"Ugh," said Quadroped emphatically.

"Such a death would be messy but honorable," said
Father Pig.

"Quadro, come *on*," said the slime mold urgently.
"There's no time to waste."

"Quadroped, stay," said Father Pig. "I forbid you to
follow this creature. You will dishonor us all."

"I'm going, Father," said Quadroped sadly. "Nieve *is*
wrong and she has to be stopped. If there is any way to
end the war, then I have to try and find it. By the time
Nieve is punished it will be too late. Thousands of people
will be dead. I don't think this will destroy society but if
it does, we can always set up a new one, with better
rulers, when peace is made."

"Then go," said Father Pig. "I will not see you again,
Quadro. Nieve will not countenance our meeting in any
of the Lands of the Dead. She will never forgive you for
what you now do. But," he added, "for all it may mean
to you, you have my forgiveness."

"Thank you," said Quadroped.

"Good luck," said Tannakin and Tantony.

"Good-bye, Quadro," said Mother Pig. "I love you.
Don't get yourself killed."

Quadroped turned and hurried away from his parents,
his eyes so drenched with tears that even if it had not been
black as pitch he could not have seen a thing. In the wake
of the sloshing slime mold he squeezed into the hole and
began to crawl up the damp path to freedom.

The walls of this tunnel, unlike those that wound
through most of the Fungal Kingdom, were hewn from
solid bedrock. Quadroped was grateful for his mail coat,
which protected his hide from the sharp abrasive walls
past which he was forced to squeeze. Only his fear of
Ferethel kept him crawling blindly on.

"Hurry, hurry," urged the Sly Mold. Being small and
of variable form, it was able to move much faster than

the round, immutable pig. "Ferethel will have summoned his guards. If they catch us they'll kill us and feast on our flesh! Quickly, quickly, all pseudopodia forward!"

"I don't have pseudopods," said Quadroped crossly. "I just have pods and they're moving as fast as they can. How long *is* this tunnel anyway?"

"We're almost there," said the Sly Mold. "See, we've reached the C horizon. The bedrock is partially decomposed."

"Oh," said Quadroped and struggled upward.

"Now the B horizon," gurgled the Sly Mold as it oozed ahead. "See? See the wonderful darkness of the soil? Soon we will reach the *humus*."

"What's that?" asked Quadroped. He could feel the damp loose dirt between the links of his shirt. He had a sudden vision of the tunnel collapsing, burying him forever in clinging soil.

"The decomposing residue of plant and animal tissues," said the Sly Mold cheerfully. "Topsoil. You grow vegetables in it."

"Yuck," said Quadroped. He wondered if he would ever be able to consume a legume with a carefree heart again.

As the Sly Mold had predicted, the soil became richer and darker, the roots thicker, until at last they broke free and emerged into the quiet, misty gloom of the woods. Quadroped shook the clinging soil from his back and took a deep, appreciative sniff of the clean, fresh forest air. The dim, diffuse light that slanted through the pines seemed gloriously bright to his blinking eyes.

"Hooray," said Quadroped. "We've made it! Come on, Sly Mold, let's find the river and get back to camp."

"This way," said the Sly Mold and once more rippled off in the lead.

Over trunk and under branch they walked, rejoicing in their deliverance from Ferethel. Soon enough their mood was broken by the distant sounds of war. All too familiar shouts and cries intruded upon Quadroped's ears. The Lost Skeggs lay before them. For the first time it occurred to

Quadroped to wonder which side of the river he was currently on.

Quadroped was just about to ask this somewhat vital question when a smooth, silky voice addressed him. Perched upon the roots before him stood, or grew, the graceful ivory form of *Amanita pantherina*.

"Where are you hurrying to, piglet?" purred the Panther. His silvery eyes gleamed in the shade. "Stay and chat awhile with me."

"No," cried Quadroped.

"Flee," said the Sly Mold, and slithered rapidly backward.

Quadroped turned and found himself face-to-face with Ferethel. Death Cap, *Amanita verna,* Fly Agaric, Fool's Mushroom, and Grisette clustered behind their lethal monarch. Filamentous hyphae of tremendous size and strength erupted from the soil, enmeshing Quadroped in slimy bonds.

"Come back with us, piglet," said Death Cap. "Out of this horrible world of lights. The Divine Mycorrhizae shall enfold you like the tender roots of the sapling tree."

I don't wish to be enfolded, thought Quadroped rebelliously. He shook his head. "No," he whispered.

"You shun our hospitality," said Ferethel. "We are not pleased." The Destroying Angel smiled, a slow, sweet smile that reminded Quadroped horribly of Goriel at his worst.

"Woe," cried the slime mold, crawling halfway under a leaf. "We are doomed!"

"Indeed you are," said the Panther. "You should not have set your will against the wishes of your Lord and Master."

"What shall we do with them?" asked Death Cap. "How shall we treat this protist and its pig?"

"I am *not* a protist!" said the Sly Mold, emerging from under its leaf in its wrath. "I am as much a fungus as any of you."

Ferethel ignored this outburst. The Panther bent so malevolent a look upon the unfortunate mold that it trembled and retreated under its leaf once more.

Ferethel waved his white hand. All around him, small nacreous globes appeared upon the roots.

"Have you ever tasted *Amanita virosa*, piglet?" asked Ferethel.

The globes sprouted. Fragile caps unfurled and shed their veils.

"The taste is pleasantly sweet."

He broke off a specimen with delicate fingers and waved it before Quadroped's nose. Quadroped shuddered and backed away.

"Of course," said Ferethel, still in smooth and honeyed tones, "it is quite, quite deadly. It contains several toxins, not all of them lethal. Do you know the symptoms?"

Quadroped did. All piglets were trained from birth to recognize the effects of mushroom poisoning. Ferethel smiled and proceeded to describe them anyway.

"There is no effect for the first eight hours or so," he said. "Why, one might even forget the mushrooms one had had for dinner the night before. And Amanitas look so edible. Death Cap looks just like a common mushroom while Panther and I resemble our harmless sister, Grisette." On the root behind him Grisette tittered and blushed the palest of pinks.

"We are delicious deceivers," said Ferethel. "Our poisons are tasty, and strong. Touch us and they seep through your skin. Dry us and keep us in boxes for years, still we can slay you at will.

"Six to eight hours and then the stomach pains begin. Meanwhile a second, more terrible toxin begins its work. Slowly, as you writhe upon your bed, it attacks your liver and your kidneys. The sickness passes, you rise from your bed. Convulsions come later, coma strikes, then death."

"All in all," Death Cap remarked brightly, "it could take you six days to die."

"There is no antidote to my flesh," said Ferethel. "Not even I can save the victim who takes that first, foolish bite."

"Be a good pig," said the Panther, stalking silently up behind. "And open your mouth." Quadroped clenched his teeth until the muscles of his jaws ached.

"Don't be so silly," said the Panther. "Your fate is sealed. Cooperate and you shall taste my flesh instead. My poisons work faster, if equally painfully."

Quadroped refused to open his mouth. The sweet musty scent of the Destroying Angel made him want to sneeze but he resisted the urge. It would be better to suffocate than to die of mushroom poisoning.

As the Amanitas began systematically to cover over his nose with moldy leaves, Quadroped knew he would fail. He would faint from lack of oxygen and his mouth would fall open. When he awoke he would have eaten an Amanita. There would be nothing left to do but wait for a painful death.

Still, Quadroped tried to resist. He kept his mouth closed despite the pressure in his lungs. He became dizzy. Though his eyes were wide open, black dots formed at the edges of his vision. His knees buckled and he collapsed on the ground at Ferethel's feet. He began to kick and convulse. His sight grew dim and black. Against his will his muscles relaxed. His mouth fell open. Reviving oxygen rushed in.

"You see," said Ferethel, "it's really quite hopeless." He began to place the amanita into Quadroped's gaping mouth. "Now, down the hatch like a good little pig."

"Stop."

Ferethel paused, amanita half lowered to Quadroped's tongue. Quadroped kept his mouth open and his tongue depressed as far away from the deadly toadstool as it could go. He fought down an urge to swallow. Little bells jangled on the wind.

"The pig is mine," said an all-too-familiar voice. Out of the corner of his eye Quadroped saw the artfully tattered hem of a multicolored garment that could only be clothing Avice.

"Nieve gave the fairy pigs to us," said Death Cap.

"Be quiet, fool," said the Panther.

"What do you want with him, Trickster?" asked Ferethel.

"Why, the same as you," said Avice with a laugh.

"I'll take him to the Fleshless Land. Nieve has a wish to see him."

"Then why not let us dispatch him there?" asked Fere-thel. "That way we both will benefit. Nieve shall have his soul to grace her halls. We shall have his porcine flesh for dinner. After a suitable period, to allow for decomposi-tion, he should make a lovely feast. We might even let his parents share the treat."

"Delightful," agreed Avice. "But I promised to bring him alive to Nieve."

"Feed the pig the mushroom," hissed Death Cap. "Quickly. The Trickster can't move fast enough to stop you."

"The Trickster is dangerous," said the Panther.

"Once the pig is dead the Trickster won't care," said the Death Cap.

"Do not antagonize him," said the Panther. "We have other pigs to eat."

"We cherish our friendship with Nieve," said Ferethel. "We should not wish to compromise such a profitable relationship." He removed the amanita from Quadroped's mouth. "Take the piglet, Trickster, he is yours."

Quadroped gave a great gulp of relief. The hyphae slith-ered across his skin and sank back into the mold. Ferethel and his court departed likewise. Quadroped rolled over and sat up. Avice was standing, hands on hips, laughing down at him.

"Thank you," said Quadroped reluctantly.

"My pleasure, hoggling," said Avice. "You know where you must go now, hmmm?"

"Yes," said Quadroped dully.

"Then come," said Avice, and held out his arms.

Quadroped quietly walked forward and allowed Avice to pick him up. In the distance he could still hear the furious sounds of the battle. His parents were in the Fungal Halls and the second Great War had begun. Mushrooms and mayhem threatened all that he loved. He would visit Nieve in the Fleshless Land. There was nowhere else to go.

Chapter Ten

Nieve's dark fortress stood high upon a towering cliff. Gray-green breakers crashed endlessly beneath its massive battlements. Black spires scratched the clouded skies. Swirling vapors poured around them like a living fog. Blood ran down the foundation rock in little spills and rivulets, cascading into the sea. The air smelled of iodine, seaweed, and salt and was loud with the wailing of gulls.

Avice glided over the waves. Each step he took carried him forward by seven leagues or more. The sea swells undulated beneath his feet. He walked as on a pane of glass that rested on the crests of the waves.

The grim fortress drew nigh. Avice shortened his stride, covering a distance more normal for mortal man. Quad-roped, tucked firmly beneath Avice's arm, looked up at the hulking edifice and bravely tried not to tremble. Grinning gargoyles mocked him from the crenellated curtain walls. On the barbican contorted demons threatened him with outstretched paws. The postern gate was thirty feet high, its doors were of sea-stained oak. Black iron vines encircled them, sheltering strange birds of prey and snarling beasts among their twining foliage.

Avice stood a moment before a smaller gate set low within the larger door. He lifted the huge iron ring and knocked. When no one came to the door he pushed it open himself, stepping lightly over the threshold into the bailey beyond.

The courtyard was empty and silent. Then, in the distance, Quadroped heard an odd clattering noise. The noise came closer. Into the courtyard flew two human skulls, grinning and clacking their teeth in a friendly, if somewhat unnerving, fashion.

The skulls bobbed in air. They rolled around and gazed at Avice through their eyeless orbits. They cackled gleefully and circled around his head. Then they turned and floated away at a slightly more dignified pace.

Avice followed the skulls across the ward. He walked on pavements white as bone, through corridors and cloistered courts, past tapestries of gold and gore.

Avice's hands were cold on Quadroped's skin. The Trickster's face was humorless. No sounds, save the distant roar of the sea, disturbed the halls through which he walked. From room to empty room they walked. They saw neither living nor undead thing, save the skulls that flew on before them.

At length they came to another great door of oak and writhing iron. The portal was open. Avice stepped inside and entered the Hall of Bone.

The windowless room was red as blood and black as death. Obsidian walls rose a hundred feet high. On the long central hearth red flames licked up. Their reflections snaked across the hall and slithered up pillars of bone.

Quadroped blinked, trying to adjust his eyes to the fitful red light. They were no longer alone. A great multitude of the dead thronged the hall. They were not, unfortunately, fleshless. Quadroped rather thought that a host of clean-picked skeletons would have bothered him less than that gaunt, decaying crew.

Avice looked around at the hollow-eyed Revenants without any evidence of distaste. He began to make his way slowly but surely through the crowd, walking down the hall to the shadowy dais set at its farthest end.

As they passed between the courtiers Quadroped saw that although their appearance was ghastly, their faces yellowed and sere, the Revenants seemed to be merry. Their rattling, hollow laughter rang out at frequent intervals and they displayed an alarming tendency to break wildly out in songs.

Quadroped's spirits began to revive. Perhaps the Fleshless Land was not so grim as it had first appeared. He mastered his revulsion and examined the strange beings who crowded the hall. He was distressed to find that he recognized some of their faces.

Many of those whom Quadroped saw had still been alive when he had left the Kingdoms. This fresh evidence that the war was on again depressed Quadroped's spirits. The Manslayer had clearly been hard at work. He looked anxiously from face to face and was heartened to find no sign of his closest friends.

Avice reached the far wall and set Quadroped down on the floor. The Revenants parted before him. A dais of living serpents rose before them. Upon a throne of milky bone sat Nieve: splendid, seductive, ancient, and deadly, Queen of the Fleshless Land.

Nieve raised her pointed chin from her hand, whereon it had been resting, and regarded Avice with a pensive eye. Long ebony hair framed a face of snow. Silver twined around her arms and dripped from her long white neck. Her frosty blue eyes fell upon Quadroped and the pensive look changed to a frown.

The room grew still. Quadroped looked into Nieve's glittering eyes and found he could not look away. He had the strangest feeling that she was saying something to him but, apart from the frown, her expression gave little away. Around her the courtiers shuffled nervously. One tittered and was abruptly silent.

Avice smiled. "The hoggling can't hear you, Nieve," he said. "You'll have to speak as mortals do."

A faint look of disgust flickered across Nieve's perfect features. Pale pink lips opened, destroying the uncanny stillness of her face. Her voice whispered through the hall like a dead leaf blown across a floor by the wind.

"Tell me, piglet," said Nieve, "how are my fairy pigs? Not too well, I trust?" She smiled a pitiless smile.

"Ferethel's killing them," said Quadroped. "You have to let them go."

Nieve's eyes flashed dangerously. "Watch yourself, piglet," she said. "I do not *have* to do anything. They are my pigs, to do with as I will. But come, do not tremble so."

Nieve leaned back indolently upon her throne. "You are a cute little thing, and too small to punish. There's little satisfaction to be had in torturing baby pigs. I would not demean myself so."

Quadroped stared warily at Nieve and wondered if he should feel relieved.

"The peace you forged between Ravenor and the Kingdoms incurred my wrath," said Nieve. "The Black Unicorn's subsequent theft of the Warlords was the final insult. I fully intended to kill you, piglet, and your Sounder with you. However, upon further consideration I conceived the idea of giving my pigs to Ferethel. The rain has worked out splendidly. My land is almost overflowing with new souls, and there seems to be no end in sight."

"So," Nieve concluded with a wave of her slender hand, "I am disposed to be generous. I am no longer angry with you, piglet. You may go."

"But . . . but what about my parents?" asked Quadroped faintly.

"Ferethel may have them a little while longer," said Nieve, "then I think I'll bring them here where I can keep my eye on them. I lost track of them in Whistlewood. I had forgotten all about my fairy pigs until you showed up with the Key."

"But it's not fair," said Quadroped. "I'm the one who stopped the war. They didn't do anything to you. You should keep me and let them go."

"Foolish creature," said Nieve. "Your Sounder is some use to me, *you* are not. You cannot even hear my voice."

"I would have freed the Black Unicorn even if I *had* heard you, you horrible evil woman," said Quadroped mutinously. He was too upset to care whether he angered Nieve or not.

Nieve raised one perfect sable eyebrow. "Now really," she said. "What was that little outburst supposed to accomplish? I'm not going to set the Sounder free, and I don't want to keep you. You are defective. You should have been drowned at birth. Now go away, and take Avice with you. I really don't know why he bothered to bring you here at all."

"I promised him to you," said Avice. "And I always keep my promises. I wonder, will you keep yours?"

Nieve regarded Avice for a long moment. "Do you think I should?" she asked. "You've brought me a pig, is that worth my hand in marriage?"

"There is also," said Avice, "the small matter of a stolen Key and this war you seem so pleased with."

"Ah yes," said Nieve. "You truly are an agent provocateur par excellence, are you not? But the Key scheme didn't work and I could have started this war without you. No, I do not think I shall take you to husband. If I want a consort I have a whole kingdom of men to choose from, and all are in my power." Her eyes strayed restlessly to the right side of the hall, where a tall winged figure stood.

Quadroped followed her gaze and squeaked. "Goriel," he said. Then, "What has she done to him?"

Avice studied the deceased Warlord. Goriel had none of the more unpleasant features of the average Revenant, being perfectly preserved. His mind, however, seemed to have suffered in the transition. He gazed blankly into space, an expression of almost bovine contentment disguising his lordly features.

"Dear me," said Avice. "A happy village idiot seems to have stolen my true love's heart."

"Don't be tiresome," said Nieve. "You are a moody, disreputable, disorderly, undependable, irresponsible, temperamental, dissolute wastrel. You would make me a perfectly terrible husband. Now go away and find some other woman to seduce."

Avice stood his ground. "You are arrogant, Nieve," he said. "And you turn from me at your peril."

Blood fell from his tapering fingertips and blossomed upon the osseous floor. "I have given you that which you desired. I have plucked crimson flowers from the warriors' field and laid them at your feet. I have filled your halls with souls."

"All very nice, I'm sure," said Nieve with a yawn. "But your usefulness is quite ended, my dear. The Black Unicorn was most upset when he learned of Goriel's death at the hands of Reander and Morragwen. He is coming west. He will reach the Lost Skeggs tomorrow and the Great War will truly begin. Not even that disruptive little piglet can stop it."

"How did Goriel die?" asked Avice. "A blow to the head? His wits seem a trifle addled."

A pale flush suffused Nieve's face. "Goriel was a trifle . . . upset when he arrived," she said. "He'll be all right presently."

"I'm glad to hear it," said Avice, eyeing Goriel's cow-like countenance with distaste. "I rather admired him when he was alive."

"I had to tranquilize him a bit."

"*Quite* a bit," said Avice. "Just how did you say he was killed?"

"In a battle," said Nieve vaguely. Her fingers began to tap a trifle nervously upon the grinning skulls carved in the arms of her throne. Avice noted her discomfiture. His gaze sharpened.

Nieve tried out a seductive smile. "I really don't want a husband," she said. "But . . . perhaps we might reach some amicable agreement later. I *am* very grateful for all you've done. My own subjects are a trifle boring. Goriel isn't as much *fun* as I thought he'd be."

"No, I shouldn't think he would be," said Avice, looking again at the Warlord. "Until later, then."

He bowed and walked out of the throne room. After a moment, Quadroped turned and followed him.

Avice left the castle and walked out into the great wooded park that surrounded it on three sides, the ocean and cliffs forming the fourth. Here there were dark cypress trees and stately oaks, whose great branches swept low upon the ground. Avice stopped beneath a mighty acorn tree and turned, noticing Quadroped for the first time.

"What do you want, hoggling?" he asked.

"You promised to help me free my parents," said Quadroped plaintively.

"I promised to ask Nieve to set them free," corrected Avice. "You've already done that and she gave you her answer. Go away."

"Go away where?" asked Quadroped. He felt rather sorry for himself. After all, he had not asked to be brought to the Fleshless Land.

"I don't know," said Avice. He lay down on the grass and closed his eyes. "Go find someone you like who's dead, or go back to the Living Lands. I really don't care *what* you do anymore. Just don't be boring."

"Oh," said Quadroped.

Quadroped looked around the park. There was no one in sight as far as the eye could see. He sat down a little way away from the recumbent Avice and began to brood. Ripe acorns lay scattered about the grass. Quadroped regarded them bitterly. It had been under just such a tree that all of his troubles had begun.

Quadroped began to consume the nuts. They had an excellent woody flavor. Life in the Fleshless Land might be bearable. He wondered how long he would have to wait before his Sounder and his friends came to join him.

Soft sobs, heartbreaking in their intensity, interrupted Quadroped's thoughts. Coming down a nearby path was the familiar figure of Goriel's wife. Glaissin looked much as she had in Goriel's tent, albeit far less transparent. Her body, like Goriel's, was healthily fleshed, with nary a bone in view. Ravenorians, it seemed, weathered death a bit better than humans.

While Glaissin did not look ghastly she did not look particularly fetching either. Her hair was wild, her nose was red, and she looked thoroughly wretched. Two small dejected figures trailed after her, wringing their hands and sniffling dolefully. Eltis and Arelis, Goriel's daughters, or so Quadroped surmised.

Quadroped got up and hurried across the lawn toward the pathetic trio. It was almost pleasant to see people who looked like they felt more miserable than he did.

"Hello," said Quadroped when he had reached a spot in front of them.

Gentian blue eyes, red-rimmed and suffused with tears, gazed down at Quadroped from a face that was, if not beautiful, quite sweet. Glaissin's handkerchief was too damp to dry off her tears. She wiped her eyes on her sleeve instead.

"Hello, piglet," said Glaissin. "We have met before, have we not?"

"Yes," said Quadroped. "That is, we weren't introduced. I'm Quadroped. I know who you are," he added shyly.

Glaissin gave a good imitation of a smile and pulled her twin daughters forward. Eltis and Arelis were as fair and pale as their parents, with the same dark eyes. Eltis's eyes were her mother's blue, Arelis's were black, like her father's.

The twins were small, their faces thin and pinched. Quadroped recalled that they had died during a period when food was in short supply. Clearly Goriel had not been one to feast his family while his people starved. Still, even allowing for slight starvation, the girls did not look any older than five or six. Their behavior confirmed this guess for they both regarded Quadroped gravely from behind their mother's skirts.

"Don't be afraid, it's only a piglet," said Glaissin. "They have never seen a pig," she explained. "There aren't any in the Fleshless Land."

"I know," said Quadroped gloomily. "But there will be soon. I hope you won't think I'm rude," he added, "but why are you crying? Why isn't Goriel with you? I thought families got to stay together after death."

"Only if they *all* want to be together," said Glaissin mournfully. "Goriel doesn't want to see us. When we went to him he turned away and said he did not know us."

Tears fell anew and this time Glaissin did not bother to

brush them away. At the sight of their mother's tears both little girls began to cry also. Quadroped stared at the lachrymose little group in dismay. It was with some relief that he saw Avice drawing near.

Avice was scowling. "Madame," he said, "if you must water the ground with your tears, could you not do it elsewhere? The sight of so much misery is unsettling. I am trying to sleep."

Glaissin gave Avice a haughty look and dried her eyes. Then she swept off down the path, her twin daughters trailing behind her.

"Attractive woman, but emotional," said Avice. "What was she crying about, hoggling?"

"Goriel," said Quadroped, looking after the Glaissin and wishing Avice had not offended her. "Those are his wife and daughters. They say he refuses to see them."

"Don't blame him," said Avice.

"You don't understand," said Quadroped. "Goriel has been in mourning for his family for thousands of years. He dresses all of his people in black for them."

"Maybe he just doesn't want to get remarried," said Avice. "Romantic passions seldom survive more than a century or two, at least mine never have. It probably came as a shock to him to suddenly be faced with a wife and twin daughters after thousands of years of bachelorhood."

"No," said Quadroped. "It's not that. You didn't see Goriel's face when Glaissin appeared in his tent. He still loves her. He hasn't changed his mind, Nieve has changed it for him. Remember how he looked in the throne room?"

"What tent?" asked Avice, ignoring the rest of this speech. "What do you mean 'when Glaissin appeared in his tent'? How did she appear? Who raised her?"

"No one," said Quadroped.

He told Avice how Glaissin's ghost had somehow possessed Sioned's body after Reander killed the Councilor on the field. Then he described how Glaissin had materialized in Goriel's tent during the peace negotiations. As he came to the part where Goriel kissed his dead wife and died, Quadroped was surprised to see that Avice was laughing.

"It isn't funny," said Quadroped.

"I know," said Avice with a grin. "But Nieve has disrupted the Balance. She's gone and meddled in mortal affairs." Avice was positively chortling.

"She's stolen a living soul," he said. "Worse, she has broken faith with one of her people in order to do it. That poor girl must be miserable. It was her kiss that killed her husband. She lured him to his death."

Avice stared gleefully after Glaissin. Then he stretched and looked around at the murky sky and shadowed woods. "Come on, hoggling," he said. "It's a fine day for a little revenge."

Avice, Quadroped observed, was quite restored to his normal good humor. His eyes twinkled, his steps were light. Glasgerion had never talked of revenge when Morragwen had refused his suit. Of course, Morragwen had returned Glasgerion's love. Still, Quadroped suspected that it was as much the thought of new mischief as the chance to hurt Nieve that had brought back Avice's nice smile.

Avice hurried after Glaissin, Quadroped trotting at his heels. When he reached her he stopped and made a low and courtly bow.

"Go away," said Glaissin. "I want to be alone."

"No, you don't," said Avice. "You want your husband back. The hoggling here has told me of your troubles."

"It was none of your business," said Glaissin, glaring at Quadroped.

"Let me help you, Lady," said Avice with his most winning smile. "You are too fair to spend your days alone. Let me return your husband to you."

Glaissin regarded Avice a trifle suspiciously. "How?" she asked.

"I need, let's see . . . a lock of his hair."

"I have that," said Glaissin eagerly. She opened a small silver locket that hung upon her breast. Inside lay a curl of white hair.

"Excellent." Avice smiled again. "And also some of his flesh and some of his blood. One of your daughters should do for that."

Quadroped gasped. Glaissin retreated, her arms spread

protectively around her children.

"Be reasonable," said Avice. "Once you have Goriel back you can always get more offspring. At their age they're replaceable, they're not quite people yet. And anyway, you have duplicates."

"Monster!" Glaissin's tears were quite gone now, it was anger that made her eyes sparkle. "Stay away from my children."

"Oh, very well," Avice sighed. "It will be less dramatic but I suppose all I really need is a drop or two of their blood and *small* piece of flesh."

Glaissin continued to glare at him but she paused. Quadroped looked at Avice and saw that the Trickster was thoroughly enjoying himself. "How small?" asked Glaissin.

"As small as you wish," said Avice. "A single cell would do if you had the means to extract it."

Avice produced a wicked-looking knife from a sheath hidden somewhere amid his artfully tattered attire. Glaissin's eyes widened at the sight of the glimmering blade but she did not leave. Avice took hold of the blade and offered her the knife, hilt first.

"Come, Lady," he said.

"What exactly would you do?" asked Glaissin.

"A simple spell," aid Avice. "No doubt you could do it yourself if the dead could do magic in the Fleshless Land."

Avice described some arcane ritual of which Quadroped could make neither head nor tail. Glaissin, however, appeared to understand him, for she nodded.

"Why would you do this for me?" she asked when he had done.

"I wouldn't," said Avice. "Nieve annoys me." He raised an eyebrow. "She is too sure of herself and she prefers Goriel's favors over mine. I suppose that you do too?"

Glaissin almost smiled. "If that's a proposition the answer's no. I *do* prefer my husband."

Avice sighed. "Well, I never wanted children anyway."

Glaissin reached out and took hold of the knife. Then she turned to her daughters and spoke quietly to them, telling them that she must hurt them, but only a little, and that it was for their father's sake.

Glaissin sat upon the ground and drew her daughter Eltis onto her lap. From the chatelaine that hung from her waist she took a small silver bowl and this she gave to the child with instructions to hold it steady. Eltis held out her hand over the bowl and gazed up at her mother, eyes wide but unafraid. With a small, precise motion Glaissin cut her daughter's hand. Blood, and some small bit of skin, fell redly into the bowl.

Quadroped watched these proceedings with great surprise. Goriel's daughter neither cried nor flinched as the knife bit her hand, although it must have hurt. With a kiss, Glaissin healed the wound and let her daughter go.

Solemnly Arelis took her sister's place upon her mother's lap and held out her small hands for knife and bowl. "Me too," she said. Glaissin smiled and repeated her actions. Arelis matched her sister in bravery and held the little bowl just as steady beneath the wound.

"My apologies, Lady," said Avice at the end of these proceedings. "I see why you value your daughters so highly."

"Theirs was not an easy life," said Glaissin. "They are more mature than their years."

"We shall have to use my hands as a crucible," said Avice. "Do you have a wedding ring? They always seem to make this mixture more effective."

"Yes." Glaissin pulled a plain silver band off her finger and gave it to him.

Avice looked at it. "A bit tawdry, isn't it?"

"It's platinum," said Glaissin defensively. "Gold isn't Goriel's color."

"No, I suppose not."

Avice cupped his hands. Glaissin placed the ring and the lock of hair in them. Then Avice spoke words whose meaning Quadroped could not understand. There was a flash of light. The lock of hair began to burn merrily away.

When the hair was reduced to ashes, and the ring a molten pool, Avice spoke more words over them and added them to the blood in Glaissin's cup. He stirred this noxious potion with a finger. His hands, Quadroped observed, were whole and unsinged despite the fire they had held.

"That should do the trick," said Avice. "Lady, do you know where your husband is?"

"By the fish pond," said Glaissin bitterly. "He's always there when Nieve does not want him at her side."

"Let's go," said Avice and stepped away, humming softly to himself.

They came upon Goriel in a weedy, secluded part of Nieve's gardens. He sat beside a scum-filled pond, eyes unfocused, staring stupidly into the middle distance. He did not look up at their somewhat noisy approach.

Eltis and Arelis immediately ran to their father and began tugging at his arms, pleading to be picked up. Goriel turned away from the fish pond and stared at them blankly.

"Do I know you?" he asked.

"Yes," said Glaissin. "Leave your father alone, girls. Here, Goriel, drink this."

She held out the bowl. Goriel looked at it but made no move to take it from her hand. Quadroped could not blame him. The stuff looked and smelled vile, it would probably taste even worse.

"Please drink it, love," said Glaissin, holding the cup to Goriel's lips.

Goriel took a step back into the muddy shallows of the pond. "No," he said. "It's not nice."

"Dear me," said Avice. "He really *is* in bad shape, isn't he? No wonder Nieve's growing bored with him. Here, give me that bowl."

He stepped up to Goriel and in one quick gesture pinched his nose closed. Goriel opened his mouth to protest and down went the potion: blood, flesh, wedding ring, hair, and all. Goriel doubled up, grasping his throat and breathing somewhat rapidly. In an instant Glaissin was by his side, arms around him, soothing him.

"Glaissin," Goriel gasped, tears in his eyes. "How could you? What *was* that stuff?"

"Goriel, my love, you called me by my name!" Glaissin wrapped her arms more tightly around her husband and began to shower him with kisses.

"How else should I call you?" asked Goriel. He looked at Avice. "Glaissin, who is that man? Why are my daughters in tears? Oh, that *taste*! Arelis, get me some water."

Arelis grabbed up the bowl and quickly washed it out. She filled it with the brown liquid of the pond. The taste of scum did not appear to disturb Goriel for he drank the water eagerly. He seemed much relieved when he had done.

"That's better," said Goriel. "Now, Eltis, Arelis, why are you crying? Had I thought you would greet my arrival in the Fleshless Land with tears I would never have kissed your mother."

"You've been here for quite some time," said Glaissin. "But that *hag* bewitched you. You did not know your own family. It's been miserable. I don't know what I would have done if this man hadn't helped me." Glaissin smiled at Avice.

Goriel looked at Avice and frowned. "Who are you?" he asked. "And how do you know my wife?"

"I am Avice," said Avice. "This little hoggling made your family's plight known to me." He indicated Quadroped with a wave of his hand.

"Ah, Quadroped," said Goriel. "You *do* turn up in the strangest of places. I'm sorry to see that you've suffered for my sudden death. Did the Manslayer send you here?"

"No," said Quadroped. "I'm not dead. Fairy pigs don't have to be."

"Then why are you here?" asked Goriel. "I cannot think the Fleshless Land a suitable place for a piglet of your tender years."

"Avice brought me," said Quadroped. "He isn't dead either. He was going to give me to Nieve but she didn't want me. She gave my parents to Ferethel the Fungus Lord to start the rain that started the war that will give her more souls for the Fleshless Land. She wanted to kill me but now that the Great War is beginning again she's not mad at me anymore so she told me to go away.''

Goriel thought for a moment about what Quadroped had said; the speech had not been unambiguous. ''Are you telling me that *Nieve* is responsible for the bloodshed between Ravenor and the Kingdoms?'' asked Goriel finally.

''Yes,'' said Quadroped. ''She wants more souls.''

''Now that,'' said Goriel softly, ''annoys me. The war must be stopped immediately.''

''But I thought you wanted a war,'' said Quadroped. ''If you wanted peace, why did you kiss Glaissin? You must have known what the Manslayer would do.''

''Well, of course I wanted a war,'' said Goriel. ''I am a Warlord after all. But I *don't* like being Nieve's pawn.''

''A shame really,'' said Avice. ''You made such a good one, almost as predictable as the Manslayer. Starting the war was child's play. It should be much more interesting to try and stop it. The Black Unicorn is about to get involved, you know.''

''I didn't,'' said Goriel. ''But as you say, it was predictable. I suppose he wants revenge for my death?''

''He does.''

''How do you propose to stop him, then?'' asked Goriel, looking interested despite himself.

''I don't,'' said Avice. ''You will. I'm sending you back to the Living Lands. Nieve will just have to look elsewhere for a lover.''

''No!'' Glaissin grabbed Goriel as though Avice might snatch him away from her at any moment. ''You can't send him back.''

''She's right,'' said Goriel. ''You can't. I'm dead. My body is probably buried or burned to ashes by now.''

''No,'' said Avice brightly, ''it isn't. The Manslayer is saving it so that the Black Unicorn can resurrect you again.''

''Too late,'' said Goriel. ''I've eaten Nieve's food and drunk her wine. I'm bound to this land now.''

''You are,'' agreed Avice. ''Unless I decide to unbind

you. Nieve broke rules to bring you here. Her actions have given me the power to send you back.''

"I've heard of beings like you," said Goriel. "Beings whose power derives from disorder. But even if you can send me back I won't go."

"I thought you didn't like being Nieve's pawn," said Avice.

"I like being yours less," said Goriel. "I'm quite happy where I am, thank you. I haven't been this cheerful in centuries. Let them fight. I am weary and wish only to rest."

"But thousands of people will be killed," said Quadroped.

"So what?" asked Goriel. "*I'm* dead and I'm enjoying it."

"That's the trouble with the dead," said Avice mournfully. "They stop caring about much of anything."

"Look," said Goriel, "if you want to annoy Nieve why don't you set the fairy pigs free?"

"Hmmm," said Avice. He stared at the ground lost in thought. "That would be very difficult indeed. . . ."

"But not impossible?"

"No . . ."

Quadroped held his breath, hoping against hope that Avice might really be willing to help him this time:

"I *did* tell the hoggling I'd help him," Avice said at last. "The pigs gave Nieve their oath of allegiance. Nieve won't release them. They can't be truly free until she does, unless . . . Unless the oath was never taken in the first place."

Goriel looked at Avice in alarm. "You'd have to warp reality completely to change the past," he said. "Can you *do* that? Has Nieve really shifted the Balance so badly?"

"I might have to bend the rules a bit," Avice admitted with a grin.

"What *is* the Balance?" asked Quadroped.

"It is a state of equilibrium," said Glaissin. "It is maintained by the proper regulation of all that occurs according to structuring laws. It is harmony and coherence."

"Umm," said Quadroped blankly.

"It is a state of *dynamic* equilibrium," said Avice. "My

powers derive from disturbances in the Balance." Avice
turned to Goriel. "The Balance has been unstable ever
since Rhiogan locked up the Black Unicorn. Something
about the proximity of Chaos has caused perturbations in
the field. Lately the oscillations have increased in magni-
tude. A year ago I could never have rewoven the past but
now . . . We'll see."

Avice stood up and stretched. He closed his eyes. Ten
minutes passed. The grass at his feet turned brown.

"You might want to move back a bit," said Avice,
eyes still closed. "This is going to be tricky. Goriel, I
might need you to hold some things."

"Right."

Goriel, Quadroped noticed nervously, was looking very
pale. It seemed unbelievable but the Warlord looked positively frightened. Quadroped supposed that he should be
frightened too, but he did not know what it was that he
was supposed to be frightened of. Avice was not *doing*
anything. He was just standing there, killing the lawn.
Even Old Magic produced greater effects than that.

Eltis and Arelis had wandered several feet away and
were now playing ball with what looked suspiciously like
a skull. Quadroped wandered over to investigate. He had
been right, it was a skull. It made quite a satisfactory toy.

"Look," said Arelis, some twenty minutes later.

Quadroped looked and saw that something interesting
was finally going on beside the fish pond. He wandered
back. Avice had produced something that looked like a
thickly matted snarl of muddy hue. Closer examination
revealed that each of the threads that wound through the
mat was, in fact, a twisted bundle of smaller threads,
which in turn were made of even smaller strands of light.
The muddy color was the result of the blending of threads
of light of every hue of the rainbow in no particular order.
The whole construction was ugly and frightfully intricate.

"What is it?" Quadroped whispered to Glaissin.

"The web of the past," said Glaissin, also in a whisper.
"Avice is going to try and unweave the part where your
ancestors first gave their allegiance to the Fleshless Land.

Then he'll have to try and reweave it so that the present isn't too greatly changed."

"I don't think," she added, "that he'll be able to do it. And if he damages it too much it will result in the total annihilation of everything now existing in the Living Lands."

"Oh," said Quadroped.

Avice began to snip through the threads with something that looked suspiciously like a pair of tiny manicure scissors. He pulled some of the shorter ones out and handed them to Goriel. As Avice dug down through the mat, and presumably deeper into the past, Quadroped saw that the horrible snarl was made up of millions of layers.

Avice located a large black thread wrapped thickly around with tiny filaments of every conceivable color. He began carefully excavating around it, detaching it and pulling it out of the snarl. Layer after layer was peeled back. At length he reached some satisfactory point and stopped.

"Nieve is this black one," said Avice with some satisfaction. "Now I wonder which threads are fairy pig threads?"

"Try pink," said Goriel. "Or brown."

"Pink, I think," said Avice. He began to snip. Quadroped was relieved to see that for once Avice was paying close and careful attention to what he was doing.

"There," he said at last. "I think that's done it. Now to put everything back together again. This is the part I'm not so good at."

Avice began twisting threads together, splicing and rejoining the mat. The layers began to build up again in their original snarled condition. Quadroped saw the pig threads still running through the mat, now no longer entwined so closely with the black one that was Nieve.

Avice took silver thread from Goriel and began to splice it back into the mat. "This is you, hoggling," he murmured. "See what a nice color you have?"

"Avice, what have you *done*?!"

Quadroped turned around in alarm. Nieve was racing toward them across the lawn like an evening shadow. Her long black hair streamed out behind her. Glaissin gathered her daughters into her arms and hurried them away from the oncoming Fury.

"Damn," said Avice. "Goriel, stall her. I'm having trouble with this splice."

"Stop," screamed Nieve.

Goriel moved to intercept her. His hands touched her, and he froze into place. All colors faded as his skin and clothing turned slowly into marble. Nieve gazed at Glaissin and her daughters. They too became motionless rocks.

Nieve grabbed Avice and spun him away from the web. "How have you done this?" she asked. "No one should be able to reweave the past."

"Now, love," said Avice with a smile, "you *know* that I gain power when the rules are broken, or at least you ought to know. You went and snatched the soul of a living man. Did you think I wouldn't find out about it? Hmmm?"

"The piglet told you," said Nieve. Her eyes shifted to Quadroped, promising revenge.

Quadroped gazed up at Nieve and wondered what she was doing to him. He began to feel faint and light-headed. With a start he noticed that he could see the grass through his front hooves. He twisted and looked over his shoulder. His whole body was transparent!

"Avice," cried Quadroped. "Help me, I'm *dissolving*!"

Avice shook his head. "No, not dissolving," he said. "Unraveling."

Chapter Eleven

Quadroped's dissipating form began to drift, like smoke, across the lawn. Avice moved to pick up the silver thread. Nieve forestalled him by grabbing his arm.

"Let him dissolve," she said. "If I'm to lose my fairy pigs let me at least have the satisfaction of seeing this one killed."

"Certainly not," said Avice. "Let go of me, woman." He pushed her hands away.

"I will *not* be spoken to with disrespect in my own Kingdom," said Nieve.

She gave Avice a mighty shove that sent him flying into the air. He landed hard on the grass some five feet away. Nieve followed up her little tour de force with an energy bolt that left Avice looking stunned, and the lawn around him scorched and faintly smoking.

Nieve smiled and brushed her hands on her black gown. Quadroped began to slip away between the interstices of the world. Glaissin, Goriel, and their daughters looked on in frozen surprise.

This is it, thought Quadroped sadly. *When I'm gone I'll*

never have been. I'm being erased from reality. His vision was blurry now but he could still see the fraying silver line slowly unraveling, becoming detached from the web.

"Enough!"

Quadroped turned what was no longer strictly his head. Avice was striding back across the lawn toward Nieve. He looked cross. As he walked, Avice began to grow in stature until Nieve came no higher than his knee. Nieve shrank back in alarm.

Avice grabbed hold of Nieve by the hair and twisted her head to look up at him. "I am going to weave Quadroped back in," he told her, "and *you* are not going to stop me."

"Damn you," cried Nieve. "Why are you *doing* this to me?"

Avice shrugged. "Because I want to," he said. "Because it's fun."

He gave Nieve's hair a playful tug and began to shrink back down to his habitual size. "You really *do* have the most beautiful hair," said Avice as the silky black tresses slipped free through his fingers.

"If I *ever* get my hands on you . . ." Nieve snarled.

"Help," cried Quadroped. His voice came out only as a thin whisper of breath.

"Later, my love," said Avice with a leer. "Coming, hoggling."

Nieve stamped off toward her palace in a rage. Avice returned to the matted web and picked up the silver thread. His nimble fingers danced through the snarl, pulling and twisting the threads back into their original configurations.

Quadroped began to feel more solid. His vision returned to normal, then his hearing, then his sense of smell. Last of all he felt the ground beneath his feet. He looked down, saw his shiny black hooves, and laughed aloud for joy.

Avice smiled. "Welcome back," he said. He patted the last thread into place and allowed the web to disappear from sight. He slipped the manicure scissors into a pocket.

Quadroped looked over at Goriel and his family. "Can you unfreeze them?" he asked.

"No," said Avice. "I've broken enough rules today. If

I break one of Nieve's spells here, in her own Kingdom, she might gain power over *me*. I'm afraid they are doomed to spend eternity as ornaments in Nieve's repulsive gardens. Now, let's see if I snipped the right threads.''

Avice walked to the edge of the fish pond and waved his hand. The scum peeled itself back, revealing a mirror of murky brown water. Images began to appear upon the surface. Pictures formed like a slick of rainbow oil. The dungeons of the Fungal Halls appeared.

With mounting glee Quadroped beheld the fairy pigs suddenly start. They looked at their prison in dawning surprise. They no longer had any memory of Nieve, or of their allegiance to her. All they remembered was being handed over to Ferethel and obediently doing his will. They could not remember why.

"We must leave here at once," Quadroped heard the great Sanglier say.

"I've been telling you all that for *weeks*," said the familiar gurgling voice of Sly Mold. "What's gotten into you all now? If you had listened to me in the first place I wouldn't be here and Quadro wouldn't be wherever that strange man took him."

"Oh dear," said Mother Pig. "I *do* hope he's all right."

"Let's get *out* of here," said Quadroped's brother, Tantony.

"Yes, *let's*," said the Sounder in a chorus.

The elder pigs huddled together in a circle, heads close together, and began to mutter an incantation. The younger pigs stood well away from them, watching in awe. The prison door began to buckle, as if under the blows of some giant fist. Huge dents appeared. The door bent and swayed. A hinge broke, and another. The great door fell down, with a thump, onto the spongy floor.

The pigs screamed out the door at a gallop. The Sly Mold had hitched a ride on the Sanglier's back and was guiding the Sounder to freedom.

Ferethel did not take the escape of his precious pigs lightly. Mushroom men, armed with spears and deadly spores, swarmed through the hallways, eager to capture the fleeing pigs. The pigs summoned a wind that blew the poisonous spores away, the spears they just ignored.

"Anastomose and conquer!" cried the Sly Mold as it rushed past on the back of the great Sanglier. To Quadroped's surprise many of the Mushroom Men took up its cry. Ferethel had a general revolution on his hands.

"Down with the ascomycetes!" cried a small band of Dead Man's Fingers. Quickly reassessing his priorities, Ferethel instructed his soldiers to ignore the pigs and concentrate on these revolting fungi instead.

The pigs galloped up through the Fungal Halls and emerged into the Upper World through a hole at the base of a tree. The day was like any other. The sky was black, the light a sullen gray. Water ran in rivulets across the sandy forest floor. The dripping branches of the pine trees deposited wet needles on the pigs' tender skins.

"Ugh," said the Sanglier. "Let's get rid of this *rain*."

The Fairy Pigs shimmered and faded from Quadroped's sight. The green and brown colors whirled away, replaced by red. Morragwen appeared, bound to a tall post by golden chains. The Manslayer was standing before her, laughing. Of Morrag there was no sight.

The tableaux revealed another scene. Warriors were splashing across the ford. Another battle was beginning, though the sun had not yet risen. Quadroped saw that Reander was again in command of the Kingdoms' army. He rode at the head of the host, Glasgerion and Eunoe beside him.

The picture began to flow, rolling over the heads of the fighters and past them into the pine woods of Ravenor. The pine woods were left behind. The high slopes of the Crystalline Mountains appeared. The vision swooped down upon a deep and ragged gorge piercing the mountains' heart. The Black Unicorn was trotting along, eyes ablaze with a sinister light, his black mane floating behind him. Behind him streamed an endless host of mounted Ravenorians, all ready and eager for battle.

"He should reach the ford in about five hours," said Avice. "Time for you to go home, hoggling. If you can get to the Black Unicorn before he draws blood you have a chance to win peace."

"But how do I get to him?" asked Quadroped.

Avice shrugged and smiled. "That's for you to decide. The game is no fun if I know all the answers."

"It's not a game," said Quadroped.

Avice shook his head and laughed. He grabbed Quadroped up, one hand upon his chest and the other upon his rump. He twisted and flung Quadroped into the air with all of his awesome strength. Quadroped hurtled away at frightening speed.

Up he flew, over the dark fantastic spires of Nieve's fortress, through a thousand veils of night. The wind whistled past, burning his face, and he closed his eyes. He landed in a heap on the mossy floor of the forest.

Quadroped picked himself up, relieved to find that he had suffered no broken bones, only a painful bruise or three. The pines whispered quietly to themselves. Away, above the green forest, hung the clouds, anchored on a void of blue. Quadroped, far below, stood still and wondering in a land of growing silence. The fern, unfurling its small fiddlehead, the errant leaf tumbling on still water, all these sounds chased loudly through the wood.

What is it? thought Quadroped. *What's different?* And then he realized that the rain was gone. The forest floor was dancing with green and golden light.

My parents are free, thought Quadroped. He began to smile. His ears perked up. Suddenly he felt very brave, capable of anything. He trotted downhill toward the valley, back to the battle below.

Quadroped's spirits rose still further when, two hours later, he heard the familiar voices of his Sounder. "Mother, Father," he shouted, running quickly through the trees. "It's me, Quadroped."

Quadroped burst out into a small glade and found himself surrounded by friendly snouts and warm brown eyes. His family crowded around him, butting their heads against his sides. Father Pig's eyes were misty as he gazed upon his son.

"Hello, hello, hello," gurgled a small voice. Quadroped looked down and beheld the amorphous green form of the Sly Mold draped elegantly over a twig.

"I have become a revolutionary," said the Sly Mold. It rippled its pseudopodia in a satisfied way. "I am organizing an underground movement to overthrow Fere-thel and the deadly Amanita. There is considerable popular support. We have every chance of success."

"Congratulations," said Quadroped.

"Ferethel has withdrawn from this world," said the Sly Mold. "He needs them to maintain order. A few still remain, but no more than is normal for the season and the weather."

A puffball came rolling up and chittered anxiously at the Sly Mold. "Oh dear, business again," said the Sly Mold, beginning to ooze away. "So long, Quadro. I'm glad you're safe. Keep in touch." The Bandit Mold followed the agitated puffball into a hollow, rotted log and disappeared from sight.

The great and ancient Sanglier came forward then and condescended to touch snouts with Quadroped. Then all of the pigs sat down in a ring around Quadroped to hear of his adventures.

"Where have you been?" demanded Tantony.

"What's going on?" asked Tannakin.

"Tell us, tell us," cried his brothers in unruly chorus.

"Hush, dears," said Mother Pig. "Let Quadro speak."

So Quadroped sat and told the pigs once more about Nieve and Avice and the war they had started between Ravenor and the Kingdoms. When he had done the pigs looked very thoughtful indeed.

"If what you say is true," said the mighty Sanglier, "then we owe you a tremendous debt. I cannot recall hearing of the Fleshless Land, or of Nieve, but it all sounds most unpleasant. It seems we must also make some amends to the Council. Let us go down to this ford on the Lost Skeggs. We shall see what we can do to end this war that we were so instrumental in causing."

"Oh yes," said Quadroped. With the Sounder and the Great Sanglier helping him he was certain that the Black Unicorn could be stopped and the Great War brought to

an end. With a sigh of relief he abandoned all thoughts
of responsibility and rejoined his herd, trotting happily
after his mother down the hill.

The Sounder made good time and soon found themselves walking along the edge of the high escarpment that
ran beside the Lost Skeggs. To Quadroped's surprise they
had come out of the woods on the Kingdoms' side. Looking around at the pine-covered sides of the valley, Quadroped realized that his assumption that pine wood equaled
Ravenor had been false. Fortunately his assumption that
downhill equaled river was not.

The escarpment ended where the valley widened. From
its height the pigs could see the great rift valley of the
Lost Skeggs. Less than a mile away lay the fateful ford,
almost completely hidden by a dark roiling mass of
humans and horses.

The din of the battle rose up, mercifully dulled by the
distance. Eagles screamed overhead, wheeling beneath the
blue vault of the sky. Sunlight gleamed off bronze feathers
and golden eyes. The Black Unicorn, Quadroped noted,
was not yet in sight. But it had been at least four hours
since Quadroped had been thrown out of the Fleshless
Land. It might take another hour for the Sounder to climb
down the bluff and reach the field of battle. There was
clearly no time to waste.

It was with some dismay, therefore, that Quadroped saw
that the Sanglier had stopped and was sitting down to
watch the battle. Quadroped timidly approached him, edg-
ing nervously through the ring of senior boars that surrounded the leader.

"The Black Unicorn will arrive soon," said Quadroped.
"Shouldn't we go down and stop him?"

The Sanglier bent his massive head and gazed at Quadroped from tiny, ancient eyes. "We shall wait here until
nightfall," he decreed. "The battle is too fierce. When
the sun sets the armies will part, then we can make our
way safely into the Kingdoms' camp."

"But . . ."

Quadroped's father edged up beside him. "Come away,

son," he said. Quadroped hesitated. "Quadro . . ." His father's voice was stern. Quadroped looked back at the battle. His friends were down there. He had to speak, and yet . . .

It was much harder, Quadroped realized, to disobey his family than to disobey even so powerful a person as Nieve or Reander or Goriel. His heart hammered uncomfortably in his breast. The old boar's tusks were chipped and yellowed, his temper as uncertain as the Black Unicorn's. A piglet just did not contradict the Sanglier. He could be gored, or worse, for such insolence.

Quadroped started to back away, ears down, then stopped. He looked at the Sanglier. "You can't wait until nightfall," he said. "It will be too late by then. We have to go down there *now*."

The Sanglier rose, the thick bristles on the back of his powerful neck began to rise. Quadroped's father quickly pushed himself between the Sanglier and his son. The two large boars stared at each other, heads to the ground, flanks quivering with tension. Then the Sanglier's bristles fell and he snorted.

"The piglet is too used to being on his own," declared the Sanglier. "He has become rude and unmannerly. We shall forgive him, this time. Where is his mother? Let him go back and stay by her side as befits a child of his age."

Father Pig roughly brushed his son back, out of the Sanglier's sight. "Don't you *ever* do something like that again," he said. "You could have been killed, or cut from the Sounder."

Quadroped's mother came running up and began to fuss over him. Tannakin and Tantony regarded him with wide eyes. His father continued to bristle and glare.

"But Father—" Quadroped began.

"Hush, dear," said Mother Pig. "The Sanglier knows best."

"No," said Quadroped, "he doesn't."

He faced his father, his own short bristles rising up. "The Black Unicorn will be here in less than an hour. He's a *berserk*. By tonight it will be too late to sue for peace. You can do what you like, but I'm going down there, now."

"You will do nothing of the sort," said Father Pig.

Quadroped did not hear him. He had turned and was running as fast as he could toward the edge of the bluff.

"Quadro, stop, you'll be killed!" cried Mother Pig.

Quadroped plunged headfirst into the thick bushes that grew on the steep sides of the escarpment. He rolled and skidded beneath their prickly branches, tripping and catching himself on their tangled roots. He could hear his parents trying to follow him. The bushes were too low and grew too thickly to let such large animals past.

Quadroped tumbled to the base of the bluff and looked up. He could see the Sounder at the top, peering anxiously over the edge. He waved a hoof to let his mother know he was all right. Then he began to trot swiftly toward the battlefield.

Quadroped began to slow down as the ford grew near. The birds of prey flashing through the air above him made him nervous. He felt vulnerable and exposed out on the open, grassy plain. He decided to walk along the riverbank where the bushes could provide some cover. It was difficult going, but at least he felt somewhat safer.

Quadroped was just trying to extract himself from a particularly dense clump of shrubbery when a shadow fell over him and a hoarse, croaking voice assailed his ears. "Ah, lunch," said the voice.

Quadroped looked hastily up into the skeletal branches of the blasted oak that gnarled above his head. A great raven had landed upon the lowermost branch, attracted, no doubt, by his thrashing. Torn flesh hung from her twisted claws.

"If you are referring to me," said Quadroped with dignity, "my name is not 'lunch,' it's Quadro. I'm not going to die here, you know. I'm going to get out of this bush in a moment."

"Too bad," said the Raven.

She tilted her head and peered sideways at Quadroped from wise black eyes. "What's a tender morsel like you doing so close to the battlefield? Shouldn't you be in a pen on a farm somewhere?''

Quadroped disentangled himself from the last clinging branch and glared up at the raven. "I am a free fairy pig," he said. "I'm on my way to try and stop the war."

The Raven eyed Quadroped speculatively. "What can you do?" she asked. "A pig, on the field of battle?"

"Stop the Black Unicorn from joining the fight," said Quadroped.

The Raven lifted her head and stared off into the distance. Quadroped moved out onto the open plain and tried to follow her gaze. Over the wide river he stared, toward Ravenor. Soft on the wind came a grumbling, rising into a cheer. Behind Ravenor's massed ranks a long dark line came plunging down into the valley.

"The Black Unicorn comes," said the Raven. "Terrible his hooves and sharp his horn. He shall kill many this day."

Quadroped did not bother to reply. He abandoned the riverside and began to run as fast as he could toward the ford. With a whirring of wings the Raven lifted off from the tree and followed him like a harbinger of doom.

"Blood spurts and stains the air," said the Raven. "The sky is crimson and the river is red. The earth groans aloud. Terrible is the work of the sword, great the carnage. It is too late for council."

"Go *away*," gasped Quadroped as he ran. "It isn't too late. It can't be."

"Too late, too late," screamed the Raven.

Quadroped reached the edges of the fighting. Past small fringe battles he ran, toward the heart of the melee. The Raven flew low above him, her great wings fanning his face. Warriors turned as they passed, startled by the sudden appearance of the bird. Their eyes fell next on Quadroped, running in the shadow of the Raven's wings.

"The White Pig," a man shouted, lifting his shield high. "The White Pig comes!"

The shout swelled, drowning out the tumult from the Ravenorian side. Quadroped gazed frantically around, wondering how he could possibly reach Reander before the Black Unicorn did. Reander would be in the middle of the field where the fighting was the worst.

Then Quadroped's eyes fell upon a familiar face, a man who had once shared chocolate with him in Essylt. He ran forward. The man looked down and smiled.

"Help me," cried Quadroped. "I have to get to Reander."

The man picked Quadroped up and lifted him over his head. "The White Pig brings us victory," he shouted. "Carry him to the Prince. Carry him to the front of the lines that he may lead us in battle!"

Eager hands grabbed for Quadroped. From hand to hand he was passed, over the heads of the Kingdoms' armies. The Raven still flapped above him, screaming her prophesies of doom. No one could hear her clearly. Her angry shrieks were taken to be a warlike, propitious omen.

Within moments, Quadroped had been carried to the front of the lines and thrust into Glasgerion's hands. Glasgerion stared at Quadroped, momentarily stunned. Then his arms tightened and he gave Quadroped a tremendous hug.

"What happened to you?" cried Glasgerion over the horrendous din. "We thought you were dead. When you didn't come back . . ."

The sounds of conflict swelled into a deafening roar. Glasgerion stopped speaking and looked up, suddenly alert. A shout arose from the Ravenorian host.

"The Black Unicorn! The Black Unicorn comes!"

Quadroped shivered and looked toward the east. Ahead of him the Ravenorian ranks were parting. Warriors fell back on all sides. The Black Unicorn appeared, moving inexorably toward Reander's standard. The Prince himself was hidden from view.

The Ruler of Ravenor was a terrible sight. Black armor, bristling with silver spikes, covered him head to tail. Through slits in his armor the wild sable banner of his mane flowed out. His fiery eyes were wild, his strong teeth bared, his lips were flecked with foam.

Warriors shifted. Reander came into sight, shield held high. The sunlight blazed from his armor as off a golden mirror. He had dispensed with his helmet and his head was bare. His hair framed his face like fire. Straight toward the Black Unicorn he rode, green eyes alive with wicked light like the eyes of some terrible cat.

"Damn that boy!" cried Glasgerion. He tucked Quadroped firmly under his shield arm. "Quadro, hold on!"

With a yell, Glasgerion urged his mount forward into the writhing crowd, leaving his guard behind him. Reander and the Black Unicorn moved closer together, separated only by a thin wedge of men. Glasgerion cursed and forged grimly on. His sword slashed down, right, left, and right again, methodically chopping a path to his nephew's side.

The Black Unicorn moved faster, breaking into a gallop. Warriors scattered from his path. Reander sheathed his sword and grabbed up a spear from a falling man. He kicked his mount into motion. With terrible speed the two rulers plunged toward each other. Reander lowered his spear.

The Black Unicorn's horn smashed into Reander's shield, almost unhorsing him. Reander's spear drove into the Black Unicorn's chest. The Black Unicorn's armor held. The spear was shivered.

Reander unsheathed his sword and wheeled his horse around. Back toward the Black Unicorn he rode. The enemies collided. Reander's sword flashed down and arose coated in blood. The Black Unicorn reared. Reander's horse shrieked as the Black Unicorn's hooves crashed down, crushing bone and slicing flesh. The gallant beast stumbled and fell, trapping his rider beneath him.

"Reander," Glasgerion cried. He leaped from his horse, Quadroped still under his arm, and ran to where his nephew lay. The Ravenorians closed in, cutting him off from his guard. Quadroped clambered on top of Reander's dying horse. The Black Unicorn reared again.

"Stop!" screamed Quadroped.

The Black Unicorn's hooves crashed down, narrowly missing Reander's chest. His fiery eyes glared down at Quadroped. "Bring that pig here," he ordered.

Quadroped squealed as a Ravenorian warrior leaped forward and grabbed him. "Put me down," he cried.

The warrior complied, placing him carefully on the Black Unicorn's armored back. Small silver studs set in the armored plates poked painfully into Quadroped's rump. He grabbed hold of a convenient spike and looked down. The ground was far away.

"Goriel was killed by Nieve," Quadroped shouted into the Black Unicorn's ear. "The whole war is a trick to fill the Fleshless Land with souls."

The Black Unicorn tossed his head. Quadroped doggedly continued his explanation. He had no idea how much the Black Unicorn believed, but the Ruler of Ravenor appeared at least to be listening. "You have to stop fighting," he said.

The Black Unicorn's dark gaze moved from Quadroped to Glasgerion, who was still kneeling beside his nephew. Reander's eyes were open but he was clearly in considerable pain. His horse was, mercifully, dead.

Glasgerion returned the Black Unicorn's gaze and held it. "It is time that we talked," he said. "I will concede this battle to you if you will agree to withdraw. We can always fight again on the morrow."

The Black Unicorn turned to where the Manslayer was butchering an unhappy Lyskerysian and called to his Warlord to join him.

The Manslayer looked up from his pleasant pastime. With terrible precision he cut off his latest victim's head and dropped the corpse upon the ground. Then he approached his sovereign.

"Set Morragwen free and signal our troops to withdraw," said the Black Unicorn. Quadroped gave a sigh of relief.

The Manslayer snarled and looked mutinous. "Withdraw?" he said. "Why? The Kingdoms are weaker than us." His cat eyes fell upon Quadroped. "If that piglet has ruined things *again* . . ."

"The piglet is not your concern," said the Black Unicorn. "You will obey me."

The Manslayer grudgingly hung his bloodied two-bladed

ax at his side. With a savage grunt he stalked off to do the Black Unicorn's bidding.

Horns cried out. All across the valley people began warily to sheathe their weapons and back away from their opponents. The noise level dropped mercifully to bearable levels. Morrag and Morragwen appeared in a puff of blue smoke. Morragwen ran to Glasgerion's side. Morrag sailed over to Quadroped, where he still sat upon the Black Unicorn's back.

Reander was pulled from under his horse. His sword arm was broken and his ribs badly crushed but he managed to stand nonetheless. Officers began to ride up, anxious to receive their orders.

Off to the left came a sudden commotion. A curdling shriek pierced the air, and then another. Isfandi soldiers were attacking. A Ravenorian captain staggered back, blood running freely from his shoulder and down his arm. He collapsed and died at the Black Unicorn's hooves.

Reander quickly assessed the situation. Th Rulers of Essylt and Ravenor, and all of their senior officers, were gathered together in one spot. "Ghola is staging a coup," he said. "He will destroy us all and win victory for the Kingdoms."

"It's treachery," chortled the Manslayer. "Now we can kill you all!" He advanced on Reander, his ax in his hands once more. Reander drew his sword with his left hand and prepared to fight.

The Black Unicorn had not moved since his captain had fallen. Quadroped felt his body begin to tremble. "I believe," said the Black Unicorn in a very calm voice, "that I am about to be angry."

The Manslayer paused and looked nervously at his sovereign. The Manslayer was not easily intimidated. All of a sudden, Quadroped discovered that it was possible to feel more afraid than he already did.

"Quadro, get down," said Morrag. "Jump."

Quadroped tried and found that he could not move. Some invisible force had glued him to the Black Unicorn's back.

The Black Unicorn's body began to emit heat. His

armor began to steam. *I'm going to be cooked alive,* thought Quadroped. It was a novel variation on the "kill the pig" theme and one he did not much care for.

The Black Unicorn's mane began to lash and writhe, as if it were horribly alive. Red light shone forth from his eyes. He threw back his head and roared. It was not a normal, horselike, sound.

Reander took one look at the Black Unicorn and began to move hastily back, pulling Glasgerion with him. Quadroped earnestly wished himself elsewhere as well.

The Ruler of Ravenor was about to do something perfectly dreadful. Quadroped was not sure what it would be but he was fairly certain it would involve annihilating everything in sight. As escape was impossible, it clearly behooved a sensible pig to try and distract the mad beast.

Quadroped looked frantically around. The attacking Isfandi warriors caught his attention. They looked odd, jerky of movement and glassy of eye. They were dying quite easily. At least . . . no, that one had picked himself up again. Quadroped blinked, the warrior's wounds had looked rather severe. Surely it was not natural that he should be grinning so maniacally or swinging his sword with such vigor?

Quadroped pounded his hooves hard against the Black Unicorn's back, making the armor ring. "Stop," he cried. "They're already dead."

"As good as," agreed the Manslayer. His ax whistled cheerfully down.

"No," said Quadroped. "They really *are*. Look at their wounds. Why, that one's missing an arm. They're corpses. Nieve must have brought them to life. I *told* you she didn't want the Great War to end."

This rather prosaic statement had a remarkably calming effect. The Black Unicorn snorted and gave himself a little shake. His temperature dropped several degrees. His mane stopped whipping around like a nest of enraged serpents. With a flick of his horn he speared a particularly determined Isfandi and began to examine him closely.

"You are right," he said. "I've killed this one before."

Quadroped glanced briefly at the ugly hole in the man's chest and hoped he would not become ill.

All over the battlefield the dead began to rise, picking themselves up from the bloodied ground and falling upon the living. Reander moved to the Black Unicorn's side.

"We must fight these creatures together," he said. He reached up and brought Quadroped down, handing him into Glasgerion's care.

The living gathered around their leaders, a small knot of mortals in a sea of the dead. With dismal moans the Revenants pressed in. Every warrior they killed increased their numbers. The island of living grew smaller.

The Black Unicorn began to falter. "The balance is shifting," he said. "Laws have been broken. The Universe is being transformed. I feel it, it tears me apart."

The living corpses gnashed their teeth and wailed. The Ravenorians collapsed as their sovereign weakened. They began to die, their life force draining back into their creator. Morragwen crumpled unconscious into Glasgerion's arms. Morrag lay weakly beside her.

More and more corpses lurched into life, each bent on mindless destruction. The balance of nature continued to tip. Eunoe fell. Reander looked frightfully ill. Those with no magical bent continued to fight but physical weakness assailed them.

Glasgerion cradled his wife in his arms. Quadroped sat down beside him. Morragwen opened her eyes and smiled up at them. "How goes the battle?" she asked.

Glasgerion smoothed the hair from her brow. "I fear we cannot win this one," he said. "This battle shall be our last."

Quadroped shivered. "There must be some way to stop them," he said. "It can't end like this. It just can't."

"You must open the Way of the Slain."

Quadroped looked around. Father Pig stood there beside the great Sanglier. Behind them came the rest of the herd, walking unharmed through the walls of the dead. The corpses had no power to harm them.

The Sanglier approached Reander and the Black Unicorn, where they fought side by side. "You must send the dead home," he told them. "The Balance must shift no further."

"It cannot be done," said Reander.

"We will show you," said the Sanglier. "Listen."

In a low voice he told Reander and the Black Unicorn and his Warlords how this magic might be done. Night fell. The white moon sailed into the sky. The sorrowful cries of the unhappy undead rose eerily into the dark. A pack of wolves wailed a lonely counterpoint. At length the lesson was finished.

Moonlight danced on the waters, sketching the world in silver. Reander turned to face the Black Unicorn. The elders of the fairy Sounder came quietly forth and circled them in a ring.

Glasgerion moved back, pulling Quadroped with him. Tannakin and Tantony, Hogni and Hogvandi, Grufin and Grundi, and all the other young pigs of the Sounder came and gathered around them. With wide, anxious eyes they waited for the spell to begin.

Reander raised his hands toward the moon. The Black Unicorn's horn stretched up between them, the third part of a cone. Little flames began to flicker around them, just inside the ring of pigs. Reander began to perspire despite the cold wind that blew off the river. The Black Unicorn's coat slowly became flecked with foam. The little flames rose slightly. A cloud scudded across the moon. The flames died down again until they were little more than embers in the grass. The Revenants gnashed their teeth. The living drew closer together.

"It's not working," said Quadroped. "Something's wrong." Then he said something he had never thought to say. "I wish that Avice were here."

Bells chimed. "Hoggling," said a silky voice, "I thought you'd never ask."

Avice appeared beside Glasgerion, hand on hip. He looked at the ring of magicians. "Goodness, how *dramatic* they all look," he said.

The Black Unicorn and Reander stepped apart and turned to face the intruder. Reander studied the Trickster with thoughtful eyes. "You must be Avice," he said. "I wondered when you'd turn up."

"Did you?" Avice smiled. "I wish you had waited for me."

"Haven't we?" asked Reander. "You've been blocking our magic quite effectively."

"Me?" asked Avice. "Now why would *I* do a thing like that?"

"To be difficult," said Glasgerion.

Avice's eyes twinkled down at Quadroped. "Your friend knows me well, hoggling," he said.

"Your habits are rather well documented in the folk literature," said Glasgerion dryly. "That's the price of notoriety."

"Will you help us?" asked Quadroped eagerly.

"Oh, yes," said Avice.

Reander looked at him sharply. "Just how are you planning to help?" he asked.

"Why, I'll open the Way of the Slain for you," said Avice. "You want to get rid of these corpses, don't you? Poor trapped spirits . . . it can't be very pleasant for them here. They'll begin to decay soon, even in weather as cold as this."

Avice raised his arms and spread them wide. Fireworks exploded from the tips of his fingers. At his feet a fire began to rise.

Flames towered up, licking the night air. Clouds of red sparks poured away on the wind. The fire thundered and roared, drowning the dismal wails of the Revenants. Low jangling filled the air, belled feet slowly started dancing. Avice grinned at Quadroped over his shoulder, mocking his own theatricals.

The flames began to move apart. Between them a gaping nothingness appeared, expanding as the fiery circle grew. The door to the Lands of the Dead was open. The dead fell to the bloodstained ground and were still.

Avice looked over his shoulder again. "Open your lines," he said. "Let the spirits pass through. It is dangerous to keep the Way open for long. Something unpleasant might decide to walk out."

Reander and the Black Unicorn issued the orders. A pathway was cleared. Through the ranks of the living a glowing mist of phantoms flowed. In slow parade they approached the Door and vanished into the void. Their half-seen faces were peaceful and calm. The spirits were glad to go home.

When the last dead warrior had gone, Avice lowered his hands. The fires died, the Door was gone. Avice rubbed his hands together and grinned. "Right," said the Trickster. "Now for some *real* magic. It's time to summon Nieve. The femme fatale of the Fleshless Land has broken the rules once too often."

The Black Unicorn quivered and stamped his feet. Reander became quite pale. "Are you *mad*?" asked Reander. "You can't pull a Queen of the Dead into the Living Lands!"

Quadroped could have told Reander that this was not the way to treat the volatile Trickster. Avice's smile acquired a dangerous edge. "Oh no? Just watch me," he said.

"Wait," cried Reander. "Don't do this! You'll destroy the Balance completely."

Avice snapped his fingers. "Nieve," he said, "come here."

The night stretched. There was a twisting sensation. Lights flashed behind Quadroped's eyes and a pulsing, aching pain began to build up in his head. Around him the other young pigs squealed in fright. Stars whirled, becoming huge silver pinwheels in the sky. The moon dipped and swung. Nieve appeared.

The malignant Queen of the Dead hung in the air, suspended against the infinite sky. Her eyes were closed. Sooty lashes fanned down on snow white cheeks. A cold dead light shone from her pallid face and her black hair fanned out around her, moving to invisible winds. Small insects and night-flying birds rained out of the air to fall, dead, at her feet.

Quadroped looked at Nieve. There was something terribly *wrong* about her. The air pressed hard upon him, pushing him into the ground. The ground rippled away from

Nieve's small feet. The Queen of the Slain looked no larger than a mortal woman but her presence filled the night. Nieve had no place in the world. Avice had managed to squeeze her in somehow, displacing reality by doing it.

The effect grew worse the closer one came to Nieve. The Black Unicorn was struggling to stay upright. Reander was pressed flat against the Black Unicorn's flank, unable to stand without that additional support.

The Black Unicorn shuddered. His mane came alive. "Trickster," he said, "send her *back*."

Nieve opened her eyes.

"Too late," said Avice with a smile.

"Why have you summoned me here?" asked the Queen of the Slain. Her lips never moved. Her autumnal voice was heard by all.

"You are summoned to an accounting," said Avice. "You have broken the laws that bind you. It is time to make amends."

Nieve shuddered and twisted. The earth quaked. The Lost Skeggs leaped high above its banks and came swirling over the plain, soaking everybody's feet.

"You cannot escape," said Avice.

"What do you want of me?" asked Nieve. All save Avice recoiled from the malevolence of her face.

There was silence. Everyone stared at Nieve. The magicians were all completely dazed by the enormity of what Avice had done. Their sensitive mental antennas were buzzing, telling them that the Balance was completely gone, that all the laws that maintained the worlds were being torn asunder.

Avice tapped his foot. "Go on," he said. "Ask her for something. I can't hold her here all night."

Fortunately there were some present who had no magical powers and were therefore completely unaware that the end of all worlds was nigh.

"Goriel," said Quadroped, recovering first. He had, after all, encountered Nieve before. "And Glaissin and Eltis and Arelis. Ask her to unfreeze them and leave them alone."

"What a miserable little demand," said Avice. "Can't anybody think up anything better than that?"

"Food," said Glasgerion, giving himself a little shake. "The famine will kill many people before spring. Let Nieve make amends by filling the granaries again."

"How about bringing everyone back to life?" suggested the Manslayer, who was a magician but not a particularly sensitive one. "Then I can kill them again."

That shook Reander back to his senses. "No!" he said. "This must stop. Avice, you are doing irreparable harm. Send Nieve back."

"Things *are* swinging a bit out of kilter," agreed Avice. "Nieve, you have heard their demands."

"Food they shall have," said Nieve. "The dead winter earth shall be revived that they may sow their fields. Goriel you shall also have. His wife and his daughters as well." She did not add "and good riddance," but her expression relayed her intent.

"Avice," Reander was almost pleading. "Don't do this. Send her home. Things must be left as they are. Order must be restored."

Avice gazed sorrowfully upon the distraught Prince. "Restore order?" he said. "I can't, for I am an agent of chaos."

Nieve vanished. With a whoosh, reality popped back into place, filling the void she had left. Avice vanished. Goriel and his family appeared out of nowhere. Shouts of joy erupted all over the battlefield. Reander put his head in his hands.

The Black Unicorn approached Reander and laid his horn on his shoulder. "It's over," he said. "Equilibrium has been restored."

Reander looked up into the Black Unicorn's fathomless eyes. "It has changed," he said. "The Balance is not as before."

"It has changed," agreed the Ruler of Ravenor. He lifted his head and looked toward the east. "The extent of the changes will not be apparent for some time. But, Prince of Essylt, I think they are not great. The worlds continue, our people live."

Reander looked around him. The moon had set. In the east the sky was pale. All over the valley warriors embraced each other or stopped to comfort the wounded.

Reander stepped back and straightened his shoulders. "It is time to talk of peace," he said. "The treaty must be redrawn, and the borders. Isfandiar and Imchadiz must relinquish your mines."

The Black Unicorn nodded. "There is much to be done."

Eunoe came up and took Reander's hands in her own. "Later," she said. Behind her, Quadroped and Morrag, Glasgerion and Morragwen, Goriel, Glaissin, Arelis, and Eltis, and all of the young fairy pigs were dancing around in a ring. Reander and the Black Unicorn looked at each other and smiled. With a toss of his head the Black Unicorn turned and galloped away toward Ravenor.

Reander put his good arm around Eunoe's shoulders. "Come on," he said. "It is time to go home." Together they walked back into camp, calling loudly for coffee and breakfast.

Epilogue

So the second Great War came to an end. The wounded
were treated. The countless dead were buried. At noon the
next day the Council of the Kingdoms was convened.

Inside the Council tent Quadroped lay, contentedly
curled up on Glasgerion's lap. Quadroped's eyes were
fixed on Reander, who had been pacing the floor for an
hour. Reander was once again looking healthy, impatient,
and arrogant. His broken bones had been healed by Eunoe,
the Council had restored him to his position as Speaker,
and he was fully in control of the political situation once
again. His only remaining injuries were a rather horrendous set of bruises, which Eunoe had refused to heal on
the grounds that too much magic was unhealthy and that
a little pain never hurt anyone.

The assembled Councilors also watched Reander, nervously. They had had difficulty accepting the reality of
the Black Unicorn. They were finding it even harder to
accept the existence of Nieve. They had lived through a
night of repeated horrors the nature of which they did not
understand. Their questions were driving Reander mad.

"I still don't understand what the pigs have to do with it all," said Aumbry plaintively.

"It's the mushrooms that bother me," said Ghola darkly.

Reander ran his hands through his hair and tried not to snarl. The tent flap lifted and a woman of Essylt came in. She looked troubled.

"Yes? What is it?" demanded Reander.

The woman licked her lips. "Sire, there's a herd of pigs outside. They're asking to talk to you."

"I see," said Reander with commendable calm. "They wouldn't happen to be fairy pigs, would they?"

"I don't know," said the woman. "What do fairy pigs look like?"

"Never mind," said Reander. He collapsed into his chair at the head of the table and waved a weary hand toward the door. "Go on," he said. "Send them in."

Quadroped snuggled deeper into Glasgerion's lap and wondered nervously how his Sounder would greet him. He had defied the Sanglier and taken things into his own hooves. Last night everyone had been too happy to comment on his behavior. By now they would have had time to remember.

The Sanglier entered the tent closely followed by the senior boars and sows, Quadroped's parents among them. The younger pigs trooped in after them and seated themselves quietly on the floor near the door. The Sanglier approached the Council table with a slow and dignified gait. He stopped some feet away and bowed, massive head down and right leg forward.

"Hail," said the Sanglier.

"Hail," responded Reander rather perfunctorily. "Our thanks for your help last night. Quadro has told us of your sufferings at the hands of Ferethel, the Fungus Lord."

"Ah," said the Sanglier heavily. His eyes fell upon Quadroped and he bristled slightly. "Then you know that we were the cause of the recent atmospheric anomalies."

"You made it rain," said Aumbry. The Ruler of Akariel had finally managed to absorb this single fact.

"We did," said the Sanglier. "We deeply regret the harm we have caused. We have come to make amends."

"No need for that," said Glasgerion cheerfully. "Quadro's explained everything." Quadroped winced.

"We bear your Sounder no ill will," said Reander. "Indeed we are grateful to you. Without Quadroped we might now be in the midst of a second Great War."

Worse and worse, thought Quadroped.

He wondered if he should be tactful and join his Sounder on the floor. The Sanglier was looking decidedly put out at being upstaged by a piglet. That that piglet was comfortably relaxing in the lap of a Prince of Essylt, while the Sanglier stood at attention before Reander, could be doing little to soothe the boar's ruffled feelings.

Glasgerion's lap was very warm. A quick peek under the table revealed that Father was looking extremely cross. Quadroped waved a hoof at his mother and decided to stay right where he was.

"If you will accept nothing else from us accept our sincere apologies," said the Sanglier. He bowed again and turned to lead his Sounder away.

"Wait," said the vixen Ilketsni. She waved an imperious paw. "You said that you made it rain, can you control other sorts of weather as well?"

"Of course," said the Sanglier with quiet dignity. "We can control *all* aspects of the weather."

"Hmmm," murmured Ilketsni. Her amber eyes acquired a sly and speculative gleam that filled Quadroped with vague alarm.

"Now what's she up to?" murmured Glasgerion, who had also noticed Ilketsni's devious expression.

"Can you bring sunshine?" asked Ilketsni.

"We can," said the Sanglier. "We have. Today's weather was one of our finest achievements. Pleasantly warm and dry, becoming cooler toward late afternoon, winds from the west."

"Can each one of you do this? Or do you all have to be together?" said Ilketsni.

"We can all control the weather," said the Sanglier.

"Except, of course, for Quadroped." He glared at the comfortable piglet.

"Oh dear," said Quadroped. "He shouldn't have told her that." He had an unpleasant suspicion where Ilketsni's line of questioning was leading.

"Do you know, I think you're right?" whispered Glasgerion. "Here it comes."

The Councilor for Ungartok smiled and preened her long whiskers. "My Lords," she said to the Council. "These pigs are a valuable commodity. Why should Jansiar have a monopoly on them? Is it fair that one Kingdom should keep all of the pigs? I think that *each* Kingdom should have one."

"Indeed," said Ghola of Isfandiar. He began counting the pigs on skeletal fingers. "There are thirty of them," he said. "That's more than one apiece. I suppose the babies should stay with their mothers . . ."

"Now wait just a minute," said Glasgerion.

Reander rose to face the Council. The boars of the Sounder formed a protective ring around their sows and piglets. The Sanglier pawed the ground. The littler pigs looked anxious.

"Hello, what's this? This place is awash in pigs."

All eyes turned to the door. Morrag had swum in and was looking around the tent in some amusement. The tent flap lifted and Morragwen entered, resplendent in scarlet and gold. "I bring you greetings from the Black Unicorn," she said. "He's taken his people home. He says he's ready to discuss the terms of the new treaty whenever you wish."

"Let us rejoice," said Aumbry, waxing poetic. He raised a brimming goblet high. "Peace and prosperity are now at hand. All ills shall grow better. The unsown fields shall bear ripe fruits. Earth's gold shall fill the granaries, the herds shall grow fat, the grass shall grow green—"

"Yes, yes," said Ilketsni impatiently. "But what about the pigs?"

Quadroped sat up and placed his front hooves on the table. "We want to stay in Whistlewood," he said. "You can't divide the Sounder up."

"Why not?" asked Ilketsni nastily. "You're not really free, you know. If you live in the Kingdoms then you have to obey Council decisions. That's the way government works."

"The pigs must go back to Whistlewood," said Reander firmly.

Ilketsni yawned and snapped her jaws together. "The war has ended, Reander. You are no longer in command and we need not obey your orders. As Speaker you don't even get to vote unless there's a tie and I don't think there will be." She looked around the Council complacently.

"Can pigs live underwater?" asked Aodh.

"How much food would they eat?" asked Aumbry.

"Can you keep them in a pen or do they need a whole forest?" asked the new Prince of Lyskerys, Sioned's heir.

Briavel looked sadly at Quadroped. "I suppose we *should* share them," he said.

"Essylt is outnumbered," said Ilketsni triumphantly. "I want those cute little piglets over there." Her pointed nose indicated Quadroped's young cousins, Betony and Campion, who were huddled miserably against their mother's flanks.

"No," said Quadroped.

"Be silent, piglet," said Aodh. "You have no voice in Council."

"I *won't* be quiet," said Quadroped. He struggled out of Glasgerion's lap and climbed up on the table. His snout quivered wrathfully as he glared at Ilketsni. "Leave my Sounder alone, you horrible fox," he said. "If you try to separate us I'll . . . I'll . . ." Quadroped tried desperately to think of some horrible threat. "I'll ask the Black Unicorn to attack you," he said.

Ilketsni blinked and stared at Morragwen. The official Ambassadress of Ravenor smiled sweetly. "The welfare of the fairy pigs is of deep concern to the Black Unicorn," she said. "I think I can safely say that he would look askance on any government that attempted to coerce or mistreat them."

Morrag unwound himself from Morragwen's neck and

flashed Quadroped a toothy grin. "If you don't want to be governed by this greedy Council," he said, "Ravenor can offer you a home. The forest of Indrasir is more beautiful than any wood in the Kingdoms."

Quadroped tried to imagine life in a world where *everyone* was magical except for himself. It sounded very unpleasant. "We'd rather stay in Whistlewood," he said. "*If* the Council will let us."

"Ah, hmm, um," said Ghola. He regarded Quadroped thoughtfully over steepled fingers. "Upon further consideration perhaps it would be best to let the fairy pigs remain in Whistlewood. We would not want our pigs to pine, eh?"

"But it's so unfair," said Ilketsni. "If Ungartok had a fairy pig we could grow our own grain. We would not have to rely on imports from Akariel and Lyskerys."

The Councilors from Akariel and Lyskerys looked startled. That aspect of fairy pig ownership had not occurred to them. "Let the pigs stay in Whistlewood," they chorused quickly. Ilketsni snarled.

"Perhaps the pigs could promise not to meddle with the weather," said Glasgerion peaceably. "That way Jansiar gains no unfair advantage."

"They have to practice their magic," said Quadroped. "Fairy pigs aren't happy otherwise."

"If *I* may speak?"

All eyes turned toward the dauntingly large form of the Sanglier. He looked upon Quadroped with an unexpectedly benevolent eye.

"Quadroped is not quite correct," he said. "We *do* like to play with the weather, but prior to our enslavement by Ferethel we had never altered conditions over the whole Kingdoms, or even over the whole of Jansiar. We are content merely to control the weather of Whistlewood itself."

Briavel stood up and flapped his wings for attention. "The Sounder is a national treasure," the cormorant said. "Jansiar is willing to relinquish all rights to it. It could be set up as an independent holding under government of the fairy pigs."

There was a murmur of voices as the Council discussed this generous proposal. "A pig could sit on the Council," said the astute Ghola. "They could be our weather advisory bureau, working to ameliorate the climate over all the Kingdoms. Perhaps the Sanglier . . . ?"

"My Lords, I should be honored," said the Sanglier.

Quadroped grunted happily and climbed from the table to Glasgerion's lap and from there to the floor. He trotted under the table toward the door, leaving the Sanglier and the rest of the Sounder to iron out all the little details of their arrangement with the Council. Morrag glided silently after him.

"Hurrah," said Quadroped when he was outside and out of hearing. "It's over."

He looked around. Nieve's promised changes had begun. The wind was warm and smelled of newly opened flowers. Tiny green shoots were pushing their way up through the trampled dirt of the camp. A flock of geese passed by, flying north. The Lost Skeggs glistened and rippled and sang.

And far to the north, in the partially melting Palace of Essylt, Fairfax the hedgehog awoke. With a bleary eye he regarded the warm golden light that streamed through the chinks in the linen cupboard's walls. His long pale snout sniffed the air. He unrolled.

"Bah," said Fairfax, "it's *spring* again."

Notes

The author would like to acknowledge the following specific works:

Anonymous. "The Waking of Angantyr," *An Introduction to Old Norse*. 2d ed. Edited by E. V. Gordon and revised by A. R. Taylor. Oxford, England: Clarendon Press, pp. 142–47.

Lucas, John, and Colin Dickinson, editors. *The Encyclopedia of Mushrooms*. New York: Crescent Books, 1985.

Milton, John. *Paradise Lost*. Book II, line 302.

Nicholson, Irene. *Firefly in the Night: A Study of Ancient Mexican Poetry and Symbolism*. London: Faber & Faber, 1959.